AF413464

Just Another Dead Boy

Just Another Dead Boy

KELLY McCAUGHRAIN

CANDLEWICK PRESS

First US edition 2026
First published by Walker Books Ltd. (UK) 2026

Library of Congress Control Number: pending
ISBN 978-1-5362-5173-9

26 27 28 29 30 31 APS 10 9 8 7 6 5 4 3 2 1

Printed in Humen, Dongguan, China

This book was typeset in ITC Garamond Std.

Candlewick Press
99 Dover Street
Somerville, Massachusetts 02144

www.candlewick.com

EU Authorized Representative: HackettFlynn Ltd,
36 Cloch Choirneal, Balrothery, Co. Dublin, K32 C942, Ireland.
EU@walkerpublishinggroup.com

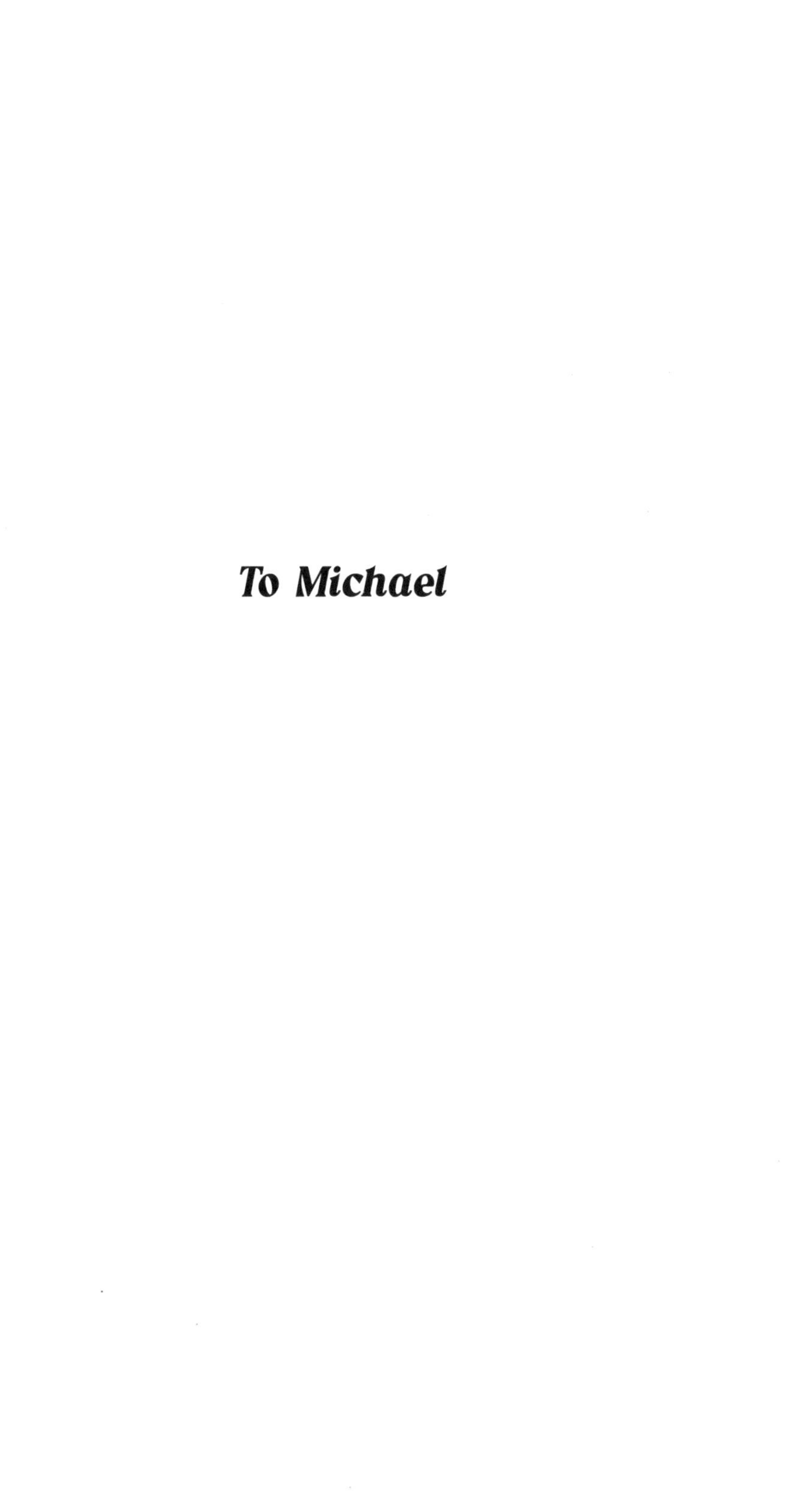

To Michael

PART I
Two
Households

Chapter 1

Our selection of Romeo-and-Juliet packages are discreet, professional, and tailored to your needs, with options ranging from meaningful friendship to true love with someone facing similar end-of-life issues.

Past clients have reported that their loved ones experienced important psychological benefits such as solidarity in the face of the unknown and feelings of fulfillment.

"Caring for another person forces you to be brave. Caring for our son always gave us strength, but it was humbling to see how his love for his 'Juliet' gave him such courage at the end. We were so grateful to her."

—Carla (mother of Sam, age 17)

"Love?" The glossy brochure in Mrs. Daly's hand trembles slightly as she examines it. Her nails are bitten, and the cuffs of her shirt hang a little loose at the wrists. Dr. Lawrence passes her a cup of jasmine tea and takes the brochure away, as if to be helpful, though it's really just that he's careful never to let the brochures leave this room.

"The appearance of it, yes," he says, sitting down again behind his huge walnut desk. Dr. Lawrence's office doesn't look like the rest of the Elite Elect Clinic. The thick rugs and wood furniture give it a warmer, homier atmosphere. There's a plush sofa, a wall of thank-you cards, and a shelf of books by Dr. Ryan T. Lawrence with titles like *The Brain Chemistry of Attraction* and *The Phases of Romantic Love*. An antique clock ticks softly on the wall.

He laces his fingers in front of him and starts explaining the different options while, in my armchair in the corner, I try not to fidget and make the leather creak as my attention wanders. I've heard the spiel before, but for the families who are ushered quietly into this room while their loved one is busy with the end-of-life counselors, this is all brand-new information. They have no idea the R&J service even exists before they're brought in here and asked if they'd be interested in an "extra option not listed on the resort website."

"So, it's not . . . real?" Mr. Daly is saying. He's a bear of a man, while his wife is tiny, and their tailored clothes are as tasteful as their English accents—cashmere Chanel for her, and I'm pretty sure his beige jacket is Armani.

I'm not supposed to participate at this point anyway.

Dr. Lawrence is the expert. But since I'm the one who'll be hired or not at the end of this interview, it's hard to sit here and say nothing. And it doesn't help that my stomach is growling, my brain is fogged, and my head aches to the ends of my ash-brown hair. I may be a *tiny* bit hungover. And by "a tiny bit," I mean we hung out with this crowd of girls from Dallas doing tequila shots and cheerleading routines on the bar top at Inferno last night. *(R-E-G-A-N! GOOOOO, REGAN!)* By two a.m., I'd lost my balance, *another* pair of heels, and the ability to spell *Cowboys*.

I silently urge Dr. Lawrence to get on with it, but he just places his chin on his interlaced fingertips, his smile the perfect balance of respectful solemnity and *this is as routine as joining a gym*. He's had variations of this conversation so many times, but he's always careful to make the appropriate facial expressions. No one wants their kid's impending death to be treated like another day at the office. No one wants to know that they're echoing the same things a hundred other parents have said on that sofa. That there's nothing at all unique about their grief.

"*Real* is a concept a lot of our clients struggle with at first," he says. "Why do we assume real is better? We've all had real relationships. We know how badly they can go. That's not something anyone needs in the last week of their life." He sits back in his chair. "We can't offer real, Mr. and Mrs. Daly, and we wouldn't if we could. We offer *perfect*. Jude deserves perfect."

The first time I did this, I expected the parents to laugh at him. Hiring someone so your son or daughter can experience "true love" before they die? It's bizarre. But you have to understand the way these people think. They're used to being able to have anything on the menu. *Anything.* From skydiving with their favorite popstar to string quartets to serenade them to sleep. Why *not* true love? That's just the kind of quality service they're used to.

But Mr. Daly frowns. "And the *full* Romeo-and-Juliet package is someone—"

"Someone in exactly Jude's position, yes," Dr. Lawrence explains. "Someone with his same Death Date—we use a special tattoo to simulate that—who appears to be here to have their end-of-life procedure, too. Of course, we never push the client into anything. We always let them be the first to suggest that they go through the procedure together. They generally do."

"So, then she would pretend to—"

"There's a sedative involved; it's all very convincing."

"Hence the name." Mr. Daly nods at the framed print of *Romeo and Juliet* hanging on the wall among the medical diplomas—him straddling a balcony, her in a voluminous nightgown, stealing a last kiss.

Dr. Lawrence's smile warms. "My wife's favorite play. You know, people think I started the Romeo-and-Juliet service because I'm a romantic." He shrugs. "Maybe I am. But make no mistake, the reason that story still resonates with us after four hundred years has nothing to do with romance." He leans forward. "It's a very primal instinct, Mr. Daly, to not want to venture into the dark alone."

The Dalys glance at each other, skepticism wavering.

Because Dr. Lawrence is right. The romance is a cute side dish, but *this* is what sells the R&J service. The parents we see in here have helicoptered over their kids since birth, and the thing they can't stand is that *this* time they can't fix it, make it better, or go with them.

Dr. Lawrence allows a pause. A brief moment for the idea to become a possibility in their imaginations. Then he says, "With your interest in science, Mrs. Daly, you'll perhaps know about the psychological benefits of companionship during difficult times. That's why our full Romeo-and-Juliet packages are so popular. And so effective. It's amazing how quickly strong bonds are formed between people in stressful situations. Ask any platoon of soldiers. Research shows that even *love* isn't implausible under those conditions. In fact, it's quite common. And it's so much easier to walk into the unknown with someone you love."

"I'm no scientist, Dr. Lawrence. I just set up the institute," Mrs. Daly says. "But you don't have to tell me about the importance of having someone to lean on at difficult times." She looks up at her husband, and they share the ghost of a smile. "But I just don't know," she goes on. "This whole place is so . . ." She looks around as if the entire resort is before her. All you can actually see through the huge sheet of glass that makes up the exterior wall is cedar, maple, spruce, and birch, then the Catskill Mountains climbing out of the tree line. The clinic is discreetly tucked away in a peaceful location in the woods, separate, as if it's not the reason everyone's here.

The main resort is completely different—a glittering cluster of hotels, restaurants, and clubs hugging the lake, a bustle of theaters, beaches, yacht parties, limos, and every bucket-list activity you could dream of. There are end-of-life clinics all over the world, but, like everything else, Elite Elect does it better, so those who can afford it choose to spend their last days here. Europeans, like the Dalys, tend to describe it as a little *flashy* when they're being polite. A little *American* when they're not.

"Well, it isn't really Jude's thing," Mrs. Daly finishes delicately, taking a linen handkerchief from her purse. Her blue eyes are red rimmed, her face pale, and her husband's square jaw is tense. But all the parents look like that. I watch them, searching for the giveaway details that tell me about *this* couple—her desk-work rounded shoulders, his deep eye crinkles, the rose-pink lining of her dress, his mismatched socks (one blue, one brown). His arm draped protectively around her is a perfect frame for her face, and my fingers twitch for my camera.

But I shake off the instinct and try to pay attention. I can imagine Dr. Lawrence's reaction if I whipped out a phone and started snapping pictures of the clients.

He's smiling at them understandingly, the tilt of his head inviting them to continue, but there's tension in *his* jaw, too. He'd like this to be going better.

"To be honest, I don't know if we did the right thing bringing him here," Mrs. Daly is saying. "It's just . . . well, what do you do with the last few days?" She spreads her hands at Dr. Lawrence, like he might have an answer to that question. "Trying to put a brave face on things, every-one pretending they're OK to spare everyone else. Do you smile? Do you cry? How do you . . . ?" She falters, takes a steadying breath, then gestures wryly at herself and her husband. "Would *you* want to spend all day, every day with people in this state?"

Mr. Daly leans a little closer to her.

"You think you're ready," she says. "But . . ." She puts her head in her hands and sucks in deep breaths that quickly become sobs, and her husband pulls her against his chest.

I look away. They've had eighteen years to prepare for this; their son was born with his Death Date like everyone else, but *no one* walks in here feeling ready. By the last couple of days, most of the mothers are on some kind of tranquilizer. They can't get through it otherwise.

"Regan?" Dr. Lawrence addresses me quietly. He nods at the coffee table. "Perhaps we could refresh this tea?"

I slip out with the tray, understanding that I'm to take my time, give the Dalys some privacy. I slide it onto the secretary's desk for a refill, wishing they were coffee drinkers. I could inject caffeine into my eyeballs right now.

"They bite?" Kendra asks, removing the used cups.

I make a face. "It's not looking good. I don't know why he's bothering with more tea." Dr. Lawrence is a good salesman, but he has more class than to pressure people. He usually just tells them the options and respects their decision.

"You don't do a rush job with people like that," she says.

"People like that?"

"The Dalys."

I look at her blankly.

"As in the *Death Date Dalys*? As in Daly *Vodka*?" she says, like it's obvious.

My mouth falls open as my eyes close. It *is* obvious. I don't know why it didn't occur to me. I haven't paid much attention to their Death Date research, but I've definitely drunk enough of the vodka. I can picture the name in curly script at the top of the label, familiar as the logo for Coke or Pepsi. There isn't a bar in the resort, or the country for that matter, that doesn't stock Daly liquor.

"Holy shit." I breathe the words. I should've guessed. I've spent enough time around rich people to spot the difference. Their clothes may be the very best, but the Dalys are understated in a way that only the truly wealthy ever are—no bling, nothing ostentatious. They have nothing to prove and no one to impress.

I suppress the urge to groan as my hands smooth the dress I fished out of the laundry basket this morning, wishing I'd had more time for my makeup.

It shouldn't matter who they are, but of course it does, and my mind races, taking in what this means. Primarily, it means a bigger tip. I work on a flat fee, but the tips vary wildly. These people think nothing of throwing a hundred at a bartender who makes a good mojito, so you can imagine how they'll tip someone who made their dying kid happy.

It also means the classier hotels. A week at the Imperial, maybe even Meadowview Lodge, while I play the part of a dying heiress. I woke up with rain coming through my bedroom ceiling, so that sounds pretty appealing right now.

I anxiously rearrange my probably *too* tousled curls as Kendra places cupcakes on the tray. "Jesus, I'm not on the ball today."

"Clearly." Kendra folds her arms over her own pristine white blouse and arches an eyebrow pointedly at my dress. I look down in panic, expecting to find it unbuttoned or something.

It's worse than that. There's a *hole* in the pale green fabric. It's tiny, but the crispy brown edges are obviously a cigarette burn and my hot pink bra strap is glaring right through it. Speaking of *giveaway details*. I put my face in my hands and groan. Did they notice? Is Dr. Lawrence going to fire me when they leave? Is that why he sent me out? *Damn it, Micah,* flicking ash around while he tells me whatever outrageous thing his latest boyfriend has done.

"Do you have a jacket I could borrow?" I ask Kendra desperately. "A sweater? Anything?"

Kendra shakes her head. "I've got nothing but what I'm wearing. Didn't you look in a mirror this morning? You don't turn up to work with these people looking like a walking thrift store, Ree. Neat and tidy is a bare minimum."

I ignore her judgy look. It wasn't my fault I was

running late. Mom's car is still outside the grocery store where it broke down last week, and I had to take the resort shuttle bus to get here. And the thing about being on a temporary contract is they don't give you regular hours. They just text when they have work for you. *Please report to the office immediately.* Whoever gets there first gets the interview. I screeched in here about thirty seconds before Samira and Katie.

And that's all the warning you get. Doesn't matter if it's eight a.m. on a Sunday morning and you're hungover, none of your laundry is done, your car is a wreck, and it rained all night through a hole in your roof, right into your fucking closet. Never mind *neat and tidy*, it's a miracle I'm even here.

"Don't look at me like that, Kendra. I have had the *worst* morning."

"And that's relevant because . . . ?" She's right. Exactly none of that will fly with Dr. Lawrence.

"What about scrubs? There must be plenty of those around."

Kendra blinks at me. "Yeah, that wouldn't look at all weird. Maybe I should just call another Juliet." She taps a button on her headset. "I think Samira is still around."

"No! Wait, please." I look around in desperation. And then spot something. On her desk is a box of yellow charity ribbons. Foundation for this or Awareness of that, I don't notice, I just grab one.

"You're supposed to donate something, Ree," she complains.

"Kendra, I don't have time. Or cash," I tell her as I fumble with the ribbon pin. "And if one more thing goes wrong this morning, I am going to go fucking postal, so how about we just let this one go, OK? Countless lives will be saved." I get it attached, neatly covering the hole, and exhale.

"There!" I tell Kendra's disapproving lips as I lift the tea tray. "Now I look neat, tidy, *and* charitable."

Dr. Lawrence pours more tea as I settle back into my chair, sitting a little straighter, smiling a little brighter. Mrs. Daly is pale but composed, and Mr. Daly kisses the top of her head and says, "Everyone told us this is where you come to make nice memories before . . . And we wanted to give him a break from all the emotion at home."

"At stressful times we all need distractions," Dr. Lawrence sympathizes. "Which is really what this service excels at. Love is actually the least of it. Of course he'll see the counselors, but a new friend his own age could be an important emotional outlet for him. Someone who's not so involved. Our own friends and family can't give us that, much as they'd like to. They're too distressed, they're not trained to listen or say the right things, and we worry about upsetting them. A Juliet offers not only a fun distraction but a source of comfort. And Regan is one of our best, highly trained and experienced; you couldn't be in better hands."

I resist the urge to check the ribbon on my chest as the Dalys turn to examine me with naked suspicion. I don't take it personally. When you need a service like this, it's only natural to resent everyone involved.

Mrs. Daly nods politely at me. "It's just that Jude is so . . ." She and her husband share an unreadable glance. "He's such an *honest* person," she eventually goes with. "He's never had a serious relationship, and of course I'd love that for him, but if it's not *real* . . ." She winces apologetically, and I feel my posture sag. Maybe they're two of the few people *real* has worked out for. Of course they want that for their son. There just isn't time.

"I'm sure some people find it very helpful," she says, but when she sets down her teacup, the gesture has finality in it, a *no* hanging in the air like the scent of jasmine tea. Dr. Lawrence leans back from his desk, Mrs. Daly picks up her purse, and Mr. Daly glances at the door. It's over. They're going to leave and I'm going to go home, wring out my damp clothes, and try to figure out how to get our car repaired and our roof fixed and our bills paid.

"Mrs. Daly?" I blurt the words without thinking, before they can even stand up, and everything pauses as they all turn toward me. I swallow, shift in my chair, and wonder what the hell I'm about to say. "Look, I totally get it. You're right; it's not real." I ignore Dr. Lawrence's warning glance and continue. "Not in the sense *you* mean." Her expression doesn't change, but she's listening. "But to be honest, I don't spend my summers doing this just to earn money. I do it because I enjoy it."

She frowns and I hurry on. "I don't mean . . . I know

that sounds strange, but . . . what I mean is . . . I enjoy their company, they enjoy mine. We have fun. We hang out. We laugh; we talk. And I'm not a psychologist or a scientist, but I *am* a teenage girl and I think . . . from what *I've* seen of first love?" I shrug. "That's real."

In the silence that follows, Mr. Daly's face relaxes a fraction, Mrs. Daly smiles a thoughtful smile at me, and Dr. Lawrence reaches discreetly for the paperwork.

"Nice work, Regan," Dr. Lawrence says when the Dalys have been shown out. "That was . . . charming."

I bob a little curtsy on my way to the untouched platter of cupcakes on the coffee table—dainty confections topped with gold leaf and spun sugar. I have my flaws, but wasting good frosting is not one of them.

"I didn't know you were such a romantic," he says as he looks through the signed contract and nondisclosure agreements on his desk. Everyone who comes in here has to sign the nondisclosure stuff before Dr. Lawrence even explains what the service is. Whether they hire us or not, they're legally obliged to not tell anyone about us. The staff signs them, too. We'd go out of business pretty fast if people knew we existed. Every client has to believe it's all for real.

I gather more cupcakes into a napkin for Micah. "Me? *You're* the one slicing up people's brains searching for love."

"Well, don't you believe it's in there somewhere?"

I shrug, weighing it up. "I'm not saying it's not a real

feeling. But so is thirst. So is hunger. You go eat a cupcake and then you don't feel it anymore." I take a large bite of mine. "I mean, you'd *like* it to last, sure," I mumble through the crumbs. "You'd *like* to eat a second cupcake and be as hungry for it as you were for the first, but it doesn't work that way."

He laughs. "You should write a paper on that. 'If Frosting Be the Food of Love' by Dr. Regan Blythe."

I swallow and grin at him. "My point is, it's short-lived. Like hunger. You can satisfy it or you can die of it, but either way . . ." I make a poof-it's-gone motion with my frosting-sticky fingers.

Dr. Lawrence lifts his head from the papers. "You *die* of it? Interesting choice of phrase, considering. Can you really die of love, Regan? *Would* you?"

I smile sweetly at him. "Only professionally."

"Speaking of which"—he laces his fingers again and peers at me over the top of them—"what do you think about this job?"

"What do you mean?"

"Think you can handle it?"

"Oh. Sure."

"Yes but *really*, Regan," he presses. "These are important clients. Of course all our clients are important. But, to be honest? Not all of them own a string of Caribbean islands. And their own research institute. And a Van Gogh that they just donated to the Met. I'm not taking any risks with this one. If you have doubts, say so now and I'll find someone else."

"Have I ever let you down?" I say, despite the flutter in my gut. A *Van Gogh*?

"Good. Because we're considering you for a permanent contract."

"Are you serious?" The cupcake stalls halfway to my mouth. R&J doesn't hire that many people permanently, because the older you get, the fewer jobs there are. Star-crossed love is really a young person's game. Anyone over the age of twenty-three probably already has a partner when they come here. Or they've been in love already and realized it's not like in the movies. But a permanent contract would mean a regular salary, and I'd be top of the list for new clients.

"Well, you're creative, versatile, you're good at making people like you, as you've proved today. And you're done with school now, right? Did you get your diploma?"

I swallow. "Uh, yeah. I mean, my grades weren't really—"

He waves a hand. "Let's see how you do with Jude Daly and then we'll talk."

"Wow, OK, great!" I straighten my face and try to sound professional. "I mean, thank you. I won't let you down, Dr. Lawrence."

He pushes the Daly contract across the desk for me to sign. "I hope not."

I take the silver pen and add my name to a document full of legal-speak and clauses. They go through it all in training, but no one really pays attention. Most of it is to protect the families, not us. I think there's even some sort of prenup in there, to dissuade anyone from eloping. I guess the parents don't want a fake widow inheriting the real millions.

"Hey, what about Micah?" I ask, handing back the pen and scooping up my bundle of cupcakes. "Is he getting a permanent contract?"

"I can't discuss other members of staff, Regan."

"It's *Micah*."

"Still. You can pick up your hotel details from Kendra on the way out."

"Meadowview?"

He allows himself a grin. "Lakeside."

I almost drop my napkin bundle. "*Lakeside?* Seriously?"

He winks. "A *string* of Caribbean islands."

I laugh, and I'm about to dance out of the office, hangover forgotten, when he says, "Remember to get your clearance from Dr. Burgess before you go."

Aaaaand the bubble bursts, short-lived as a frosted cupcake.

Chapter 2

Still no reply. In the corridor outside Dr. Burgess's office, I text him again, leaning over the balcony to watch the clinic reception area four floors below where families are being checked in or taken on tours. The building is arranged around a huge open atrium in the center, the corridors of each floor circling it. There's a lot of polished steel and glass, but the floors have thick carpets, and the place inspires you to speak in hushed, respectful tones, so it's somehow always quiet.

I pace the corridor, waiting impatiently for Dr. Burgess and wishing I could skip this part, but her sign-off is non-negotiable.

A family on their clinic tour approaches, and I move aside for them. Two parents, two teenage boys scrolling on phones, a little girl in a Cinderella dress, and a grandfather wheeling a portable oxygen tank with googly eyes stuck on it.

"Each suite contains two rooms," the nurse is telling them. I can almost hear the starch in her pale blue uniform. "A family room with sofas, refreshments, et cetera, and a procedure room with a large bed, space for everyone to gather around, and views over the mountains." The grandfather sucks hard on his oxygen mask, and they pause to let him get his breath back. "The suite is yours for the day so you can do things at your own pace. You can also control the temperature, lighting, and sound system. Some people bring favorite photos or blankets or flowers from their garden, to make it feel like home."

"Can we bring our own nurse?" the mother asks. She's wearing huge sunglasses indoors, clutching a Prada purse like a shield. "They said we could bring our own nurse. I can't do this without Sheryl." Her voice is shrill compared to the nurse's soothing one.

People are always nervous about seeing the procedure suites. But there are definitely worse ways to go. The people who come here with painful terminal illnesses, weeks or months before their Death Date, are grateful there's such a gentle and dignified way out. If I ever get that sick, it's what I'd want.

"You can bring anything and anyone," the nurse is

saying. "We had one family who brought their pet horse! Animals can be very soothing."

The boys snicker at something on their phones as they move on, and the mom says, "Did you get my directions about bedsheets? The violinist will be arriving at two. I want all the staff to wear the perfume I designed. And I'm allergic to dust, kiwis, and purple so—"

"I'm sorry?" Even the nurse, who I guarantee has seen *everything*, is taken aback by this. "Purple? As in . . . the color?"

"Yes!" The woman throws her hands up like this should be simple enough to understand. "Also anything lavender scented. The last thing I need is . . ."

Wow. They've moved on down the corridor, the nurse assuring them that everything will be to their specifications. I guess you have to make allowances—they're about to lose their grandpa—but I'm glad I'm not a nurse here.

I lift my phone again.

REGAN: Micah, I swear to God, I know you're reading this, I can see the ticks

REGAN: I'm not going away

Still no sign of Burgess. I think she makes me wait on purpose because she knows it gets me edgy and then I talk too much.

Cinderella is trailing listlessly behind her family and she stops to stare at me as she passes, chewing the ribboned end of her wand like the world's saddest princess. She's too young to understand what this place is, but kids know when their parents are upset.

"Cinderella is my favorite, too," I tell her. She doesn't reply so I produce a cupcake from my bundle and hold it out, but she's too shy to take it. I shrug and take a big bite, making sure to leave a huge gob of frosting on my nose. Her lip twitches and I'm like *What? What?* looking behind me like *What's funny?* She giggles and points to her nose. I go cross-eyed, trying to lick the frosting off, and she cracks up. Her mom calls her as the group disappears around the corner. She dashes after them, ribbons flying, as I wipe my face.

My phone pings. Finally.

> MICAH: It is with deepest regret we must announce that Micah is no longer with us
>
> REGAN: Get out of bed, Micah
>
> MICAH: Donations of Advil will be accepted in lieu of flowers
>
> REGAN: Get down here now
>
> MICAH: The family has requested privacy at this time and kindly ask that you fuck off

I grin, tapping in the words, *I got Lakeside.*

The phone rings instantly and I answer, saying nothing, as Micah's laughter explodes in my ear. "*Fuck* off!"

I laugh, too. "Fourth floor, baby. And a *big* expense account."

"I hate you."

"Full R and J." I lower my voice and glance around, but the corridor is empty now, and the people in reception are far below.

"What's he like?"

"Haven't met him yet. But the parents seem OK."

"Good-looking?"

"Don't know. Don't care. It's a job. I can bat my eye-lashes at anyone for a week. Listen, you should get down here and see if they've got something for you. I'll wait. I have to see Burgess anyway."

He hesitates. "Ugh. I can't deal with Burgess right now."

I wince. "Me neither. What does Dante put in those cocktails?"

"I think it was the tequila that did the damage." I hear Micah tilt the phone away and yell, "All *right*, I'm *up*!" Then he's back. "Elena. Gotta go. Inferno tonight?"

"Can't. Immediate start. I have to move today."

Dr. Burgess pokes her head out to tell me to come in, and I say, "I'm coming home to pack; meet me there," before hanging up.

Dr. Burgess's office is nothing like Dr. Lawrence's. There's a lot of metal and glass and the furniture is minimal. Micah calls it there's-nowhere-to-hide chic.

Today she's wearing a plain gray pantsuit, hair scraped back as always. Her desk is clear except for a stack of folders. She makes me wait some more while she scans one of them. I force my jiggling leg to stay still in the uncomfortable chair across from her. She'd read way too much into jiggling.

"Can we make this quick?" I ask. "I have kind of a busy day so . . ."

She looks at me over the rims of her glasses. "I could say *no*. That would be super quick."

I sit back in the chair.

"So. New client. Jude Daly. Eighteen," she reads from the paperwork. "Full R-and-J package?"

"If he seems into it. I don't think they're on a budget or anything."

"And how do you feel about it?"

"Great! Looking forward to it." I take the smile down a notch. "I mean, they seem like nice people."

"Sometimes that can be harder," she says.

God, I hate shrinks. But I don't have a choice. I'm supposed to come here every week to talk about *the emotional impact of interpersonal relationships with clients of near terminal status*, as Dr. B would say. Or *hanging out with Dead Boys*, as I would. Though not to her face.

I dial the smile up again. "No, I feel very positive about it. I have a lot of positive emotions. I think helping them will be uplifting and . . . positive. I mean, I always learn a lot about my own emotions, my feelings; I relish the opportunity to get in touch with my inner . . . emotions . . ."

Dr. Burgess looks at me and straight through my bullshit. I roll my eyes.

"Come on, Burge, you know I can handle it; I always do. I keep the journals, I do the reflective exercises, I'm like a psychological *athlete*."

She continues to stare over the rims of her glasses and I give up. I've never yet made her laugh.

"Look, can you just sign the papers? I have to pack some stuff from home before I relocate."

She just says, "How's your mom?"

I shrug casually. "She's good. Fine. Why do you ask?" *Breezy.*

"I heard she was . . . no longer working for Dante Colucci."

"She wanted a change. Who wants to work in a bar at three a.m., right?" *Upbeat.*

"You know you can talk about anything in our sessions, not just work."

"And I appreciate that, thank you." *Open and non-defensive.*

Burgess sighs.

"Hey, is Micah getting a contract?" I ask. "He finished his last job a couple of weeks ago. Don't you have anything for him?"

"Not at present." But she glances at the stack of folders on her desk as she says it.

"What about those?" I nod at them. "I can get him down here right now if you have something."

"Perhaps in a few weeks. I'll discuss that with Micah myself."

"A few *weeks*?"

"How *is* Micah?" she says. For someone who demands you answer her questions, she excels at dodging mine.

"What do you mean, how is he? Aren't you supposed to be the one who knows how we all are?"

"I know you well enough to know that you need the

money and you tell me what you think I want to hear," she says.

"You give us actual training in how to bullshit people. You can't complain if we're good at it."

She hitches one eyebrow. "Did Dr. Lawrence tell you he's considering offering you a permanent contract?"

"Yep! Excited about that, too."

The second eyebrow joins the first. "Are you?"

"Of course. It's a hell of a lot better than waiting tables."

"It's a hell of a lot better *paid*. And that's not what I asked. I want you to think carefully about your options, Regan. Your future. You're young, this is the time to be ambitious."

I bristle at that. "I *am* thinking about my future. You think I want to live in Staff Town forever? If I get a permanent contract, I'll be staying in the resort full-time. Living like an actual billionaire. How would *you* define *ambitious*? Most kids my age are flipping burgers."

"Or in college."

"Why would I waste time studying or climbing some boring corporate ladder when I can go straight to the top rung right now?"

"It may seem boring, but long term—"

I hold up a hand. "Believe me, Dr. Burgess, if you learn one thing doing this job, it's that life's too short for long term. Or being bored. And by the way, *that's* why my clients like me. I have a good time and I make sure they have a good time, too. That's my job and I'm good at it."

"Well, it's part of your job. The other part is to help them face dying young. Which can bring up difficult feelings. And it's hard for me to assess how you're doing when you won't let me in."

I unconsciously cross my arms, irritated, then consciously uncross them. Shrinks are always so determined to find some deep, dark trauma. They're supposed to listen to you, and then they totally ignore you when you tell them you're fine.

"There *is* no 'in.' I'm sure it's hard for some people, but I'm just not one of them," I reassure her.

"Nevertheless, you've had a lot of clients. Perhaps you could do with a break."

"What?" My face falls. "No, you can't do that. The Dalys already signed up. Do *you* want to be the one to tell the Dalys there's been a change of plan? Do you know who the Dalys are? Daly Vodka? The Death Date Dalys?"

She looks unimpressed. "I'll do whatever I need to do to look after the psychological well-being of our employees. That's *my* job. I can and will pull you out of any contract at any time."

I fold my arms again and attempt to stare her down. "Well, *I'm* a professional, too. The Dalys liked me and I don't want to disappoint them."

She wins the stare-down. If I photographed her, her stare would probably break the lens.

"Please, Dr. B? Honestly, I'm fine. Better than fine. I love this job."

"You do?" She tilts her head, interested.

"Why wouldn't I? Making people happy is pretty rewarding."

"You don't find spending time with someone who doesn't have long to live difficult? Your last job was tough."

I scoff. "It wasn't even a real R and J—she only wanted a friend to go bungee jumping with and paint her nails at sleepovers."

"*Chloe*," Dr. Burgess says, like she's pointedly introducing the name.

"Chloe," I repeat, meeting the challenge.

She waits. And waits some more. The waiting is the worst. She has a PhD in it.

I throw my hands up. "Ugh. Look, it's sad, yes. I do get that, obviously; I'm not a robot. It's sad that they're young, but young people die every day, and to be honest, I've kind of gotten used to it."

It's true. This place is full of them. You'd think a resort for end-of-life procedures would be dominated by an older clientele, and sure, there are plenty of people who come because they have some horrible illness. But most old people actually die of natural causes in the hospital, or at home, heavily medicated. They don't need the clinic.

But say you're *not* old. Say you're young and in perfect health and your Date is a couple of weeks away. You can't assume you're going to drift off in your sleep or have a quick and painless heart attack. For young people, the leading causes of death are things like car wrecks, drug overdoses, homicide, drowning, and other random, nasty accidents. Who'd stick around for that when you could come here, have the vacation of a lifetime, make beautiful memories, and then have your family gather around your bedside to say a proper goodbye? Beats bleeding out on your way to the ER, and your relatives getting a call to say it's too late and that viewing the body maybe isn't a good idea. It's not nice to have to organize your own death, but given those alternatives, coming here is a no-brainer.

If you can afford it, that is. When my grandparents or my mom dies, it'll probably be in some grimy retirement home that smells of soup, or a basic end-of-life clinic with a fake-leather recliner and a fluorescent strip light, and *dignity* won't be on the menu, never mind champagne breakfasts. So, no, I'm not going to get all weepy over someone having a perfectly nice death.

"And the romance?" Dr. B is saying. "*True love*, no less. I'm sure that can be intense."

"Not really. It's pretty easy."

"Is it?"

"Sure. Haven't you ever read a romance novel? Or seen a romantic movie? Didn't your mom read you fairy tales?" I smile as I remember Cinderella in the corridor.

Dr. Burgess blinks at me. I guess she was never eight years old. "My mom used to love fairy tales," I tell her. "The princess ones. The same movies over and over. I never really understood why she liked them so much. But I do now. It's because they're *fun*. Falling in love is *fun*. The start of a relationship is the best part. It's . . ." I search for a way to describe the adrenaline, the tension, the obsession, the whole heady, flirty, fluffy, dizzy mess. I grin. "It's the first bite of the cupcake."

She glances at the napkin bundle I've left on the side table, confused.

"Never mind. The point is everyone loves the falling-in-love part. But most people only get to *read* about it or watch it on TV. *I* get to do it for real. Over and over. And if most people were honest, they'd jump at the chance, too."

She studies me for a few moments, then sighs again and says, "You set for birth control?"

"Dr. Burgess!" I feign shock, and then primly quote the brochure at her. "'The Romeo-and-Juliet Experience is an elite service providing meaningful end-of-life companionship and emotional and spiritual connection with a skilled professional. We politely remind clients that physical relationships are strictly off the table.' Didn't you write that?"

"I did. I also live in the real world."

"Well, don't worry, I definitely consider *that* to be a scene from a disappointing sequel to the fairy tale. From what I've heard."

Her lip curls a fraction, which is as much as you ever get from Dr. Burgess.

"Can I go?"

She grimaces and shuts the file. "Fine. Clearance approved."

The "briefing" email is in my inbox already as I wait for the elevator, impatient to get home and pack. This is the best part. When it's all about to begin. Already there's a buzz of anticipation humming like a generator beneath my skin. I hug my cupcake bundle to my chest so I can open the document on my phone.

In theory this tells me everything I need to know about my new client—background, hobbies, favorite movies/foods/music, information from the family, plus anything Kendra could pull from the internet that I might be able to use to bond with him. In practice, I usually find that the things you *really* need to know about a person aren't on the internet, but the brief is useful for the basics. And, most important, it'll have photos. Sometimes you can learn a lot just from those—the expression, the posture, the clothes. I scroll quickly as I step into the elevator, skimming the text, stopping as I reach a photo of my new client.

He's tall with chestnut-brown hair, a square jaw, long limbs, and good skin. His mouth is a wide, straight line and there's a deep crease between the eyebrows as he frowns off at a point beyond the camera, as if he'd like to be somewhere else. He looks familiar, but if his family is that rich, I've probably just seen him online somewhere. Or maybe it's that he resembles his parents so much. He's got his dad's build and his mom's angles—her cheek-bones, his jaw, only a slight bump to the bridge of his nose ruining the symmetry. The eyes are his own, though, so dark brown you almost can't see the pupils.

It's one of those faces you can't take a bad photo of, but he's not giving a lot away, and I find myself lingering on the eyes, noticing the warmth of the color, the coolness of the gaze.

Of course, what my clients look like is irrelevant, but I'm only human; I appreciate a cute guy as much as the next girl, and I admit to being distracted as I hurry out of the elevator, still studying my phone screen, completely oblivious to the figure stepping in.

"Watch where—"

Too late. We meet in a head-on collision of my cupcake bundle with his hot coffee, and the unholy mess of cappuccino foam and frosting splatters all over his plain navy sweater while I watch my phone hit the marble floor with a sickening crack. Everyone in the foyer turns to stare at us, and there's half a second of stunned silence before I dive for my phone where it rests facedown in a pool of coffee, already lambasting him with "What the actual fuck! Are you *blind*? My phone!"

"Am *I* blind?" The furious voice comes from above me as I crouch on the floor examining the smashed screen. "If I *was*, I couldn't have done a better job!"

A glob of wet frosting detaches itself from his sweater and lands in my hair.

"Ugh!" I scramble to brush it out but only smear it all over. I look up, opening my mouth to really let him have it.

Except . . . I'm staring up at dark brown eyes, a square jaw, chestnut hair, and a frown line that's rapidly going from annoyed crease to furious furrow above the bump in his nose.

Fuckfuckfuckfuck*fuuuuuck*!

Jude Daly is towering over me, staring incredulously down at his sweater as if he's not sure where to start. "I realize nothing is more important than the latest bloody TikTok video," he snaps, his English accent clipped, nasal. "But if you can't look at your phone without being a walking liability, maybe it's a good thing it's broken."

"I wasn't on—" My brain switches back on as I remember what I *was* looking at, and I swallow, grateful it landed facedown. That was *way* too close for comfort. Flustered, I stuff the wet phone in my purse and fuss with retrieving his paper cup and mopping up a lake of spilled coffee with a single thin tissue.

"I was . . . I didn't see you, I . . ." I ramble as the receptionist hurries over. I stand as she takes over, mopping around our feet with a towel, but to be honest, Jude Daly is wearing the worst of the mess, frosting smeared right into the weave of the wool.

"Who wears a sweater in June anyway?" I say, dabbing helplessly at him with my wet tissue and making it worse.

He bats me away. "Yes, *that's* the lesson we've all learned here. *Knitwear* is a public nuisance."

I cringe at him. "Sorry," I mumble finally.

He exhales and drops his arms, as if accepting there's nothing to be done. "Forget it," he mutters.

"No, really. Let me get you another coffee at least."

"I said forget it."

"But your sweater . . . I feel bad. It'll only take a minute! Please, let me—"

He holds up a hand. "Look, no offense, but if you want to even *register* on the shit-o-meter of this bloody day, you're going to have to try *much* harder. So, unless you've got a vat of ice cream you'd like to add to this cake, I think we're done here."

He turns to walk off, taking with him my chances of ever working for R&J again, but then he immediately slips on a wet patch of floor the receptionist hasn't gotten to yet and lands on his ass in another puddle of coffee.

The receptionist freezes in horror, probably envisaging being fired, sued, and arrested all at once. Jude Daly just glares up at me, teeth grinding visibly.

I stand over him, wincing. "Do I register now?" I squeak.

"You're getting there," he growls.

"The café will have napkins," I offer weakly.

He inhales deeply, then grits out, *"Fine."*

"It's just back here, right?"

Of course, I know exactly where the café is, but I follow Jude there as if I'm not sure, still stammering apologies. His expression doesn't relax any and my heart is pounding, my hungover brain racing as I try to focus. I don't usually have to switch to "Juliet mode" so abruptly, and the last thing I want to do is blurt out the wrong thing. I don't even have my backstory worked out, I haven't read the rest of his file, and I am in no way prepared for a conversation with him.

Not that he seems interested in talking. As we enter

the café, he grabs a pile of napkins from a server and heads for a table by the window, already peeling off his sweater to reveal an equally boring T-shirt underneath.

The café is at the back of the clinic, enclosed by glass, and looks out onto the woods. Sometimes deer walk right past the windows, and there are birch trees growing in huge planters between the tables, blending with the outdoors. Everything about it, from the soft classical music to the scent of baking bread, is designed to be soothing for people who are upset, stressed, grieving. I wonder if it works for "mad as hell."

I go to the counter to order, still glancing surreptitiously at him. His hair is a little longer than in the photos, fluffy on top, like he used to have a hairstyle but he's since lost interest in it. He takes a paperback book out of his back pocket and sets it on the table before sitting down to wipe the worst of the gunk off his sweater and shoes.

My attention is drawn back to the counter when my turn comes, and the server, Jodie, recognizes me and opens her mouth to greet me. But she takes in the look I give her and realizes I'm working. The other resort staff know about the R&Js. They have to so they know to treat me as a "guest" when I'm working. It's more than their jobs are worth to blow your cover. Almost every hotel, bar, or restaurant in the resort is owned by the same few people, and if you get blacklisted by one, you'll never work here again.

Jodie's smile oozes hostility as she says, "What can

I get for you today?" Two months ago, she was being crowned prom queen while Micah kissed her boyfriend in the parking lot. Now she's wearing an apron and filling coffee orders for a girl she used to be mean to in the halls. That's gotta sting.

I'm not in the mood to spar with her today, though. I need coffee so badly I might beat Jude Daly to the pearly gates. "Two cappuccinos. To go," I add. I need to get out of here as soon as possible. Go home. Regroup. Make a real plan to meet him when I'm not so flustered. I tap my new R&J credit card impatiently on the counter.

Jodie glances at the card and says, under her breath, "Paying for these yourself, Ree? You'd think he'd at least buy you a drink first."

"First?" I say, still distracted.

"Or are you giving it away for free now?" Her smile is snide as she pushes the coffees at me.

My scattered thoughts immediately snap into focus and I turn my full attention to her. "On second thought." I push the take-out cups back across the counter. "I'll have a quad-shot skinny caramel macchiato, two pumps of hazelnut, one pump of peppermint, extra hot, extra foam, extra caramel drizzle, and can I get a little heated milk on the side?"

Her lips thin while I smile like butter wouldn't melt. "Make that two. You can just bring them over. Oh, and congratulations on the new job, Jodie. I heard you applied to R and J; sorry that didn't work out." I wrinkle my nose sympathetically. "They're picky, I guess."

"You heard wrong." The lips vanish altogether. "*I* don't fake it with guys for money."

A customer comes up behind me to pay, saying, "That pie was just delicious, great recommendation!"

Jodie flashes him the full set of pearly whites. "You're welcome! Enjoy that cruise, y'hear? I wanna see the pictures!"

"You betcha!" He throws a big tip on the counter before sauntering out, and Jodie pockets it as she turns back to find me watching, amused.

She sours, cheeks flushing. "There's a world of difference between what I do and what you do," she mutters.

"You're right," I agree as I walk off. "*My* tips are bigger."

I make my way over to Jude Daly like I am completely in control of this situation. I'm completely *not*. But you can't plan these things anyway, I tell myself. And a good Juliet is always ready for the unexpected. An *excellent* Juliet can turn any situation to her advantage. This one wasn't a great start, but surely I can do something with it. After all, it's amazing how often a good meet-cute involves a mistake or a disaster of some kind. I've engineered lots of them. You can reach for the same item in a store, mistake his towel for yours at the pool, look lost on the street, or trip over his bag. I once stumbled right into the lap of a guy on the resort bus as the driver pulled away from the curb. I think he fell for me while I was still brushing pretzel crumbs off his shirt. You can't argue with something that . . . well, cute.

Just because this one wasn't planned doesn't mean I can't use it. Improvising is actually one of my skills. I was recruited for this job because Dr. Lawrence saw me in a school production of *My Fair Lady* where I forgot all my lines and ad-libbed the entire thing (in an English accent) to rapturous applause. My drama teacher wasn't impressed, but Dr. Lawrence loved it.

If I can get my head together, I can have Jude Daly eating out of my hand by the time our coffees arrive. And Jodie Clements can go polish her fucking prom queen crown with her dish towel.

When I reach his table, Jude has given up on the sweater and he's dabbing at the stain on a pair of otherwise pristine sneakers.

"I thought you were ordering coffee," he complains.

"On its way. And I ordered extra caramel drizzle, so hey, your day is looking up!"

"I doubt it," he says with a huff. Jesus, it was only a sweater. It's not like he can't afford a new one. He's in a plain gray T-shirt now, his long, pale arms a fuzz of dark hair over taut sinew. I can see the edge of his Date, an elegant black line unrolling across one bicep. He sees me notice it and folds his arms awkwardly. Ah. That explains the sweater in June, then. Some people would rather show you their bank statements or their journal than their Date.

"Have you just arrived at the resort?" I ask, trying to steer the conversation into friendlier waters.

"Yes."

"Would you like something to eat?"

"No."

"Is that an English accent?"

"Yes."

Not the talkative type, then, which means I have to stop asking him yes/no questions. "What do you think of the resort?" I try.

He makes a face. "If the intention is to make you pray for death, then I guess it's a triumph."

I laugh, although I don't think he's joking. "Are you on your clinic tour?"

"I'm in a counseling session."

I glance around at the café, confused. "You are?"

"Officially. Unofficially, I left to use the bathroom half an hour ago."

"Oh. You know, you kind of *have* to go to the counseling sessions. It's, like, a legal requirement."

"I doubt it'll be a problem," he says. I guess people aren't in the habit of saying no to a Daly.

"Where are you staying?" I persist, but it's hard to keep up a chatty tone when you're getting *nothing* back. He's not even looking at me, just staring out the window, arms still folded across his chest, and I'm starting to sweat. "My mom and I chose one of the smaller hotels," I go on when he doesn't answer. "Less crowded. A little more exclusive. Lakeside, I think it's called?" If he thinks I'm not good enough for him, he's got another thing coming. I could be Hollywood royalty for all he knows.

"I've stayed in better," he says, glancing at his watch.

"Oh." The soothing track on the café's sound system

changes abruptly to Madonna's "Material Girl." Jodie's doing. I can feel her eyes on my back. I lean across the table, so it at least *looks* like this is going well, and mentally run through my R&J training—*relate with his experiences, use humor, share feelings, enthuse about his interests, empathize.*

"Well, I guess no one *wants* to be here," I say, empathetically as hell. "I admit, I've been nervous about seeing the clinic. I know it's the right choice for my"—I lower my voice a little—"*procedure.* But still, actually *being* here is kind of . . . real."

He finally looks at me, but only to frown. "Your procedure?" he says.

"Oh. Yes. It's . . . soon." *Brave but vulnerable.* He continues to watch me, as if trying to work out something complicated. *It's really not complicated,* I want to tell him. The correct response is *You too? Sucks, doesn't it? Hey, why don't we hang out sometime?* But he says nothing. OK, he's a bit of a loner; I can work with that.

"I'm looking forward to spending some quality time with my mom, though. It's been a tough year for her. How are your parents coping?" Nothing. He actually looks almost irritated now. I start to wonder if he's not just a loner but a *fuck off and leave me aloner.*

"There's so much to do in the resort, though. I'm not sure where to start. What are your plans?"

"Reading mostly." I glance at the paperback on the table. People don't come here to read. There isn't even a bookstore.

"Sounds . . . great! Nothing better than just lying on the beach with a good romance, right? What are you reading?"

"French philosophy," he says. "Camus."

Jesus, I think I preferred the yes/no answers. How do you *enthuse about his interests* when his interests are French fucking philosophy? "Wow. What's it about?" I ask weakly, out of my depth already. He couldn't have been into waterskiing?

"The absurdity of existence." He looks at his sticky sweater and makes a face. "Turns out I didn't need a book about that."

"True!" I laugh too loudly. "Well, when you've figured out existence, are you planning on doing any of the resort activities? Have you ever gone skydiving?"

After a long pause, and a stare that could only be described as *penetrating*, he says, "You ask a lot of questions."

I shift in my seat. "I do? Oh. Well. Just being friendly. Passing the time." I try to run my fingers idly through my hair, but they get stuck in a mat of frosting. "I have a counseling session myself in a few minutes, actually. I guess I'm nervous. I hate counselors, too. It's weird, right? Talking to a total stranger about my pro—"

"Your procedure, yes. You mentioned," he says, unfolding his arms and leaning forward across the table. I resist the urge to lean back. His eyes are flat brown now, cold. "And what is it you're dying of?" he says, head tilted like he's interested. "Some sort of verbal dysentery?"

"W-*what?*" I falter.

"Well, you talk *a lot*. I assumed you had some sort of unfortunate condition."

I exhale, too stunned to reply. Where did *that* come from? Is he trying to be funny and he's just really bad at it? Or is he actually that rude?

With impeccable timing, Jodie appears with two elaborate coffees on her tray, and I wonder how much she heard.

"Can I get you folks anything else?" she says with a smile that suggests it was more than I'd have liked.

Jude just looks disdainfully at his ridiculous coffee and its overdone caramel drizzle. "Actually, I have to go."

"Oh. Really?" I say.

He stands, leaving the untouched coffee on the table and lifting his book and sweater. "I'm afraid so. It's still possible this day could get worse and I don't want to miss it."

"Uh . . . yeah. That shit-o-meter could still go higher, right?" I attempt a little laugh, as if we're sharing a private joke. "Maybe we'll run into each other again!" I add, looking up at him through my lashes and giving him my most flirtatious smile.

He responds with a smile that's *almost* pleasant. "Oh, I'm sure we can avoid it if we *really* try," he says before walking away, leaving me staring after him with my mouth open.

Jodie sets the check next to my ludicrously fussy coffee and says with a shit-eating grin, "You're gonna earn that tip, Ree."

Chapter 3

MY BRAIN RACES AT A MILLION MILES A MINUTE AS I PANIC ON THE way home, making the shuttle bus's infuriating trundle around the resort feel even slower. The recorded tourist information tells us about the sailboat cruises on the lake, horseback riding on trails from Silver Pines Ranch, white water rafting on the river, *followed by a hot-air balloon back to the resort at sunset!* I could walk faster, but I've reached peak hangover now. My head thumps like the music at Inferno last night, and I have flashbacks of doing high kicks with the cheerleaders on the bar. Maybe if I take some painkillers, all this will be clearer, but I have a horrible feeling I've fucked up and I don't even under-stand how. *Did* he see something on my phone? No, I'm sure he didn't; the screen was dead. But then . . . why was he so hostile? No one is that attached to a sweater. I'm used to people in his situation being depressed, weepy, anxious, irritable even. That's why their parents hire me, to lift their mood. But this was *beyond* irritable.

I lean my head on the glass with a groan and let the dappled sunlight strobe my face as we head out of the woods and the main resort begins to glide past.

There's always been a resort here, but it wasn't always an end-of-life location. Bergman's was just a vacation resort that opened in the 1930s, one of many in the Catskills. Wealthy New Yorkers would come up to the mountains to escape the heat and spend the summer in log cabins, doing wholesome family activities and being entertained by famous singers like Frank Sinatra and Dean Martin. My grandparents met here, but they weren't guests. When my grandma was my age, she'd get sawed in half by a magician on a nightly basis and spent the rest of her time serving drinks. My grandpa was a singer with one of the bands.

But by the 1980s, air travel was cheaper and people stopped coming to places like this. Most of the resorts folded. Bergman's would have, too, but then Elite Elect swept into town with their team of doctors and developers and made Mr. Bergman an offer he couldn't refuse.

I give up my seat to an elderly woman as we pass through Old Town, where the seniors hang out, going for lake cruises and expensive lunches. Some families board the bus at the waterfront area, where sailboats and swimmers dot the lake and tanned bodies are already stretched out on the shore, waiters adjusting beach umbrellas and carrying elaborate drinks over the sand. Finally, we reach Downtown, at the southern end of the resort. No seniors here; this is where the nightclubs and hipster coffee shops are, and the people on the water are Jet Skiing and Flyboarding. My stomach growls as we pass the tall, circular spike of Inferno, its gothic iron gates firmly shut until the sun goes down.

None of it has anything to do with the clinic, really. But the resort developers knew what they were doing. The thing is, this isn't a drive-through. You don't come all this way to die or watch someone you love die, all in one day. In fact, part of the legal requirement is that you have an established relationship with the clinic doctor. And have several sessions with a counselor. Your Date has to be verified; you have to sign a euthanasia directive and a living will in the presence of lawyers. You have to express the desire to die, consistently, more than once, and that has to be witnessed by professionals. All of which takes time. And if you're going to spend your last nights on earth here, and you happen to be pretty wealthy, you're going to have *really* high expectations of your hotel room.

So it made sense to build some luxury accommodation with views over the lake. It made sense to have some restaurants. It made sense to open a spa, offer designer shopping options, develop the beach, build a jetty, do boat tours. It snowballed very quickly. Michelin-star chefs, skydiving, skiing, a bungee bridge, private helicopter flights. If you wouldn't spend the last day of your life doing it, it's not good enough for Elite Elect. Sure, you could have your procedure at a normal clinic close to home. But if you can afford it, why wouldn't you come here?

The new resort shifted about a mile north to where the beaches are better, while the original Bergman facilities were quietly abandoned. But the Bergman staff got new jobs at Elite, and they even got to move into the fancy log cabins the Bergman guests used to stay in. Mom and I have one just a couple hundred yards from the lakeshore, where vacationers used to swim and drink rum out of coconuts. I think the area with the cabins is officially called Bergman Village, but everyone who lives there just calls it Staff Town.

The bus drops me off near the entrance to the resort, where it circles back for the return journey. Two sleek black limos swish past as I turn off onto a forest trail and hurry into the shade of the trees, barely noticing my surroundings, still trying to make sense of Jude Daly. Maybe Micah can help. He's been a Romeo for as long as I've been a Juliet; he must have come across difficult clients. As I pass his cabin, I consider knocking to check if he's left yet, but his foster parents don't like me. They think I'm a bad influence. If they only knew how little influencing Micah needs. They're his third foster family in five years because no one can deal with him.

The Acostas keep their place immaculate. Elena has a vegetable garden and Luis even built an extension off the back. There's a tire swing and a jar of wildflowers on a table on the porch. The only room that's not beautifully decorated is Micah's. He won't even paint the walls because that would suggest he's staying. He and the Acostas do nothing but argue, and it's fifty-fifty who'll crack first. There's no sign of him, but the bedroom window he regularly crawls out of is open. I keep going, hoping he's at my house already.

Our cabin is *not* immaculate. Mom and I do our best, but it's astonishing how fast a coat of paint can go green beneath the shade of the trees. How fast new wood can rot in the dampness beneath the tree canopy in winter. By the time I was born, these cabins were already run-down, and no one manages the trees anymore so they've encroached on the whole area, obliterating paths and shading us out. As I run up our porch steps, I notice a bag of recycling I left outside two weeks ago, already submerged in the weeds from a few weeks of summer heat. The car is still missing, so I guess Mom didn't find anyone to tow it this morning.

These cabins were luxurious when they were built, sure, but that was decades ago, and they were never meant to be year-round accommodation. It was more important that they *looked* like luxurious mountain cabins than that they actually functioned as such—they're drafty, they're damp, they're prone to leaks and hard to heat, the verandas rot, the walls are thin. When it rains you can't hear the TV, and when it's windy they rock like ships in a storm. None of the cabins were ever meant to be a permanent place to live. And yet this is where I live. Permanently.

"Mom?" The pink tunic of Mom's uniform is still on its peg by the door, her name tag, CATH, dangling from the pocket. The living room is chilly, and a sickly green morning light exposes the peeling wallpaper and thread-bare rug, and the scratches in the coffee table made by a cat who died six years ago. It's always a downer coming back here after being in the resort. I mute the blaring TV and replace the remote on the shelf of Mom's old princess movie DVDs.

"Micah? *Mom?*"

She comes down the hall, dressed but still wearing a bathrobe on top, tugging a brush through her unruly red curls.

I glance at the clock above the TV. "You're going to be late for work."

"I'll make it," she says, giving up on the hair and tying it back with an elastic.

"Is Micah here?"

She shakes her head. "Haven't seen him. Did you get the job?"

"Uh, yeah." No point telling her I might have gotten it and blown it all in one morning.

She doesn't congratulate me. Instead her face does that pinched thing. *I don't approve, but I can't really say anything because we need the money.*

"It's fine, don't worry," I say, preempting the lecture as I head to the kitchen for some breakfast.

"Someone has to," she mutters, picking up the pile of clothes I frantically tossed out of the laundry basket this morning. I could say *someone has to* about bringing in a regular paycheck, but I don't.

There's only cereal dust at the bottom of the box, and

I curse Jude Daly for ruining my cupcakes. "I thought you went to the store. You said the car broke down there."

There's a fractional hesitation before she says, "Well, I couldn't carry the bags home, could I?" She doesn't look at me, just grabs a cookie as she searches for her shoes.

"Mom. That was the last of my paycheck; I don't get paid for this job till the end of the—"

"Ree, it's fine," she snaps. Then, more gently, "I'll figure it out. Don't worry. Anyway, you won't even be here."

"Exactly. Just . . . make sure you eat while I'm gone."

"I know, I know."

"And don't lose your keys."

"I won't."

"And don't be late for work."

"I *won't*. Jesus. Where are you staying this time?" she asks, heading back to the living room and peeling off her bathrobe.

I wince and tell her, reluctantly, "Lakeside."

She barks an unamused laugh as she pulls on her Lakeside maid's tunic. "Figures," she says. "So I get to pick up after you this week, too! I am *not* calling you ma'am."

I jab a finger at the clock. "Five more minutes and you won't have to."

"I'm *going.*" She steps into her ugly Lakeside shoes, then turns to the mirror by the door and mutters, *"God."* I'm a head taller than her, and, apart from my green eyes, my face is nothing like hers in the glass. I have no idea where my features came from.

"Hey, is it true that Lakeside sends their concierges on

a course to learn how to tame wild horses?" I ask, dipping a finger into the sugary dust at the bottom of the cereal box.

"Yep." She grimaces as she dabs on some blush. "It's supposed to teach them to empathize with difficult guests or some shit."

"Wow. How about they send the guests on a course to teach them how to, y'know, *not behave like animals*?"

"I'll suggest that." She fishes a lipstick out of her pocket. "You know, you don't have to do this job," she says. "I'm working now and I'll . . . it'll be fine this time."

I turn away to sit on the couch and start emptying the contents of my purse onto the coffee table. I won't need most of it this week. "Mom, every girl in school wanted this job. What do you want me to do instead, wait tables?"

"Well, if you'd worked harder in school," she mutters.

"If I'd worked harder in school, I could tell the customers about my GPA while I pour their coffee."

"You gotta have reasonable expectations, Ree. People work their way up. Elena Acosta started out washing hair in the salon, and now she practically runs that place. She'd hire you, that's always an option," she says, searching through her own bag for her keys.

"So is a slow death," I mutter. "Anyway, I *am* working my way up. Dr. Lawrence said they might give me a permanent contract." I grin triumphantly at her.

"Ree!" She abandons the keys and stares at me. "I don't know, honey, a vacation job is one thing, but I don't think that's a good idea."

"Are you kidding? A regular salary isn't a good idea? Health care? *And* big tips? We can fix the leak in the roof. Get a better car, maybe. We could do another road trip to Florida, see Grandma."

"I know, but it's just . . ." She comes to sit on the arm of the couch beside me. I glance at the clock. She was lucky to get the job at Lakeside, and the guests may be allowed to behave however they like, but they don't take any shit from the employees.

"I worry about . . . I mean, those resort boys . . ." She gives me a look that's almost pitying. "They won't take you seriously, honey."

I tut and stand up, irritated suddenly. "Jesus, who wants to be taken seriously?" I mutter, sweeping my things back into my bag. "It's not like I'm angling for a husband here; this isn't Jane fucking Austen."

"Just don't get involved with—"

"I never get involved with them. *I'm* not that stupid."

It's a low blow, but she just takes a breath, stands, and walks to the door.

"Mom, I—"

She waves over her shoulder. "I've gotta go, honey. I'll be late." She doesn't look back as the screen door slams behind her.

Annoyed at myself, at her, I stomp back to the kitchen. I know I shouldn't have snapped. But it's true—I'm *not* that stupid. *I'm* not the idiot hooked on fairy tales. I've seen enough of those princess movies to realize that, yeah, the falling-in-love part is fun, but after the couple finally kisses, the movie always ends. Because after that, every-thing goes south. No one wants to see the part where the prince gets her pregnant, ditches her for a princess in the next kingdom, and she starts drinking in the afternoons. No one wants the second bite of *that* particular cupcake.

I toss out the empty cereal box, knowing what I'll find in the trash can before I even open it. An empty wine bottle and the usual quart of vodka. *Daly* vodka. Guess I know where the grocery money went. I push it deeper into the bag, toss the box on top, and slam the lid, won-dering how much of that string of Caribbean islands Mom has paid for so that Jude Daly can swan around being an asshole to total strangers.

My room is the way I left it this morning—bed unmade, curtains closed, last night's outfit on the floor. But with a new smell of damp coming from my closet and a wet stain on the carpet. At least it's stopped raining through the ceiling. On the desk there's a mess of makeup, which I push aside so I can pack my bag on the cleared sur-face. The only neat thing in the room is the shelf above the desk, where there's a row of high-end magazines like *Vogue* and *Zeitgeist*, the ones with the best photography, and then my Lakeside brochures, arranged chronologi-cally. Lakeside publishes a new brochure every season, and I've been collecting them since I was six. Thick and glossy, like a catalog to choose a perfect life from—the executive suites, the private lodges, ice sculptures at the summer parties, fire dancers at the winter gala, the spa treatments, celebrity chefs, the helipad, the Bentleys, the private yachts.

Mostly I collect them for the pictures of the Midsummer Ball. Last year they had my favorite photographer from *Zeitgeist*, Yvette Scholes, take the photos. I love red carpet fashion; I can name the designer of every important award-show dress from the past five years, but red carpets have nothing on Lakeside. The women take it as a personal challenge to outdo one another.

I've never been to the ball, of course; the tickets are wildly expensive. Dr. Lawrence would never spring for that, but it's this week and maybe I can hang around the lobby and see the gowns in person. Maybe even take some Yvette Scholes–inspired photos.

I turn the radio on, throw the curtains open, and almost jump out of my skin when the tangled lump of sheets and blankets on the bed shifts and groans.

"Fuck! Micah! How long have you been there?" I close the window Micah has obviously crawled through as a dark, tousled head emerges from the blankets and blinks deep blue eyes at me. "You know, these cabins have doors," I tell him.

Micah Lowry is eighteen, very beautiful, and *very* hungover. "Ree, can you turn the light off?" he whimpers.

"It's daylight, Micah. It doesn't have an off switch. And no, I have to pack."

I start stuffing a few things into my bag. I won't need much, just clothes for coming home.

"Why are you all"—Micah flaps a hand at me—"intense?"

I let my shoulders drop. "Sorry. Mom."

"Ugh. Luis threw out my cigarettes. You got any?"

"You're not smoking in my bed."

"Like you even need a bed. I hate you, by the way. You're dead to me."

I grin. "A whole week at Lakeside." I relish the words. "And the ball is this week. I'll be able to spy on them and play designer bingo. I'm predicting a lot of Versace."

"Go ahead, rub it in."

I make a face. "If I haven't struck out already, that is."

"What do you mean?"

"I mean, I think I fucked up." I turn to face him, leaning on the desk and chewing my lip. "I ran into him at the clinic. My new client. Literally, I walked straight into him and spilled his coffee."

Micah's eyes widen. "Oh shit, what did you do?"

"Nothing! I mean, apart from ruining his clothes, I don't think I did anything wrong. I didn't give anything away. I think. But I don't know. He was just, kind of . . . off."

"Off?"

"I mean, I guess it wasn't a great day for him; he was on his clinic tour. It's understandable he was irritable. But he wasn't just rude, he was . . . well, he didn't seem to like me. Like, *at all*." I try to make that sound like a professional problem and not the personally wounding insult I suspect it might be. I mean, what's wrong with him? Apart from the coffee-frosting debacle, I was fucking charming!

"He's gay," Micah says flatly.

"His parents don't seem to think so."

"Yeah, and they always know."

I cross my arms and chew my thumb. "What do *you* do if a guy just isn't into you?"

He looks blankly back at me. "That's never happened to me."

"Oh, go fuck yourself." I throw a hairbrush at his head and he dives back under the blankets, laughing.

I flop down on the bed and he peeks an eye out.

"If he's that bad, just tell Dr. Lawrence you want out," he says. "They'll give you someone easier."

My grin fades. In theory, if you get someone difficult or someone who makes you really uncomfortable, you can bail. The parents get a refund, it's no problem. In *practice*, if that happens too often, they start looking at you like *you're* the one being difficult, and pretty soon you stop getting new clients.

I shake my head. "I'm supposed to be impressing Lawrence."

"Why?"

"He said if this one goes well, they'll give me a contract. A permanent job."

His whole head emerges. "Seriously?"

"Seriously. You need to get down there. Burgess has work on her desk; I don't know why she hasn't called you already. Did you piss her off?"

"No," he says, but he sounds cagey. "Why, what did she say?"

"Nothing. But whatever you did, just apologize. Micah, if we can *both* get permanent contracts . . ." I squeeze his knees under the blankets. "We could be living in the resort full-time! Hotel after hotel. Expense accounts, wardrobes, every night at Inferno, every day on the beach. We could be living like—"

"Like today is our last!" Micah completes the quote this entire resort is founded on, throwing his arms out melodramatically, and we both laugh.

His laughter fades and he says, "Ugh. I am *not* in the mood to be brain-groped by Burgess right now. The woman has no boundaries." He dives beneath the blankets again.

"Phillipe?" I ask.

The blanket nods.

"Shit, I'm sorry, Micah. I forgot. When did he . . . ?" I wince sympathetically.

"This morning," he whispers.

I kick my shoes off and climb into bed beside him. He cuddles into my shoulder and I stroke his dark curls. In my best Dr. Lawrence voice, I say gently, "Grief is natural at times of loss, Micah. We need to mourn. Remember, Phillipe has gone to a better place." There's a beat as he raises a tear-stained face to look at me. "Paris," I finish flatly.

He snorts a laugh that's half sob.

"This is the trouble with foreign guys," I tell him. "They have this tendency to fuck off back to their foreign countries."

He sniffs and nods. "It's très inconsiderate."

"Hey, you learned some French!" I squeeze him. "Wasn't a total waste, then."

"Non."

"You shouldn't get so attached, mon ami. You know everyone here is just passing through, one way or another." I plant a kiss on his forehead. "I've gotta go pack." Micah's boy-hangovers are shorter lived than his tequila ones; he'll be fine.

He pushes me out of bed. "Fine, abandon me for your fancy hotel room. Heartless wench."

"Suite," I correct him.

"Kill me."

"You could be coming with me if you'd just get your ass out of bed and go see Dr. Burgess." I throw a pillow at his face and start pulling clothes out of my closet, item after damp item, dumping them on the floor. Some are obviously ruined, streaked with filthy water. It's not like my clothes are resort-worthy, but I do spend a chunk of my paycheck on secondhand designer stuff, and it's not easy to replace. The only thing I don't spend money on is shoes. I've lost too many pairs at Inferno.

"Maybe he was just having an off morning." Micah sighs, pushing the pillow off. "Or he's just a jerk. Who is he anyway?"

"Jude Daly," I tell him. "Eighteen. Parents own half the Caribbean or something. Daly as in the vodka. You'll have to google him; I can't even read the brief until I get another phone. *Thank you, Jude.*" I show him my smashed screen and he winces.

Micah googles for a moment. "Thomas and Julia Daly. London, England. It says his alcohol fortune funds her research institute. What are they researching?"

"Death Dates, I think."

"Ooh, I've heard of these guys!" He scrolls excitedly. "They're trying to find out how to survive your— Oh." He winces again and lowers the phone. "I guess we know why now."

"And we know it didn't work. Big surprise." I remember Dr. Lawrence talking about their "interest in science." I'm not sure I'd call it "science." How dumb do you have to be, how *arrogant*, to think you can take on *death*? And to waste billions of dollars doing it?

The only way you can change your Date is to preempt it. Checking out early is always a possibility. If it wasn't, the clinic drugs wouldn't work. You can always do something stupid like step in front of a bus. Your Date doesn't necessarily tell you when you're going to kick it; it just tells you the date you can't live beyond. It's not a prediction. It's more of an expiration date.

But most people do end up dying on their Date—it just seems to work out that way, probably because most people take care to live as long as possible and not step in front of buses. And everyone knows you can't *survive* your Date because no one ever has. *No one. Ever.* It must be weird to grow up like Jude Daly, being told there's a chance. I can't imagine that. I can't imagine what kind of person that would turn you into. An entitled one, I'm guessing. It would explain his attitude.

"Maybe Jude is involved in the research?" Micah says. "Maybe he's a Death Date geek."

"Fine," I say. "The more of a gullible idiot he is, the easier my job."

He scrolls farther, eyes growing wider. "Um. I don't think he's an idiot."

I stop sorting through my clothes. "What? Oh God, what? Is he a psycho?"

Micah reads aloud, still scrolling. "Child prodigy . . . two University of Oxford degrees at sixteen . . . founder of the Young Scientist Scholarship program . . . junior chess champion . . . UNICEF Goodwill Ambassador . . ." I nudge him over so I can sit next to him. "Plays piano, speaks four languages, three TED Talks. You said eighteen, right? Not eighty?"

But he's definitely not eighty. The pictures attached to all these articles are of the tall, broad-shouldered guy with chestnut hair I met this morning. The articles go back years because there he is at age seven, twelve, fifteen, seventeen. The hair changes style and length, the gangly limbs become more defined, the chest fills out, the jaw squares, until the awkward, grinning boy is gone and a very serious-looking young man takes his place.

"Hot" is Micah's considered assessment. We study a picture of Jude Daly in gym shorts, playing soccer with a ten-year-old cancer patient at the new hospital his parents have funded. "Those are the worst." Micah sighs. He watches me study the picture and grins. "Careful, Ree."

I tut, scrolling firmly past it. "My curiosity is purely in

the interests of research," I say primly. "Oh my God, Yvette Scholes did a shoot with this guy in *Zeitgeist*! *That's* why he looked familiar! There was a whole article about him." I grab the magazine from my shelf. He's been sitting there all along.

"About what?"

I wave a hand as I flick through to the article. "I didn't read it; I just like her pictures." The *Zeitgeist* photos are black-and-white, from a low angle, making him even taller and more imposing, and again, he doesn't smile or look at the camera, just stares into the distance like he has better things to think about. Scholes's portraits always say something about the sitter. These ones all scream aloof. Standoffish. *Don't even try.*

"Hiked the Andes. Founded the Make a Difference charity." Micah goes on scrolling, but I stop him as images of a little yellow ribbon logo flash past. I touch the one pinned to my dress: MAKE A DIFFERENCE, it says in tiny letters. He *founded* that charity?

Micah clicks on a video link of Jude giving some sort of lecture to a packed hall, pacing the stage, his voice level despite the sea of eyes watching.

"*. . . don't deny that these wish-granting foundations have great intentions, but I must admit, when they asked me to contribute to sending kids to theme parks, I thought, How is a roller coaster and too much sugar supposed to make anyone feel better about dying young?*"

That gets a ripple of laughter from the audience,

but he doesn't smile. When the room goes still again, he continues.

"The thing is, people aren't afraid of death. They're afraid of evaluating how they've lived. I set up Make a Difference to enable people with early Death Dates to do something meaningful with their lives. We've funded thousands of people to go to college, do scientific research, write novels, create sculptures. To leave the world a better place. To face death without fear because they've lived intentionally and . . ."

"He set up an entire charity to make dying kids go to *school*? He sounds like a riot," Micah says, scrolling on. "Jesus, is that him with *Obama*?"

I roll my eyes as I get off the bed. "He's loaded. You know what they're like. Someone else probably did all that stuff and he just stuck his name on it."

"Well, he's kicking the shit out of that bucket list. Wonder what he's doing here? What could there possibly be left to do?"

"Something fun?" I take his phone and gesture at the screen. "Seriously, this is all committees and fundraisers. No girlfriends, no friends. This guy needs to loosen up." I hand Micah his phone and turn back to my clothes. My heart fractures a little as I toss a white, but hopelessly stained, silk blouse in the trash. "*That's* my angle. His whole life's been about work. I'm the fun-loving girl he never knew he needed. Easy."

"Except he hates you already," Micah points out.

"He just caught me off guard," I protest. "I wasn't ready for him; I wasn't even looking my best. I had frosting in my hair!"

"Yeah, but . . ." Micah makes a face. "Look, nailing an easier job might not be that impressive, but it's more impressive than fucking up with Dr. Lawrence's most important clients. Ree, what happens if this *doesn't* go well?"

I stop packing and look at him. He has a point. And for the first time, it occurs to me that the alternative to that permanent contract might be losing my job altogether. If I mess this one up, Dr. Lawrence won't be happy. And I can't deny that this morning did *not* go well.

Instead of answering Micah, I grab the phone back, shut the browser, and open the camera, framing him stretched out in my bed. He pouts like a supermodel, and my mind stills as the light rearranges itself to suit his cheekbones. Micah can have anyone he wants; he just tilts his head, looks up from beneath his lashes, lets one corner of his lip curl. His black hair flops over one eye and he can look charmingly helpless or dangerously sexy depending on how he pushes his hands through it. Makes R&Jing a breeze. Love is so much easier for the beautiful.

So how come Jude Daly is single? I zoom in on Micah, but what I'm seeing is Jude in the café, sitting there like a photo by Yvette Scholes, backlit by the windows, staring out into the shadows between the trees. And I can't help it. There's something about *Don't even try* that makes me think *Watch me.*

I take the photo and toss the phone back. I'm not going to freak out about this guy. There's more than one way to get under someone's skin. People think they're so complicated, but they're not. They never *tell* you they're insecure, afraid of commitment, bored, shy, sensitive, lonely, but they give it away all the time. You just have to watch. Like a camera.

I zip my bag and tell Micah, "Don't worry. I can handle this."

The thing is, this is not normal dating. These are not normal people in normal circumstances. Normal people might have alarm bells in the back of their head. *Is this going too fast? Is it really OK that he's into geocaching? Maybe I should be focusing on my exams.* Not these kids. *These* kids have switched off all the alarms and they're desperate to believe that you're the One, because if you're not, then they don't get the One. Ever. It's actually pretty easy to give people something they desperately want.

I still have time. Five whole days. And next time I meet him, I'll be ready.

Chapter 4

LAKESIDE, IN THE OLD TOWN AREA, IS THE JEWEL IN ELITE ELECT'S crown. There are plenty of luxury hotels in the resort, but this one is smaller, more intimate, more exclusive. It's on a peninsula that juts out into the lake, only connected by a narrow strip of land, so it's almost its own island. A wide, Adirondack-style building in gleaming white wood, five stories, a terrace, and then a lawn sloping down to an infinity pool, private beach, private jetty for the private yachts. The dining room of the hotel is a semicircle protruding onto the terrace like a big belly with wraparound windows and a huge roof garden on top. Behind the building is a golf course, tennis courts, and a spa surrounded by trees and nature trails. And if you've still got cash to burn, you can stay in one of the seven private lodges in the woods around the hotel, which is where the Dalys are, of course.

I've never even been inside the hotel, but I know all this from the brochures.

One of Lakeside's chauffeured Bentleys purrs down the drive as I walk up it, enjoying the gentle sounds of tinkling glassware from the terrace as I approach the hotel, the tapping of the rigging on the sailboats. Even the background noise here says *quality*. And everything from the doormen to the prices is designed to intimidate people like me.

I straighten my posture, lift my chin, and walk up the steps like someone who belongs here.

The door to my fourth-floor suite opens with an elegant swish. It's a corner room with windows on two sides, and from here you can see the lake and its little islands and the mountains beyond. There's a living room, dining area, office, two bedrooms, two bathrooms, steam room, two balconies, even a kitchen for families who bring their own cook. The decor is done in pale fabrics, deep rugs, glass chandeliers. Everything exudes taste, serenity, and comfort. I generously tip the bellhop carrying my lone weekend bag, close my eyes, and inhale deeply.

When I open them, a woman is standing in the doorway to the kitchen, grinning at me.

I throw my arms out. "Mother!"

"Darling!"

We laugh and Naomi flings herself at me, bouncing me up and down as she hugs me.

"Ree! This place!"

"I know!" We squeal like kids on Christmas morning.

Naomi almost always plays my mom for R&J gigs.

Someone has to stand by my deathbed looking sad, and she makes a very classy weeping mother. She has green eyes like me, a tall slender build, the same pale skin with freckles. She looks more like me than my real mother, so it's a good fit. The rest of the time she works at the grocery store in Staff Town, but if I get a permanent job, it could mean more work for her, too.

"We have our own butler!" She points excitedly at the CALL THE BUTLER button on the wall. "Imagine! A *man* at your beck and call. Won't that be a change." Naomi has a husband and two sons. I think half the reason she does this job is to get away from them.

"Have you looked yet?" I ask, gripping her hands.

"No, I was waiting for you!"

We dash to the larger bedroom, with its four-poster bed and gauzy curtains, and stand before the dressing-room doors. I take one sculpted copper handle; Naomi takes the other.

"Ready?"

She nods.

We pull them open in unison.

The R&J stylist team provides all our clothes for each job and puts them in our rooms in advance. How you look is all part of what the parents are paying for. Even though it's temporary, they still want you to look like the kind of girl they'd expect their son to bring to dinner and eventually marry. In reality, these are teenage boys, and given the timescale we're working with, a more effective strategy would be a pair of short-shorts and an exposed midriff, but we have to go with whatever the stylists think is appropriate.

To be fair, they're *very* good stylists. And they must have decided the Dalys have high standards because this particular wardrobe is extremely classy.

The lights in the dressing room come on when the doors open, and soft music plays somewhere over our heads. There's a wall of mirrors, a makeup table lit with a row of bulbs like a Hollywood dressing room, and ceiling lights designed to flatteringly illuminate the rails of clothes and racks of shoes. We stare in reverential silence for a moment before stepping in to swish our hands along the edges of the fabrics. My skin registers crisp linen, the scratch of sequins, feathery cashmere, clouds of chiffon, waterfalls of silk as the garments sway and dance like they're already at a party.

"Oh my God!" Naomi moans, pulling out a shimmering, open-backed evening dress in a 1920s style, slit to the thigh and in a color I could only describe as *midnight*. "This will look incredible on you!" She drapes it against her and twirls before the mirrors. Naomi gets a wardrobe, too, but it's never as extensive as mine, and she spends most of her evenings trying on my clothes.

"That's Gucci," I say. "It cost more than our car."

"God, I'd sell my eldest for these heels." Naomi cradles a pair of yellow Mary Janes like they're a newborn baby. "It's the shoes that get me. Every time."

"Look at these!" There are dresses by Alexander

McQueen, in shades of blue to complement my fair skin and green to match my eyes. A Valentino minidress. A Dolce & Gabbana peasant top, an Alberta Ferretti maxi dress in a geometric print, a silk Hermès skirt, a Brunello Cucinelli linen jacket. And then casual items—Dior jeans that will fit me like they've been painted on, Vivienne Westwood floral T-shirts, Balenciaga sneakers and Burberry strappy sandals in gold and silver, movie-star sun hats, a multitude of silk scarves, shorts, bikinis. I won't have time to wear half of it.

It's completely ridiculous, total overkill, but it's also completely necessary. This is what the daughters who come here are wearing, so I have to look like my wardrobe resembles a fashion-week catwalk, too.

"I bet Marta put this together." She's my favorite stylist. She doesn't just create a wardrobe; she creates a *story*. You can totally imagine the girl who wears these clothes. You know her. You like her. You'd like to *be* her.

Just seeing the clothes makes me feel better about this job. The girl Jude Daly met was just Ree from Staff Town with a hole in her dress. No wonder he wasn't interested. Marta hadn't waved her magic wand yet.

In a drawer we find a jewelry box full of necklaces, bracelets, rings, earrings, all nestled in plush velvet and sparkling beneath the lights. Cartier mixed in with hand-crafted artisan stuff—lots of silver, a few tasteful gems, nothing ostentatious. There's a range of Mulberry and Dior purses, a cute little tartan backpack, a drawer of underwear so light and pretty it could float away. And, *thank God*, the latest iPhone, preloaded with shopping apps, playlists, photos of me, Naomi, and other members of my "family and friends." It has a *fantastic* camera, and I immediately start playing with the settings.

"Let's do the products!" Naomi squeals, running to my en suite, a sapphire necklace still swinging around her neck and Louis Vuitton sunglasses in her hair.

This part's maybe even better because, while all the clothes are itemized and have to be returned next week, no one cares about the leftover beauty products. The bathroom cabinet is vast and filled with bottles of the most expensive hair and skin products you can buy.

"Smell this." I waft a bottle of shampoo under Naomi's nose.

"Jesus, I would put that on a salad and eat it."

I start trying out the makeup, all in perfect shades for my skin. I dab a shimmering gold eyeshadow on one eyelid, sky blue on the other.

"I'm going to check out the refrigerator," Naomi says. "Forget the shoes, *that's* my favorite part." She heads to the kitchen, calling over her shoulder, "You wipe that stuff off your face right now, young lady!"

"Yes, Mom!" I call after her, grinning.

I stretch out on the floor, sinking into a rug so deep my body will leave an imprint, and in the crystal chandelier above me, a million Regans smile contentedly.

Dr. Lawrence wasn't wrong—the R&Js really do help people; I've seen it. And Dr. Burgess wasn't wrong, either; the job is a *lot* better paid than anything else I could get in the resort. But the truth is, people don't do this job for the money, and they don't do it because they're saints. They do it because it's a fucking blast. A week in the lap of luxury, living every day like it's your literal last? If they were honest, who would say no to that?

Dr. Lawrence said there was a reason people still love the story of Romeo and Juliet four hundred years later. Well, I tell him silently, *the story of Cinderella is even older*.

When the butler has drawn a bath in the claw-foot tub, complete with six inches of fragranced foam on top, I send a picture of it to Micah, slide in, and scrub myself with the loofah, like I can exfoliate Staff Town right off my skin. I extend one bubble-coated leg in the air to admire my shiny calf, wiggling my toes at the girl in the mirrored wall across from me, wondering who she's going to be this week. Shy? Bubbly? Studious? Adventurous? Everyone's Juliet is different, and it's not just Dior and Valentino I get to wear this week. Once I figure out what my client is into, I get to try that girl on like a dress.

I sit up and turn, craning to see the reflection of my back, where my own Date has adorned the skin just below my shoulder blade since I was born. Mine is in a wobbly, childlike script, like it was done by a drunk tattooist, much less elegant than Jude Daly's.

But they're not tattoos at all really, and no one gets a choice about what they look like or where they appear. They're there when you're born, part of your skin, as unchangeable as your blood type. I know mine by heart, of course, but it's a very long way away, so I never think about it.

By the time I see Jude again, it'll be gone, covered with a color-matched skin patch. Someone is on their way to the hotel to apply it, as well as a henna tattoo with a new Date, the same as his.

A reply comes from Micah. *Are there dolphins in the tub?* I take a photo of my monogrammed bathrobe and send it back to him.

I felt superstitiously freaked out the first time they gave me a fake Date tattoo. As if it might change something. Of course it didn't. I don't know what the Dalys hope to achieve with their research; people have been trying to survive their Death Dates forever, and no one's ever managed it. People have locked themselves in abandoned subway stations and then died when an earthquake brought the ceiling down on their heads. They've gone to the desert only to be bitten by something toxic or struck by freak lightning. Someone once set up camp in a hospital for his Date but got stabbed by a drunk guy in the emergency room. There's a whole website—Death by Irony—devoted to stories about the stupid ways people have died trying to avoid their Dates. Most people just accept it's impossible. The end-of-life clinics are a much better option.

It does mean sacrificing a day of your life, of course. No one's allowed on resort grounds *on* their actual Date. Because that's a disaster waiting to happen. We'd have broken bungee cords and people choking on gourmet fish bones all over the place. Your procedure is always scheduled for the day before. One day is a lot to give up when it's all you have left, but most people think it's worth it so you can be sure you get the peaceful death of your choosing and not a random accident on the way to the clinic. If you change your mind, you're escorted off the premises before midnight, and whatever happens to you on your Date won't have any effect on the resort's insurance.

It's Sunday now, and Jude's Date is Saturday, which means his procedure, and hopefully my fake one, will be Friday. It's not a lot of time, and we haven't gotten off to a good start, but I'm confident I can turn it around. Adrenaline makes you smart, and I usually get a feel for what they want pretty quickly.

While I'm swaddled in my bathrobe and toweling my hair, wondering whether to go for sleek, curls, or tousled, Naomi pokes her head around the door, sniffs the air, and smiles a blissed-out smile. "I always wanted a daughter. There's nothing more disgusting than sharing one bathroom with a husband and two teenage boys. The tattooist is here."

I decide tousled will be quicker. "Almost done. How's the kitchen?"

"Amaaaaazing. Though, actually, I kind of wish they wouldn't stock it. I love going to the Old Town delis and thinking, *I can buy anything I want in here. Anything.* What do you want for dinner? Something expensive that I can go and buy?"

I laugh. Naomi doesn't have to cook for me, but she can't help being a mom.

She lifts a bottle of Dior perfume and sprays herself liberally. "Mmm. Smells like—"

"Money," I finish for her.

"Money." She sighs. "Assholes?"

I make a face. "Actually the *parents* seem OK." It's true. The Dalys could have made me an offer for my *soul* that I'd have seriously considered, and for that reason, I want to dislike them. But there was something about the mismatched socks, the bitten nails.

Naomi looks disappointed. "That's a shame," she says. "It's my one consolation when we have to return all this stuff. Rich people are assholes. I have to fake cry over my fake daughter to feed my real kids, but at least I'm not an asshole." She holds up a tiny jar of skin cream. "A half ounce. I bet it cost a week's worth of groceries."

"A month's," I tell her. "And if you're looking for an asshole? You're in luck."

By the time I've stopped ranting about Jude Daly to Naomi, the tattooist is gone, and Micah has arrived.

"Wow," Naomi says once I've repeated the whole conversation.

"I know!"

She passes a quinoa salad decorated with edible flowers across the suite's glass dining table to me. Micah is already halfway through his. She's ordered nearly everything on the restaurant menu, but I can't eat.

"And he was only as polite as *that* because he thinks I'm a guest here! If he knew I was from Staff Town, he'd be ordering me to fetch him something while staring at my chest. I'm not surprised he doesn't have a girlfriend. Or boyfriend. Or *friend*. Apart from his parents, he seems to be here all on his own."

Naomi's face crumples. "Oh no! Maybe he just needs someone to talk to, poor kid."

"Poor kid!"

She shrugs and pushes another plate at me. "I can't help it, I feel so bad for these families," she says. "Believe me, every mother's got that moment seared on her heart. When they hand you the baby and you don't even see his face, you just look for the Date. Trying to do math after forty-eight hours of labor. I misread Finn's at first, he came out so scrunchy. I had to throw up." She shudders and starts gathering Micah's empty plates, even though there's a maid who'll do that. "It's not their fault some of them are spoiled," she says. "They're not just rich, they're *ill-fated*. How do you raise a child like that?"

"Let me get out my violin," I mutter.

"Maybe he's shy," Micah suggests.

"He's not shy, believe me."

He taps his water glass on his teeth (Naomi refused to let him order champagne). "Then he just needs to get to know you. We should get him down to Inferno. It's still early."

"That's your solution to everything. I'm not getting him drunk, Micah." That's a last resort, and I like to think

I'm better than that. "Anyway, I don't think Jude is an Inferno kind of guy."

"Yeah, but I am. And you need a drink. Come on, let's go, Ree. Pretty please?" He stretches his arms across the table and does puppy eyes, this morning's hangover forgotten. "Text Mrs. Daly to say you'll be there, and if he shows up, he shows up. What else can you do tonight?"

I twist my lips at him. "I guess." He probably won't come, but the idea of thinking about nothing except how to dance in heels for a few hours sounds extremely appealing right now.

"You need me?" Naomi asks.

"Probably not. Jude Daly isn't interested in meeting *me*, let alone my mother."

"Well, I'll be at the spa if you do. I'm getting everything down to my *aura* exfoliated."

"Don't overthink it, that's my secret," Micah says as he pushes me toward my dressing room. "Jude Daly just needs someone to remove the stick from his ass." He wags his head. "And maybe replace it with something else." He winks. "That's another of my secrets."

I snort and Naomi flicks her napkin at him. "You'll get yourself in trouble one of these days, young man."

"God, I hope so," he says.

"What should I wear?" I call from the bedroom, overwhelmed with choices for a moment.

"Glasses!" Micah shouts back. "He's an intellectual," he explains to Naomi.

"Do you think this dress makes me look smart?" I pull

out the Valentino halter neck minidress with its glittering hem of petal-shaped sequins.

She laughs. "Just be yourself, Ree."

"Yeah, that'll impress him."

I disappear into the dressing room and an hour later step out of the hotel lobby wearing an impenetrable armor of lotions, potions, oils, and creams. Not to mention the minidress, a Fendi bag, Jimmy Choo heels, and the thick veneer of total confidence that comes with them. Naomi's wrong. With this outfit, I don't *need* to be myself.

The gates of Inferno are an iron lattice of grotesque, entwined bodies, contorted limbs beckoning as we approach. They slam behind us, swallowing us in a cathedral of blue smoke, strobe lights, and a ferocious drumbeat your heart instantly syncs to.

The place is heaving already, the crowd moving like one great undulating beast as Micah and I head for the bar, and I feel my muscles relax into the heat from hundreds of bodies sweating through their couture outfits.

Dante's Inferno was the first club Dante Colucci opened when he came to Elite Elect ten years ago, and it's still his flagship, although he owns most of the entertainment venues in the resort now. It's located in the heart of Downtown and the decor is hell themed, with a focus on sin, decadence, living fast, and dying young. When it opened, a lot of people thought it was in poor taste, considering the location. But as with all things that old people think are in poor taste, it was an instant hit with the younger guests.

The hell theme isn't cheesy skulls and Halloween decorations, either. The club is a circular, concrete column with a dance floor at the bottom and then four levels of balconies—the "circles of hell"—winding like a silver snake from the bottom of the club to the top. The ceiling is lit with the projection of a lightning storm in blue and red strobe lights, and neon electric chandelier sculptures descend through the space almost to the ground. The dance floor is a giant 3D interactive LED screen that mirrors your movements but turns them into writhing, shadowy creatures beneath you, while projections of the seven deadly sins are cast onto hanging strips of ghostly, gauzy fabric that undulate lazily in the air, and moving frescoes of dancers adorn the walls, lit by jets of blue flame that lick at their feet. The bar curves in a semicircle along one wall, and the racks of designer liquor bottles are lit by a heavenly golden light and swathed in clouds of organza, with the bar staff dressed as "fallen angels"—black, low-cut cocktail dresses, corsets and fishnets, tight leather pants, little black wings perched on their shoulders. The head bartender blows fireballs with vodka and occasionally pours a line of high-proof alcohol along the length of the metal bar top and lights it in a whoosh of flame while the crowd goes nuts. Wealthy people choose Elite Elect for the high-end luxury. But young people come here to party at Inferno.

I sent Mrs. Daly a text to let her know where I'd be tonight, and she said she'd do her best, but there's no sign of Jude.

"Stop stewing," Micah says, watching me scan the crowd. "I have had *a day*. I need you on form."

"Fine, no stewing. No moping, either," I order him. "We're going to have a few drinks . . ."

He salutes.

"Do some very risqué dancing . . ."

"Sir, yes sir!"

"And by midnight I demand that you hook up with a guy who's twice as hot as Phillipe."

He cocks his head. "Phillipe who?"

At the bar, drunk teenagers are throwing their platinum credit cards at the staff. Others are pooling pills and powders at the tables like it's a buffet. No one even gets carded here; the whole resort is lawless. The cops turn a blind eye to all kinds of stuff because it's not a good look for them to arrest a sixteen-year-old cosmetics heiress with twenty-four hours to live. Micah and I hang out here even when we're not working. It's easy to attach yourself to a group of kids drinking $300 cocktails. Our bill gets added to theirs at the end of the night and they don't even care.

And I swear, these kids are the *best* to hang out with.

No one talks about homework or college plans for a start. And they're up for *anything*. Tequila slammers? Mystery pills? An impromptu striptease on the bar top? Midnight cliff diving? Sure, why not? And they don't care that their mascara is sweating off or their underwear is showing, they don't care who they hook up with, they don't care how late or how dangerous or how expensive it is. Because life's too short.

And the club does everything it can to reinforce that message. Every time a celebrity dies young, they invent a new cocktail. The wall art features James Dean, Kurt Cobain, Marilyn Monroe, Jimi Hendrix, Aaliyah, Heath Ledger, John Lennon, along with slogans like *Burn Out, Don't Fade Away.* As if death is a party only the popular people are invited to.

And I guess it works, because everyone here, whether they're here for their own procedure or a friend's, drinks and dances and snorts like there's literally no tomorrow. After a few cocktails, I start to imagine I'm dancing in a room full of ghosts. Future legends. There will be shrines to some of these people in their high schools. Their families will light candles and their friends will get matching tattoos of their names, and while everyone else gets old and boring, they will be forever young, forever gorgeous, forever here, dancing themselves to death with Kurt and Marilyn. And with Micah and me.

We order two El Diablos on my expenses credit card and I don't even look at the prices. The girl in this outfit never looks at prices. We toss the drinks back, then go for Flaming Zombies. Jude Daly is still nowhere to be seen, but a group of college guys are doing a hip-hop routine in the center of the dance floor, the crowd roaring for more, and after another Flaming Zombie, I'm ready to join them. I want to dance. I want to dance until I've sweated the water out of my system, along with every last thought in my head, and all that's left is the alcohol.

I drag Micah with me, and the crowd absorbs us into the belly of the beast. The music gets louder, faster, the air a fug of sweat and aftershave. The dance floor goes from ice blue to blood red, pulsing beneath us with vibrations from the dancers, and the bass is a living thing now, a demon possessing the crowd, an inferno sucking up the oxygen, pounding my brain to oblivion so there's nothing but the next beat. *No tomorrow.* No hangover, no leaking roof, no car repairs, no vodka bottles in the trash can. *Fuck* tomorrow. I give my body to the demon and watch tomorrow go up in flames.

Someone hands me a shot and I throw it back without even looking. Micah spins into my field of vision, yelling something about the college guys.

"What?" I yell back.

"Is it too late for me to apply to college? No! Let's get some champagne and see if you can pour it off the balcony right into my mouth! *Then* I'm going to college."

I laugh. "I love you, Micah!" I yell back, pulling him in so our sweaty foreheads are pressed together. "You make me feel like the responsible one."

"Well, it's no fun if you're not doing *something* stupid." He grins and spins me around, and I let my head fall back, gazing up into the lightning storm crackling above.

I stagger away, dizzy. "I'll be back in a minute." I hold a hand up and stumble toward the elevators. I can't do stairs in these heels.

On the top balcony, four floors up, I lean over the rail, peering down into the thrashing mass of bodies below and breathe for what feels like the first time all day.

It's less crowded up here. There's actual air and a few tables dotted around. Part of this floor is roped off because that's where Dante's offices are. But I want a shot of the bar from directly above, so I duck beneath the ropes and position myself so I can hold my phone over the edge, looking straight down. I kick my heels off because I don't trust myself not to lose my balance and topple right over, then I lean out and wait. The music ramps up, building to a frenzy, but I wait. I wait, wait, wait until it can't get any louder, any faster, until the drumbeat is a machine gun and, at its peak, I'm rewarded with an explosion of flames soaring up from the bar top as the bartender throws his lighter onto a line of alcohol, the bar staff's black wings illuminated as they lean over to take orders, the crowd going wild. *Yes!* I punch the air; it's perfect. Yvette Scholes did something similar with a fireworks display shot from a helicopter, families picnicking below—it was stunning. This is no family picnic; it's a murkier, grimier scene. *My* scene.

I'm lining myself up for a shot of the dance floor when a door behind me opens.

"Nice view."

I roll my eyes as Dante Colucci comes to stand next to me—ridiculous arm muscles on display as usual, black hair slicked back, and that wolfish smile on his fake-tanned face. The "view" he was referring to was *not* the one over the balcony.

Despite owning a chunk of the resort, Dante spends most of his time at Inferno, occasionally appearing behind the bar to mix cocktails (to wild applause, like squeezing a lemon is hard) or in the DJ box to get the crowd worked up. I have a theory that he really wanted to be a TV host or a movie star, but it didn't pay as much as owning a string of overpriced bars in a resort where people have more money than time.

He leans farther out and I say, "Is your hair thinning, Dante? You know, there are products you can get for that." It's not wise to antagonize him, but I'm too drunk to be wise, and anyway, I'm pissed at him. I haven't seen the scumbag since he fired my mom from her job at another of his bars. And now he has the nerve to perve on me? I should push him over the fucking balcony.

He says he fired her because she was drinking at work. *She* says she'd just gotten too old to look good pouring cocktails for rich businessmen. Either could be true, but if he fired her for being old while he hangs out at Inferno, flexing his muscles at teenagers in short skirts, he's got some nerve.

His eyes narrow, but he only says, "How's Cath?"

My lips tighten and I try not to slur my words as I say, "Fine. New job's going great."

"Good, good. I'm hiring, if you're interested."

I snort disdainfully but tighten my grip on the rail so I don't ruin the dignified effect by falling over. "Bar work? No thanks."

He gives me a sympathetic grimace. "Actually you're

too young to work behind the bar. I was thinking more collecting glasses?"

My own eyes narrow. "Very amusing. Anyway, I have a job."

"Oh yes, I heard you got a new client."

"Where did you hear that?" I snap. But the big cheeses here are all friends.

"I thought you could introduce me," he says.

I turn to look at him properly. "Why?"

He shrugs. "It's smart to make contacts with important people."

"Well, I hate to disappoint you, but I don't think Jude will be interested in drinking in your VIP area."

He laughs. "I meant his parents."

"Oh. *Oh*." My alcohol-soaked brain finally catches up. Of course Dante's aware of the Dalys and their alcohol empire. Some sort of endorsement deal involving their vodka and his bars would line his pockets nicely.

He turns to face me, still leaning on the rail. "You know, there's a lot of money floating around this resort. We could be useful to each other. You could introduce me to certain clients, that kind of thing."

"Me? Why me?"

"You're good with people. And you're good at getting them to do what you want. I admire that."

I draw my head back, a little repulsed by his assessment of my job. "That's not what I do."

He looks amused. "Don't look so offended. Networking is a perfectly legitimate business practice."

"How could I even introduce you? I'm not supposed to have met you myself. I'm a 'guest' here, remember?"

He waves a hand. "You'll think of something."

I shake my head at him. "I can't believe you'd even ask me for a favor. After what happened with my mom?"

He smiles and spreads his hands. "Fair enough. I can make it worth your while. I heard you were having car trouble."

Jesus, he really has done his homework. Which makes me think this vodka thing is a big deal.

I fold my arms and look like I'm considering it. "That shit heap's not worth repairing."

"True," he says. "How about you take my BMW instead."

I almost drop my new phone over the balcony. "What?"

"I'm upgrading, so you can take the old one off my hands. Runs like a dream."

I stare at him, wondering if this is another joke, while the alcohol seems to suddenly evaporate from my bloodstream.

"Are you serious?" I ask.

"Deadly."

"And all you want is an introduction?"

"That's all."

I chew my lip, not sure what to say. I was relishing the opportunity to disappoint him, to summon everything I learned today from the Jude Daly charm school and fire it at him. But now . . .

Before I can answer, he nods down into the club and says, "Speak of the devil."

I look over the balcony. He's not hard to spot. Almost a head taller than everyone else and twice as upright, wearing faded jeans and a plain gray shirt, and making his way into the club.

"I'll be behind the bar," Dante says, walking toward the stairs.

When I get back to the dance floor, Micah is having a dance-off with the college guys. I close in on him, throw my arms around him, and start grinding against his hip.

"*Whoa,* Miss Sexual Harassment! You know, consent is freely given, informed, enthusiastic, and—"

I pull him closer. "Jude Daly is over there!" I whisper urgently in his ear. His eyes widen as he peers over my shoulder. "Don't look! OK, look. Is he watching?"

"He's standing by the wall. He's looking at us. You want me to grope you?"

"Thanks, but no," I deadpan, although I keep my arms around him. With some guys, all you have to do is show them something they can't have.

"He's even hotter IRL," Micah says. "If you don't want him, I'll take him."

"You're welcome to him," I mutter. "How's my hair?"

"Sweaty. But in a sexy way."

I roll my eyes and leave Micah on the dance floor as I summon all the "sober" I've got and make my way to where Jude is leaning against the wall, watching the dance floor like he's making a documentary about us.

I *can't* go over there and simper at him again. No

one with any self-respect would give him a second chance after he was so rude in the café. Instead, I plant myself directly in front of him on one hip, arms folded, look him dead in the eye, and say, "This is you avoiding me, is it? Or do you just get a kick out of standing around in clubs looking like a department store mannequin while people are trying to have a good time?" If he likes antagonism, I can do antagonism. Especially when slightly drunk.

His lip twitches at one corner. "Am I distracting you?" He feigns innocence.

"Not as much as you'd like to think."

He laughs. Maybe he likes a girl with a bit of backbone.

I relax my fighting stance. "OK, Camus, at the risk of asking you another *question*, I know you hate those, what the fuck was that earlier? You seemed . . . upset."

"Really? I was going for laceratingly rude. That's disappointing."

"No, you pretty much hit the mark."

"Doesn't seem to have put you off though."

"I'm thick-skinned."

He slowly stands up straight, and I notice that his eyes have gold flecks when the strobe light catches them, but the gaze is no more welcoming than it was this morning. "It's Jude. Daly," he introduces himself. "And actually, I thought you were a journalist," he admits.

"A *journalist?*" Of all the explanations for his behavior, that's not one I was expecting. "Why?"

He shrugs. "Call me paranoid. But they're fairly

devious. Bribing our staff, harassing us in restaurants, that sort of thing."

"What do they want?"

"Information about my parents' research into Death Dates. They even tried to tap my phone once."

"Jeez, that's pretty shitty."

"Isn't it?"

"So how do you know I'm *not* one?"

He shrugs. "A professional would have been better at the flirting."

"Ouch!" I feign outrage, mainly to cover the *actual* outrage. The fucking nerve. "And for the record, I was *not* flirting," I add, flirtatiously.

"Ah. That explains it, then." The gold flecks are crackling with amusement now. Which I guess is an improvement, except that it's all at my expense. "But I shouldn't have jumped to conclusions this morning. It's perfectly possible that you *are* just a klutz with zero spatial awareness."

"Thanks," I deadpan.

"And probably even a journalist wouldn't stoop to pretending to flirt with someone at an end-of-life clinic. I mean, who does that?" He huffs at the idea.

I swallow and force a coquettish laugh. "Yeah, I guess that's pretty unlikely."

"I'm just . . . on edge, I suppose," he goes on. "Ready to lash out. You got in the way."

I move over to lean against the wall beside him and give him a grudging shoulder nudge. "Understandable.

Let's start over." I hold a hand out. "Regan Albright." I give him my fake surname. "*Not* a journalist. I'm here with my mom. We just flew in this morning from Philadelphia."

"Just the two of you?"

I let my smile fade a little as I lean closer to be heard over the music. "My dad can't be here. He had a stroke a few years ago."

"I'm sorry to hear that."

"I'm not sure he understands what's happening, but maybe that's better for him now. And I don't have brothers or sisters. They never said it, but I think, after seeing my Date, my parents couldn't face having another kid. I wish they had now, though, because my mom will be . . . Anyway, I have cousins and friends, but I didn't want a lot of people around this week. Too emotional, you know? We had a big party before I left, it was nice. But I just want my mom with me for, y'know. We're very close. My aunts are flying in to bring her home after, so she won't be alone, but you can't help worrying, right? Although sometimes I think it's easier to worry about her than to think about . . . everything else. Is that selfish? That's probably selfish. Sorry, I'm rambling. I'm just . . . I'm on edge this week, too, I guess."

I glance helplessly up at Jude, who's just listening, nodding, the amusement all gone now. I've used this backstory a few times; it's pretty effective. Enough detail to be believable, nothing so specific you'd question it, and enough emotion to discourage anyone from probing.

But he says, "It's OK. My grandfather had a stroke

before he died. Has it affected your dad's speech?"

"Huh? Oh, uh . . . yeah. Yeah, he can't say much. He points at stuff."

"So his mobility is OK?"

"Well. I mean, he can point a bit. With one arm."

"Couldn't he spell out words, then? That's what my grandfather did."

"Right, yeah. He does that, but sometimes he gets confused so . . ." And *I* ask too many questions? I make a mental note to research strokes. "Ugh!" I shake myself, as if to shake off the moment before he can start asking what medication he's on. "I came out tonight to *not* think about all this! Sorry."

"It's OK."

"No really, I'm being a huge buzzkill. Hey, technically I still owe you a drink. You never got that coffee. How about a cocktail instead?"

He shrugs. "Lead the way."

We push through the heaving crowd toward the bar, which is three deep, the bar staff frantically trying to keep up. I hold up a hand, trying to get someone's attention, and get completely ignored. Jude comes up behind me, tilts his chin at the bartender, and gets served instantly. One of the fundamental laws of the universe is that confidence is directly proportional to the number of dollars in your bank account. This guy has an unfair quantity of both.

Dante is behind the bar, and I groan inwardly as I remember his offer. It occurs to me that Jude must get a lot of this. Apparently everyone from reporters to club owners wants a piece of him. I don't want to be part of that, but he's right there and it really *isn't* every day someone offers you a BMW, so I hear myself say, "Wait, isn't that . . . what's his name? The guy who owns this place? Dante something?" I wave the bartender away and start calling, "Excuse me?" at Dante. He does an excellent job of ignoring me for a few seconds before coming over.

"Hi! You're Dante, right?" I turn to Jude. "This guy is *amazing*. I read an article about him when I was researching the resort. He's like some sort of cocktail *virtuoso*."

Dante waves a hand and says, "Just years of practice. What can I get—"

But I interrupt him. "Don't be so modest! I read that he can invent the perfect cocktail to suit your personality, like *on the spot*," I tell Jude. "Could you do that for us?" I smile sweetly at Dante, whose own smile has tightened. He told me to "think of something." He didn't say I couldn't make him work for it.

"It would be a pleasure," he says. I can almost hear his teeth grinding. "Let's see now. For you . . ." He looks me over slowly and then starts lifting bottles and splashing them into a cocktail shaker. "I'm thinking something fun. Light. A little spicy, a little salty, some gold leaf to garnish."

"Mmm, sounds perfect already," I say.

"And definitely boozy," he finishes smugly, upending a bottle of tequila into the mix. I narrow my eyes, feeling sick at the sight of it after last night, but he's moved on to Jude.

"And for you . . ." He looks Jude over thoughtfully and says, "Not too sweet. Plenty of ice. And . . ." He grins. "Daly Vodka, obviously." He holds a hand across the bar for Jude to shake. "Jude Daly, right? I was just reading about your parents' company in *The New York Times*. Their new line of whiskeys are pretty good, I hear."

"Thank you," Jude says, shaking his hand. He's polite to assholes like Dante, apparently.

"You guys having a good night?"

"It's an . . . interesting place," Jude says.

"Thank you. You enjoying the resort?"

"It's also . . . interesting."

At the other end of the bar, the bartender yells, *"Stand back!"* Then he sloshes alcohol on the bar top and lights it. There's a roar from the crowd.

"Our little party trick," Dante says. "Listen, I know the resort inside out. If you kids need anything." He slips Jude a business card. "And the VIP balcony upstairs is free."

"Thank you, but I'm not planning on staying out late tonight," Jude says.

"These are on the house," Dante says, pushing the drinks across the bar. "Tell your parents to come visit the club. I think they'd love our new range of Paradise cocktails."

"Hmm, I don't know if anyone's *parents* would enjoy Inferno," I say, reaching between them to take my drink. I've done my bit, and he never said I had to be nice to him. He was probably lying about the car anyway. "It seems like it's for a younger crowd," I go on. "People in their thirties or forties would be *way* too old." Dante is at least thirty-five.

The smug look hardens as I thank him for the drinks, smile innocently, and turn away.

Jude and I watch the dance floor for a while. It's difficult to talk, which is usually one of the advantages of taking a guy to Inferno.

"This place doesn't seem like your thing," I shout.

He shrugs. "I've got a week to kill in this resort." He sniffs the drink in his hand suspiciously and adds, "If it doesn't kill me first." He sets it on the bar again. Mine reeks of tequila and I try not to grimace as I sip it. "My mother recommended I try this place. It was this or a tea dance in the ballroom. And I believe there's a singing circle?" Maybe nothing in this resort is Jude's thing.

"It's not really my thing, either," I lie. "But I felt like blowing off some steam. I found someone to dance with anyway. Just before you arrived. Seems like a fun crowd. Maybe you should ask someone to dance. You might get lucky. Meet someone interesting." I smile up at him, sipping from my straw.

"Yes, I'm sure true love awaits," he says drily.

"What's that supposed to mean?"

"I mean, what kind of person wastes their time in a place like this?"

As the kind of person who wastes a lot of time in a place *precisely* like this, I find it hard not to take offense at that.

Someone lurches off the dance floor and almost crashes into us, and Jude tuts and takes a step backward. He's going to leave any minute.

I decide to go for broke. I set my drink down and say, "Well, since we're here and at least one of us is drunk, do you want to dance or do you want to stand there looking like someone's dad?"

"I don't dance," he says.

"You don't dance?" I'm incredulous. He has two legs and two feet, doesn't he? "Don't be shy, I can't dance, either. Who cares?"

"You *can* dance."

"Oh, were you watching?" I grin at him. "Come on, if you fall on your ass, it just makes for a better story."

"Thanks, but no."

I shrug it off. "Fine, suit yourself. Maybe I'll go find that guy I was dancing with earlier. He was kind of cute." I look at him like, *this is your last chance, Daly.*

"You should do that," he says. He nods at the far wall. "He's over there." Then he walks off toward the exit as I turn to see Micah, his back against the wall in a corner of the club, hair wrecked, lip-locked, and hands groping the ass of one of the college guys.

Chapter 5

THERE WAS NO POINT YELLING AT MICAH; HE WAS TOO WASTED. I took him back to the Acostas', waking them both up, and they looked at me like it was my fault he was climbing the porch steps on all fours. Luis insisted on driving me back to the hotel even though I was totally fine by then. Humiliation is very sobering.

After Inferno, my room was so quiet I couldn't sleep, so I went back down to the hotel guest lounge in pajamas and a fluffy bathrobe and curled up in an armchair to watch it get light outside.

Hotels are different at night. The staff put away their welcoming smiles and get out their paperwork and cleaning tools. They collect room service trays and start tomorrow's breakfast. The lighting is lower; the phones are muted. A maid drags a vacuum cleaner along behind her like a reluctant puppy. Mom will be here in a few hours for her morning shift.

Beyond the windows, the lake is a black mirror, the shadowed mountain peaks outlined by a pale light in the sky. I take my phone out and open the camera, waiting for that weird instinct that tells you when to press the shutter. But it doesn't come. The shot is beautiful, but it isn't interesting until the silhouetted figure of a maid walks into the frame, a dustpan in her hand. She stretches her back as she pauses to look out at the lake, then pushes the hair off her face and lets her shoulders drop.

The sound of the shutter startles her.

"Oh, it's you!" She laughs. I vaguely know her from school. She was a few years ahead of me and Micah. It's weird sometimes, having your school friends and neighbors serve you coffee and make your bed. Awkward. Partly because I know I'm only one job away from being where they are.

"Sorry, it was too good."

"Can I see?"

I turn the phone and she comes to bend over me. Her name tag says KRISTEN. "Hey, that's nice!"

I shrug. "It's surprising what you can do with a phone camera if you play with the settings."

"I didn't know you were a photographer."

"Oh, I'm not, it's just . . ." I stuff the phone into the pocket of my robe. "Couldn't sleep."

"Ugh, I wish I had your problems. I could drop right now. I hate the night shift. And someone walked mud all the way up the stairs." She brandishes her dustpan. "My supervisor turns into Vladimir Putin before the Midsummer Ball."

"How are the preparations going?"

"Oh my God, you should see the flowers! They delivered them today; the whole back-of-house area looks like a wedding. And we're all getting extra training on how to carry a tray. Who knew there were so many ways to get it wrong." Someone calls her name from the lobby and she sighs. "Better go. G'night!"

She hurries off and I curl up on a sofa, watching pale light creep into the sky high above the mountains, and wonder what it's like to be Jude Daly. To get to go around saying exactly what you think, doing exactly what you want.

I take my phone out again and google him, because winging it doesn't seem to be getting me anywhere, and I think I need to do some homework.

Micah was right; he's not normal. There are a million search results, but not in the usual way there are a million search results for wealthy teenagers. There are no paparazzi shots of him falling out of clubs or vomiting on his limo driver. No sordid affairs with Hollywood actresses. No reality-TV series about how he spends his money. No British tabloid–splashed pregnancy stories, no plastic surgery gone wrong, no red-carpet outfits, no skincare line.

Instead, there are articles about how he set up a scholarship program for science students from underprivileged backgrounds, adopted eight rescue dogs, flew aid supplies to earthquake victims in his family's private jet. He's on a list of Twenty Under Twenty in *The New York Times* and *The Washington Post*'s Ten Most Influential Teens. Everyone seems to worship him.

Which just proves that you can look any way you want on the internet, especially if you have your own PR team, and still be an asshole in real life. If *I'd* grown up rich, I could have saved earthquake victims, too.

The *really* annoying thing is that him being an asshole is irrelevant. Assholes fall in love every day. It should still be possible for me to do my job. But so far, I'm not doing it very well. And I'm running out of excuses. We had a meet-cute so classic it was actually *real*. And he no longer thinks I'm a reporter. And I looked great tonight—I was witty, I was fun, I flirted, I even tried to make him jealous. I've deployed every weapon in my arsenal, and the truth is . . . he just doesn't like me.

I'm woken early in the morning by a loud, nasal voice with an accent that's 90 percent English, 10 percent disgusted.

"No, not the parachuting, but the archery is fine. And the climbing, I suppose."

At first, I'm sure I'm dreaming, or that he's infiltrated my hotel room specifically to annoy me. Then I realize I fell asleep on the couch in the guest lounge last night. Jude is in the lobby, just outside, booking activities with the concierge. When I poke my head up, I can see him standing there, leafing through the brochures.

He turns and I duck down quickly, cursing. But it's too late. Next thing, he's leaning over the back of the couch, where I'm lying flat, trying to hide beneath a throw cushion. Apparently he *is* interested in me, but only when there's an opportunity to humiliate me.

"I thought you had a room here. How much do they charge for a sofa for the night?" He's hovering above me, visually pinning me to the upholstery.

"I do have a room."

"Are you on a stakeout?"

"Just . . . waiting for the sunrise." I gesture at the big windows.

"I see. East is that way though." He jerks his head over his shoulder.

"Right. Yes. That would be why I missed it." I struggle up from the couch. My hair is a mess, my face is one big makeup smudge, and I'm feeling those cocktails. "You're up early."

"I'm always up early. Just checking out what there is to do at this theme park of the damned." He looks in amusement at my pajamas as I tug the robe closed, kind of prudishly for someone who was twerking in a mini-dress last night. I attempt a dignified expression and his lip twitches.

I can't take his smug face at this hour of the morning. "Would you excuse me?" I push past him and head out of the lounge, bypassing the elevators in the lobby where guests are starting to gather, because I'm still in my bathrobe and bare feet. I head down a long corridor toward another set of elevators there. I know I should be using this opportunity. I should be suggesting we do something together. I should be inviting him up for breakfast to meet my "mom." But I'm half asleep and flustered and I just want to get away from him.

But he walks alongside me, flicking through the brochures and asking if I've done any of the activities. I suspect he's just doing it because he knows I'm uncomfortable. I need my makeup armor, my couture shield. I can't do this in fucking pajamas.

"Apparently there's a twenty-four-hour Cirque du Soleil, in case you felt the need for clowns at six a.m.," he drawls. "Or they run classes. I'll admit I've neglected my basket weaving and macramé skills over the years. Maybe I should go to some of those."

A maid passes us and the familiar uniform gives me a jolt. But it's not Mom. I recognize her from Staff Town, but her eyes slide over me like I'm any other guest.

"Sure, good idea," I say through gritted teeth.

"Everything OK?" He blinks innocently at me. "You seem tense."

I force a smile onto my face. "Just not really a morning person."

"That's a shame. I thought . . . maybe we could do something."

"You did?" Freak storms are more predictable than this guy.

"There's a hiking trail up into the mountains. It's steep, but apparently the view is worth it."

"Riiight. That sounds . . ." Oh God. The last thing

on earth I want to do is hike up a mountain. But what choice do I have? "Sounds like fun!" I could not sound less enthusiastic.

I stab the button for the elevator when I notice another maid pushing her cleaning cart along the corridor that runs at right angles to us, picking up shoes and dry cleaning and last night's room-service trays from outside the doors, humming softly, her red hair clashing with the pink tunic. Mom. I feel awkward suddenly, standing here with Jude. The elevator is taking forever to arrive, stopping at every floor for people coming down for breakfast.

Jude turns to look in the direction I'm staring. She's just a few doors along from us, stooping to load a couple of trays onto her cart, and she hasn't noticed us. She picks up a tray in one hand, and then my stomach drops like an elevator as she quietly palms a half-full miniature of gin with the other and slips it into her tunic pocket.

Oh my God.

She stands, glances around quickly, and almost drops the tray when she sees us. Sees me. Standing there in my fluffy Lakeside bathrobe with Jude fucking Daly. Forget the elevator—if the *floor* opened right now, I'd gratefully jump in.

She opens her mouth automatically, but what can she say? What can *I* say? I have to stand here and pretend I don't even know her while Jude, as if to prove that he can be even ruder, just stares pointedly at her and then mutters, completely audibly, "Well, I can understand a person being driven to drink by this place, but that's a *little* unprofessional."

She blushes, fumbles to put the bottle back, makes a lame excuse about there being no space on these stupid carts. Then she hurries off, scarlet-faced, and the whole, horrifying time I just stand there, watching him look down his crooked nose at her, saying nothing.

When she's gone, Jude turns back to me, as if nothing happened, and says, "Do you think we'll need a map for the hike?"

The elevator doors have finally opened and people are pouring out. But they're ten seconds too late.

"Actually I do have a recommendation for you." Everything in me is telling me to *shut up, shut up, shut up.* "I suggest you try the advanced skydiving. The one where you leave the parachute *on the ground!*"

"Excuse me?" He looks confused about why I'm mad. "Have I upset you in some way?"

"Do you ever meet anyone you don't upset? Are you *trying* to be an asshole, or does it come naturally?"

That wipes the amused look off his face. He draws himself up so he's even taller and says, "*I'm* an asshole? Do *you* verbally attack every guy who won't dance with you?"

I scoff. "Yeah, that's it, I'm heartbroken. I literally have nothing better to do with my time than dance with enti-tled, arrogant, rude, uptight, *judgmental—*" I can't help glancing down the corridor, and his confused expression clears as he realizes what I mean.

"I'm judgmental because I object to people drinking at work?"

"What would you know about what people do at work?" I step into the elevator and punch the button for my floor. "Have you ever worked a day in your life? Oh no, that's right, your parents do the work." The doors slide shut as I spit, *"They sell liquor!"*

Fuck, fuck, *fuck!*

I've really blown it now. I'm already imagining Jude telling his parents about the "really rude girl" he met at the hotel. Never mind the permanent contract, I'm going to get fired when they tell Dr. Lawrence about this. And if Jude talks to the Lakeside management about Mom, we could be a no-income family any minute. Being fired once was bad enough, but twice? Who would hire her after that?

I turn the shower up as hot as it'll go, and three rainforest showerheads douse me in massaging jets that fill the bathroom with so much steam I can't see myself in the mirror as I slide to the floor and let the water beat down on my head.

I close my eyes, tell myself it was nothing. But my brain's taken a photo I can't delete.

Mom's always enjoyed a drink in the evenings, wine with dinner, or a couple before bed. When you're a single parent, that's probably the closest you get to having a social life. My grandparents left for Florida in their camper when I was six and she couldn't afford childcare.

And OK, it's more than a glass or two these days, it's more than wine, and I guess she spends more of the grocery money on it. There's always a bottle in the trash and she opens them earlier in the day. The rent's been late a few times recently, and there's been a drunk-dialing incident or two involving old boyfriends. And if she's been on a real binge she can be a little . . . argumentative. But only if you make the mistake of talking to her.

But who hasn't done or said something stupid when they're drunk? It's not like it's ever been a major problem; she's *not* an alcoholic. Alcoholics are people who pass out on the lawn, beat their kids, crash their cars, end up homeless. My mom's not like that. She always made it to work every day, she made it to parents' nights at school, there was food in the fridge. It's never been a problem, so there was no need to talk about it. There was nothing to talk *about*. Talking about it would have *made* it a problem.

But then Dante fired her. Which I guess counts as a problem, but she was feeling down enough about being out of work; it wasn't the right time to bring it up.

She didn't sit around feeling sorry for herself, either. She tried a bunch of other bars; she even applied for the job of my "mother" at R&J. Lawrence turned her down.

"She's my actual mother!" I told him. "Who could pretend to know and love me better than my actual mother?"

"I just don't think she has . . ." He winced. "The emotional range."

"You think she can't weep at my deathbed? Come on,

if we're honest, she's probably had that fantasy more than once."

He just laughed.

When she finally got the job at Lakeside, I thought everything would be OK. Things would be better, in fact, because she wouldn't be surrounded by alcohol at work. But I forgot about the minibars, the room service, the things people leave behind.

I shut off the shower and watch my reflection emerge from the steam, makeup gone, bare skin beaten red by the water. Then I dress and slip out before Naomi is up. I don't want to tell her what happened. I don't want to tell anyone. Ever. I think about texting Mom to check she's OK. But what would I say? What do you say about something you don't talk about?

Outside, the air is hot already, and too still, the lake blinding in the sun as the doorman opens the front door of the hotel for me. I could swim. Or have iced tea on the terrace while I wait for Dr. Lawrence to fire me. Anything would be better than sitting around stewing. As my eyes adjust to the light, I notice Jude perched uncomfortably on a deck chair on the lawn, like he's not sure how it's supposed to work.

Almost anything.

I walk straight past him, assuming we'd both like to pretend we haven't seen each other. But when I'm a few steps down the drive he catches up.

"Regan. I was waiting for you."

I look warily at him. "You were?"

"I thought I should apologize. For"—he shrugs—"whatever it was I did that put you in such a foul temper."

I lower my sunglasses and look at him over the rims. "I'm not sure the word *apologize* means what you think it means."

"Look, I'm at a loose end this morning, and it's dangerous to hike alone, so . . . do you want to come?"

I blink at him in amazement. I really, really don't, no. But I thought I'd blown it and here I am being offered another chance. Only so he can push me in front of him if we meet a bear, but that's still more than I expected. Maybe there's still hope. Ugh. I almost wish there wasn't.

I should be going home. I should be checking on Mom, because there is no way she went back to work like she wasn't just humiliated in front of her daughter, and I worry about what she's doing now. Instead, I have to smile sweetly at the asshole whose fault it all is and say, "Fine. Life's too short to hold grudges."

I don't say much as we start up the steepest trail out of the resort. I'm too out of breath already. Anyway, everything I say to him ends in disaster so I'm going to let him take the lead now. I limit myself to swatting mosquitos and commenting on our surroundings, like I haven't seen the view a million times. He doesn't say much in return, but he seems to pick up the pace every time I open my mouth. My Balenciaga sneakers were not made for hiking.

He's wearing boots, as well as baggy jeans and an

open shirt over his T-shirt, and he doesn't appear to sweat. The son of a bitch is *whistling*. As we climb higher, the trees thin and there are glimpses of the lake far below and I'm grateful for a cooler breeze.

I beg him to stop so I can sip water from one of the bottles the concierge packed in Jude's backpack. Of course, the concierge thought of everything and there's also a picnic blanket, breakfast, sunscreen, a magazine, and a paperback book in there. I sent a quick text to Mom while Jude was getting the picnic. *Hey. You OK?* Most inadequate text message ever. No reply yet.

"I love the smell of books, don't you?" I say, nodding at the paperback as if I spend a lot of time in libraries. I'm basically stalling so I can catch my breath.

He raises an eyebrow. "I prefer to read them, but . . ." He lifts the book out, opens it, sniffs the pages. Then he looks up, eyes narrowed, and says, like a wine connoisseur, "European history, eighteenth century. I'm getting France; I'm getting revolution. Hint of deposed monarchy, trace elements of disgruntled peasantry."

He snaps the book shut and we look at the cover.

"*The Great Gatsby*," he reads the title aloud.

I can't help but laugh. "Well, you were close." I shrug, and he smiles. A nice smile, not the mocking one. I guess that's progress.

"Come on, then: onward and upward."

I sigh and follow him along ever narrower and more overgrown trails. But the steepness is leveling out now, the fresh air clearing my head, and I tell myself that if he wants us to be alone, that's a good sign. My phone vibrates and I check it quickly while he's ahead of me, but it's not from Mom. It's a selfie of Micah with the college guy in one of the private cabanas on the beach. That's what I should be doing right now. That's what R&Jing is supposed to be all about. Instead I'm discussing literature and being eaten by mosquitos.

"*Tender Is the Night* was better," Jude's saying. "And I've heard *This Side of Paradise* is good, but I haven't read it yet." His whole body hesitates for a microsecond, like a computer with a glitch, and he repeats, "I haven't read it."

For a moment I feel sorry for him. "Jude?" I say. "I could live to be a hundred and I wouldn't read *This Side of Paradise*. There are billions of books. You could never read them all anyway."

"Of course not," he says. "It's just . . . onism, you know?"

I do *not* know.

"Onism. It means the feeling of frustration from being limited to one body, one place, one lifetime," he explains.

"Oh. That." I grimace like *yeah, totally.*

"What does it for you?" he asks.

But I have an answer ready for this. It always comes up. "I guess it's the places I'll never go." I look out over the lake as we walk, into the distance where the air is hazy with heat. "And little things. Stupid things. Foods I'll never try. The end of the series I'm reading. She hasn't written the last book yet so I guess I won't get to see if they get together in the end."

"I can tell you now, they will," he says.

"Yeah, but *how*? That's the fun part."

"Getting to vote for the first time," he muses.

"Music I'll never dance to."

"People I'll never meet," he says. I look at him and he adds, "You know, wondering if there was someone out there I might have really . . . connected with?"

My ears prick up. "I get that. It's easy to feel lonely at a time like this." Maybe Naomi was right, maybe just talking to him *is* the best strategy. Maybe I've been over-complicating things. "Look, I know we don't really know each other, but I do get it, Jude. So, if you want company this week . . ."

He looks thoughtfully at me. "You know, when we met, I really *didn't*. I didn't want to get to know another person. Someone else to leave behind. Maybe that's why I was—"

"Laceratingly rude?" I supply.

"Let's say . . . touchy. But you're right, it *is* lonely. And my family's great but . . ."

"But they can't understand."

"No."

As we emerge from the trees into a clearing at the top of the cliff, it feels like things have shifted a little—the air between us freshening like the breeze up here. I can't help feeling relieved. And a little smug. Only took a day and one sleepless night but maybe we're finally on track. For all his standoffish exterior, this guy wasn't so hard after all.

I wander over to where the cliff edge drops away. The whole length of the resort is small and peaceful beneath us and the sky is vast above, and suddenly the week feels full of possibilities again.

"You should come see the view," I call back to Jude.

"In a minute," he says. He doesn't come to the edge to look out, just sits down on a flat rock in the middle of the space and starts stripping the bark off a twig. "I admit, meeting you has been a welcome distraction," he says. "And . . . I don't know. We keep running into each other."

"I guess that must mean something." I walk over to flop down beside him, grateful for the rest. I check my phone again, but I'm not even getting reception up here.

He laughs quietly. "I think it means I keep seeking you out. I don't *want* to need support through this, but . . ."

I touch his arm gently. "Jude, everyone needs support sometimes."

"I usually get all my moral support from books. Philosophy mostly. Have you read Camus?"

I look blankly at him, and quip, "I'm waiting for the movie."

He smiles. "Camus said there is only one truly philo-sophical question to answer, and that is whether to live or die."

"Cheery."

"*To be or not to be.* Shakespeare said it long before Camus."

"Well, we're all here, aren't we? *Being.*"

"Doesn't mean you've answered the question. Camus said you have to look at your life objectively and decide if it's worth living. Then"—he points the twig at me, and grins—"and this is the kicker, you have to *act* according to your answer. You have to die or you have to live."

"Whoa. Intense. So did he do it? Did he kill himself? Camus?" I ask, interested despite myself.

"No."

"So he thought life *was* worth living?"

"He thought life was absurd. Meaningless. But he also thought the correct response to that was revolt, not suicide. To find your own meaning. Enjoy life anyway."

"Oh. Well, *I* could've told him that," I say. "I thought philosophy was hard."

Jude laughs. Then he tosses the twig away and says quietly, "He also said that, in reality, even the most miserable people usually don't kill themselves. One thing gets in the way."

"What's that?"

"Hope. There's always the hope that something might change." He looks thoughtful, gazing down at the boats on the lake, as if he's talking to himself now, not me.

I shake my head. "I think I need some breakfast. You don't do small talk, do you?"

He turns a little more toward me. "The thing is, we don't have any," he says.

"Any what? Breakfast? There's some in the backpack."

"Hope." He reaches over and takes my hand in his. His

palm is cool despite the heat and I shiver involuntarily. "But isn't that kind of liberating?" he says.

"I'm not sure I—"

"All the complications just stripped away."

"Yeah, I guess. When you put it like that." God, I need to lie down for several hours. I don't even know what we're talking about now.

But he's searching my face as if there might be answers there, the flecks of gold in his eyes picking up the sunlight as he says, "So why wait?"

My scattered thoughts snap into focus.

"What?"

"Camus said you have to act on your decision. He didn't say decide, go on a luxury spa break, *then* act."

"Yeah, but—"

"I mean, what is the point of prolonging things at this stage? I would have done it already," he says. "It's just—I guess it's like you said. It's hard to be alone right now. I have this thing about being alone. *Dying* alone."

"Right. Yeah," I say uncertainly. If this is the part where he suggests we have our procedures together, then I guess that's good. But something about this isn't right. It's too fast. Something about *Jude Daly* isn't right, and I just can't figure out what it is. A minute ago I thought he might ask me to a movie or something, now he's talking about death?

He squeezes my hand tighter, then stands, pulling me up with him. "You're right, there must be a reason we kept running into each other." His dark eyes have become intense, and I'm suddenly aware of just how far away all the speedboats and sunbathers are.

"Uh . . . Jude?"

"I'm glad we're on the same wavelength, Regan. I didn't really want to come to the resort. I just wanted to get it over with. And now there's nothing to stop us."

"Stop us? Stop what?"

He looks out at the view again. No. Not at the view. At the cliff edge. The sheer drop about fifty feet from where we're standing. I instinctively try to take a step back, pulling away from him. But I can't. Because he's still holding my hand. And he's not letting go.

"Jude? Jude, stop it, you're scaring me." I try to tug my hand back but he barely notices. His eyes flick to me, freezing me to the spot.

"Really, this is the perfect place," he says. "They're set up to deal with this stuff here."

"But your parents—they'll be devastated!" I pull harder, tugging at his fingers with my other hand.

He tilts his head, as if considering. "Obviously they'll be *upset.* But what difference does a few days make? I think they'll be relieved to get it over with. It's been so hard for them for so long already. And I know they're dreading being there when . . . you know." He looks back at the edge, as if he's calculating the distance.

"Jude!" My sneakers start to scrabble in the loose earth, losing grip as I pitch my weight backward. But he's so much stronger than me.

"I'm sure your mother feels the same," he says, ignoring my struggling.

"*I* don't feel the same! I don't want to do this!"

He looks back, genuinely confused. "Why not?"

"Because I don't want to die!"

He snorts. "No choice about that, do we? I mean, no one does, when you think about it. But especially us."

"But—" I can't breathe, let alone think. Burgess is supposed to fucking screen these people!

"But what?" He takes a step toward the edge, and my feet slide forward in the dirt.

I hold up my free hand. "Look, this isn't what you think!"

Another step. "What isn't?"

"Me! I'm not . . . I'm not what you think. This is a mistake!"

He frowns. "I don't understand. You said you felt lonely. I hoped . . . I hoped maybe you felt—"

"Well, I don't, OK?" I pull backward desperately, so he has to turn and hold on with two hands. "I don't even know you! I don't give a shit about fucking Camus! What the fuck do you think this is? People don't just jump off a cliff with a complete stranger because they read some stupid book!"

He crows a sudden laugh at that. "Oh, but they *do*!" he says, delighted. "It's a classic plot, isn't it? Not Camus, not many people have read that. But there's . . . I don't know . . . *Romeo and Juliet*?" He lets go so suddenly, I flail backward, landing on my ass in the dirt, panting. He tilts his head. "Have you read that one?" His eyes are narrowed now, ice-cold, as he stands over me, arms folded across his chest.

I falter. "W-what?" I breathe.

"It's pretty good. Sort of unrealistic, though; you're right about that." He gives me a sarcastic sneer. "Come on, a couple of teenagers who go on one date and then off themselves because they can't be together? I mean"—he laughs harder, shaking with it—"what kind of . . ." He throws his head back and guffaws. "What kind of *moron*"—he roars the word, and I flinch as he leans down into my face—"would fall"—closer still—"for *that*?"

There's a long beat where we're both just breathing heavily in each other's faces. Then he straightens and steps back.

"You're . . . you're *joking*?" I whisper. The word couldn't be less appropriate.

He takes deep, shuddering breaths. "How does it feel to be lied to over a matter of life and death?"

I stagger to my feet, then double over again, trying not to puke. He just watches. When the nausea has passed, I stand up, still shaky, and yell, "What the fuck is *wrong* with you?"

He turns on me. "I could ask you the same question! This is how you get your kicks, is it? Preying on vulnerable people?"

"What? No! It's just . . . it's not like that! And if you

knew, you could have just said so. You didn't have to go all fucking serial killer on me!"

He snorts. "Think of it as Method acting. Now that you've been face-to-face with death, you can use it with your next . . . client? Is that what you call us?"

"That was fucking cruel!"

"Oh, *I'm* sorry," he says with exaggerated emphasis. "I guess I was just a little pissed that you were planning to make the last days of my life a fucking joke!"

"It's not like that! It's supposed to be . . . fun, I don't know. It helps people!" I don't know why I'm defending myself to this guy.

He steps closer. "*It's a job. With a big expense account. Full R and J. I can bat my eyelashes at anyone for a week.* Was that how it went?" He quotes my own words back at me, dripping scorn.

"You heard that?" I breathe, remembering my conversation with Micah in the corridor outside Dr. Burgess's office. "Where— How did—?"

"I was on the floor above. Looking over the rail. But I didn't realize *I* was the job until your appalling little seduction routine in the café. All that bollocks about your *procedure*. I actually did think you might be a journalist. But then my mother starts suggesting *nightclubs* to me? It didn't take much to work it out. You're in her phone under *Juliet*."

"So . . . So you've just been fucking with me this whole time! Being rude and—"

"Wondered how much you'd take before you'd quit. You're persistent, I'll give you that."

"And all that stuff about being lonely and wanting to end it!"

"Total BS. You think I'd do that to my parents?"

"I don't know what you'd do! You're a fucking *psycho*!"

"And you're a fucking *parasite*." He practically spits the word. "I hope you're well paid. What's the going rate for someone's dignity these days? And you had the nerve to judge my parents for what *they* do for a living?"

Shit, this is bad. This is really, *really* bad. His parents signed a nondisclosure agreement, but Jude didn't. What if he talks to the other guests? What if he talks to the fucking *Tonight Show*? Never mind my contract, he could bring down the whole R&J program. And it would be all my fault.

"Jude, I—"

"Don't speak to me. You're disgusting." He hurls the word in my face before walking off, leaving me to collapse in the dirt.

Chapter 6

I came straight back to the hotel and found Naomi on our balcony in her robe and slippers, tapping through the brunch menu on her electronic guest handbook.

"I can't tell Lawrence! I'll get fired!" I pace the balcony while she frets on the edge of her lounger. "They're supposed to be supervised in the clinic. Why did they let him wander off by himself? Why didn't Burgess realize he was nuts? Why is there nowhere in the building you can have a private conversation without being overheard?"

Naomi lets me rant, because she knows I need to blame everyone else, including the architects of the building, before I face the fact that this is all my fault.

"Maybe he won't say anything. I mean, if he was going to, wouldn't he have done it by now?" she suggests.

"He's not exactly predictable. He just threatened to throw me off a cliff, who knows what he'll do next." A horrible thought occurs to me. "Do you think Lawrence could sue me? For, like . . . loss of earnings or something?" R&J only works because the clients have never heard of it. And I signed all those nondisclosure things, too.

She thinks about it, which is not reassuring. "I don't know."

I sink down beside her, head in my hands. "It was going terribly anyway. At least now I know why."

"You don't have to win 'em all, Ree," she says, rubbing my back. "It doesn't matter."

But this one *did* matter. It'll matter to Mom if I get fired. It'll matter to Micah, and Naomi, and all the other Juliets and Romeos if the R&J service gets shut down. It'll matter to Dr. Burgess and Dr. Lawrence if they lose their business. And it'll matter to me if I have to crawl back to Dante and beg him for a job. How are normal people supposed to get anywhere when there are assholes with so much power that they can get you, your mom, and everyone you love fired from their jobs in one fucking morning?

The worst part is that his words are still earworming in my head. *Parasite. What's the going rate for someone's dignity?* I'm used to people having opinions about this job. I'm used to how the parents in Dr. Lawrence's office look at me. How the kids from school look at me. But I've never had a client's take on it.

He just doesn't understand. He thinks my job is entirely fake because it's not entirely real. But there are shades of gray. I've never felt guilty about what I do. It helps people; I've seen it. But I'm a parasite because I get *paid*? Nurses get paid. Social workers get paid. It would be great to be able to help people for free and then get praised for it on the covers of magazines, but we don't all have that luxury.

I'm not a parasite; I just live in the real world. And I won't be judged by someone like him.

I start to shiver. I think I'm still in shock. Naomi brings me a glass of milk and tucks a blanket around me, and I curl up next to her, let her wrap her arms around me, stroke my hair, and murmur that *everything's going to be OK, honey*. As if she really is my mom and I have nothing worse to worry about than a fight with my boyfriend and which of my designer shoes to wear tonight. The thought is comforting and I let myself sink into it for a moment.

Why is everyone so hung up on *real* anyway? Sometimes it's OK to pretend. Sometimes people want the fantasy. What's wrong with giving it to them?

Damage limitation is the best I can hope for now.

I might not be able to change anything, but I have to at least know what he intends to do. So, I promise Naomi I won't be alone with him, and head out of the hotel and toward the Hermitage.

Lakeside has seven private lodges dotted around the little peninsula. The Hermitage isn't the biggest, but it's got the best view of the lake. It's right on the shore, facing away from town, so you could believe you're out here alone in the wilderness. It's done in a kind of "rustic" style, all wood and shingles and exposed beams, but there's nothing rustic about it. It's a two-story luxury cabin with a veranda, pool, hot tub, steam room, sauna, staff, and your own boat moored at a private jetty.

I make my way along the woodland trails, wondering what I'm going to say. There's nothing in the training manual about psychopaths who try to throw you off a cliff. And what if his parents come out? What do I say to them? I hesitate outside the building. On the table on the veranda there are a couple of wineglasses, a blanket, some books. Maybe they sat out here last night while Jude was at Inferno. How *do* you pass the time until your son dies? I guess this entire resort is an answer to that question.

The screen door opens, but it's not the Dalys. It's Jude. I instinctively take a step backward, and he has the decency to look ashamed of himself. He holds a hand up, as if I might get spooked. "It's OK," he says. "I'm not—"

"Psychotically dangerous?" I shift my weight to one hip, glaring at him.

"Quite so pissed off," he finishes, sounding only moderately pissed off. "Do you want to come in?"

"Not if you paid me."

He comes down the steps, though we're no less alone out here. I glance at the house behind him. "My parents are out," he says. "They have a counseling session."

"Oh." It's annoying to be reminded that you're not supposed to be mad at someone who's dying young. Who wouldn't act a little crazy in those circumstances? But on the other hand, no one else has ever threatened to throw me off a cliff, and why should I feel sorry for Mr. *I've stayed in better*? Everybody dies. Not everybody gets to live.

"So, what can I do for you?" he says. Neither one of us is apologizing, it seems.

"I just need to know . . . Look, I get that you want nothing to do with all this. Fine, that's your call. But you should know, if you talk about it, to anyone, it could put a lot of people's jobs at risk."

He snorts. "Morally reprehensible people."

"You don't know them. Naomi—she plays my mom. Her kid is sick. Like, really sick. She has medical bills." This could be true for all he knows.

He just folds his arms, his expression giving nothing away.

I take a breath and count to three. "You have to admit, that was kind of crazy behavior back there. But hey, I get it. You're upset. Who wouldn't be a little . . . unstable?" I try to sound like I'm being understanding, instead of totally gaslighting him, as I say, "But I'm willing to let it go, I won't say a word to anyone, we can drop the whole thing."

"Is that a threat?"

I throw my hands up. "That's me trying to be nice! But

fine. OK. How about this? How about I tell the fucking cops about that dumb stunt you pulled? I have a friend who's a lawyer. He says I could sue for emotional damage."

He frowns at me. "You just can't help yourself, can you? Do you even know the difference between reality and bullshit anymore? Keep going. I genuinely can't wait to see what's next."

I clench my jaw. Even if I did have a lawyer friend, the cops would probably take his side. "You don't know anything about the R-and-J service, you haven't read the brochure, you don't—"

"The brochure!" He pours derision all over the words. "See, this is exactly what's wrong with this place. Do people really think you can buy yourself a girlfriend? You can't *buy* love. Everything is cheapened and worthless because of people like you."

"You can buy a personal appearance by a Hollywood actor at your dinner table in this place, of *course* they think you can buy love. *People like you* think they're entitled to everything, why *not* love? My job wouldn't exist if people like you didn't demand it, so don't look at me like *I'm* some moral vacuum."

He opens his mouth to retaliate, but I hold up a palm. "Look," I say, jaw tight and teeth grinding. "This may come as a shock, but I don't actually *care* what you think of me, so spare me the lecture. I just need to know what you're going to do. Because if you talk about this, then . . ." But I'm all out of threats and tactics. "Then I'm going to get in a mountain of trouble," I admit, folding my arms sullenly. "You want reality, *that's* the reality. Not that you'd care, but that's a one hundred percent fact." I scowl at the ground, finally deflated and waiting for him to deliver the death blow.

After an agonizing moment, he mutters, "You don't have to worry. I won't say anything."

"What?" I look up, still suspicious. "You won't?"

He shakes his head.

I exhale. "Good. Great. Thank you." I step back. "Well. I'll stay out of your way, then." It's the best I could hope for. There's no way I'll get my permanent contract, and I might still lose my job for failing with this guy, but at least I won't be responsible for everyone else losing theirs.

But he says, "No."

I stop. "No?" Oh God, what now? If he's playing me again . . .

"You're paid for the week, aren't you?"

"Yeah, but—"

"Then that's what we're doing."

"What? Are you serious? Hey, if you mean . . . sex, it's really *not* that kind of deal."

He laughs. Sort of insultingly.

I spread my hands. "Then . . . *why?*"

"Because I said so," he snaps. "And you need a favor from me."

He looks down at me, dark eyes unreadable. "We're going to go through the motions of this farce and no one is going to know that we're pretending. Or that you're *not* pretending, or whatever fucked-up version of the truth we're at now." He rolls his eyes. "You can have my silence in exchange for yours."

He walks up the steps and calls back before he shuts the screen door, "I've booked a bunch of stuff for today. We're starting with archery at noon. Don't be late."

PART II

Pretty
Piece of
Flesh

Chapter 7

JUDE'S PARENTS ARE WAITING WITH HIM AT THE ARCHERY RANGE. It's in a clearing in the woods behind the Imperial Hotel, and the staff wear Robin Hood–style green livery. You can do falconry and jousting and other medieval sports, too, followed by a medieval lunch banquet. Some people have very weird bucket lists.

I'm dressed like someone who's up for a day of activities—Ralph Lauren loose pants and white shirt, a swimsuit in my bag—but I don't know why I've bothered or who I'm fooling. I don't know what I'm supposed to be wearing. I don't know what I'm supposed to *be*. How do I act around Jude if I can't, you know, *act*?

He barely looks at me anyway, while Mr. and Mrs. Daly do an impressive job of pretending we haven't met before. Mrs. Daly's wearing huge sunglasses, but I imagine that beneath them, her eyes are as red rimmed as last time I saw her. They're putting on an Oscar-worthy performance of "fun family day," though.

"Rachel, was it?"

"Regan."

"Regan, so nice to meet you. Have you tried archery before?"

"No, but, you know, anything once!"

"That's the spirit," Mr. Daly says as a guy from my school fits my usual armguard.

Jude is already kitted out, and he hands me a bow with perfect civility. I know that Jude's proposal is a good thing for me. Technically, it makes getting that permanent contract easier because I don't even have to make him like me. All I have to do is put up with him for the rest of the week. But that might be worse.

When I told Naomi and Micah about his plan to fake it, they were as confused as I am.

"But . . . *why*?"

I threw my hands up. "That's what I said!"

"I don't know, Ree. It's weird," Naomi said.

"What choice do I have?" And her expression conceded *not much*.

Jude carries my equipment out to the range. I'm still wary of him, but he looks relaxed as we listen to the instructor and take our places at the waiting line.

"OK, so what are we doing here?" I whisper while Mr. and Mrs. Daly step forward to take their shots. Mr. Daly impales a tree at the far end of the overshoot area, and Mrs. Daly can barely pull back the bowstring.

"It's called archery," Jude replies. "We're going to attach these pointy stick things to this long bow thing and—"

"I know what we're doing! *Why* are we doing it?" He knows exactly what I'm saying; he's just being a dick. But I'm used to working to a brief. I need to know what I'm here to achieve.

He just shrugs. "When I start something, I finish it."

"I'm not interested in being some checkmark on your to-do list."

"I thought that was your entire job," he says as the Dalys start back toward us, laughing at their terrible shots.

I put on a big smile for their benefit while saying, under my breath, "Please fuck off into the sun."

He matches the smile as he waves me forward to the shooting line with an exaggeratedly polite, "After you."

The Dalys move back to the waiting line to watch. We have three shots each. I'm so distracted, I only hit the outer circle of the target the first time. Three points. He hits the blue ring for five.

"If you know so much about my job, tell me this," I say as he comes back to the waiting line. "If you wanted to go through with this whole charade, why not just go on pretending not to know? What was that stupid stunt with the cliff about?"

"I *was* going to go on pretending, but apparently I have too much human decency to con someone for a whole week. *I'm* not that dishonest. Anyway, there was a serious risk of me vomiting all over your manic-pixie-dream-girl act."

I open my mouth, shut it, turn it into a smile for Mrs. Daly, who's beaming from ear to ear at what must seem like quite an intimate conversation from a distance.

I remind myself that Jude Daly might know I've been hired, but he doesn't know anything about *me*. He doesn't know, for example, that I've spent a lot of time on this archery range with a lot of teenage boys. He doesn't know that, when I'm not fuming with rage, I'm actually a pretty good shot. In fact, no one knows this, because I always make sure to let the boy I'm with win. Usually I let him show me how the bow works, as well, while standing too close to me and mansplaining basic physics.

This time, I don't do that. I take my place at the shooting line, raise the bow, and imagine Jude standing in front of the target.

"Bull's-eye! Nice job, Regan!" His parents jump up and down and punch the air while Jude gives me a tight smile.

"Not bad," he says. It's clearly painful for him to compliment me. His next shot is a mere six.

"I *think* that means I'm winning, then." I bat my eyelashes at him.

"I didn't realize it was a competition," he says.

"Oh, I suppose you're not competitive."

"Of course not, that would be childish. I'm just . . . in the habit of succeeding at whatever I set out to do."

"Finally," I say, drawing another arrow and stepping

up to the shooting line again. "Something we have in common."

We spend the rest of the afternoon trying to annihilate each other while smiling charmingly and being outrageously polite.

It's liberating, being able to let loose and show what I can do, instead of pretending to be a newbie, and I take every opportunity to wipe the floor with him. I win the archery by a mile, but he holds his own at beach volleyball. He's good at horseback riding, but too careful a driver for dirt track racing. It strikes me that he hasn't really gone for the adrenaline rush activities. No skydiving or bungee jumping, no wingsuit flying, and—ironically— no cliff diving at Bergman Island. This place is wasted on him. Or maybe it's so his parents can participate. They're both game, if not exactly sporty. His mom almost throws a parade every time Jude lands a point.

But there's a desperation to their attempts to make everything super exciting, and Jude responds in a stiff, forced way. Like he's decided to "have fun," but he's acting it out according to a manual. The longer the day goes on, the more on edge everyone seems, and there's a hysterical undercurrent to the laughter. I feel sorry for them. And I feel helpless. They're paying me to lighten the mood, but I can't even do that because Jude knows the truth. The thought of keeping this up for a whole week suddenly seems exhausting.

"OK, one more before dinner!" Mr. Daly says, and I

try to look enthusiastic instead of despairing as we say goodbye to the staff at the stables. "We have ten minutes to get to the rock-climbing area. It's not far."

A little golf cart comes to take us there. Jude sits in the back with me. I check my phone quickly. Still nothing from Mom.

"Are we keeping you from something?" Jude says quietly, seeing me tuck it away.

"Yes, I have an unanesthetized root canal I'm suddenly looking forward to," I mutter.

"Well, don't forgo unimaginable pain on my account."

Mrs. Daly leans back to smile at us, like she can't bear to take her eyes off him for too long. Jude pastes on a grin and I feel like a jerk, intruding on his last days with his family. But this was his decision, I remind myself. I didn't ask to be here.

The rock climbing is just a couple of small outcrops with handholds embedded in them, and they strap you into a harness so you can't hurt yourself. It's only about fifty feet, but since you start near the top of the mountain, the view is pretty great when you get up there.

The rock-climbing guy straps us in, but Jude seems to be having trouble with his harness, checking and rechecking it. As I tap my foot, waiting for him, he takes the helmet off and starts tugging all the straps on that, too. Jeez, if he hadn't come here for his procedure, what would have killed him? A random accident doesn't seem likely for someone that careful. And I can't see Mr. Do-Gooder having any murderous enemies. Except me, obviously.

Eventually he's ready, and we start climbing side by side while the Dalys watch from below. I'm expecting a race, but when I'm only about twenty feet off the ground, I realize Jude is lagging behind already. For the Dalys' sake, I slow down. When he reaches me, he's sweating.

"You OK?" I ask. Maybe his harness is too tight.

"Fine," he says, teeth gritted.

"You sure?"

"I said I'm fine." He looks over his shoulder toward the ground, then quickly back at the rock in front of him and leans his forehead against it, breathing hard.

It dawns on me. He's afraid of heights. I'm incredulous. Doesn't he have a private jet? But I guess that explains why we're not skydiving.

He slowly pulls himself up to the next rung. I could race ahead and sit at the top, lording it over him, but there's not much glory in winning a competition with someone who's having an aneurysm every time he looks down. So instead I say, "Look, if you don't want to—"

But he reaches for another rung with grim determination. Then another. I keep pace, making it look like I'm finding it tough, too. We're thirty feet up now. Thirty-five. There are only fifteen more before we get our *I Beat the Rock! (intermediate level)* certificates and souvenir T-shirts. Which we might need because Jude is sweating through his shirt. It's honestly fun to see him looking less than completely smug and dignified for once. He keeps glancing back to where his dad is beaming like it's graduation and his mom is standing with her hands clasped beneath her chin like he's tightrope walking over Niagara Falls.

He swears as his foot slips out of its toehold and he has to scrabble a little. Someone below yells, "Go, champ!" and he rolls his eyes.

At forty feet up, he seems to hit a wall. He just freezes, knuckles white and his body pressed against the rock like he's Velcroed to it.

"I can't . . ." he breathes.

"Jude?" I draw level with him. He's just shaking his head.

"I thought I could but . . . this whole thing was a stupid idea," he says.

"It's OK, we just have—"

But he ignores me. "I'm sorry I got you involved; it was crazy. I can't do this. I can't." I wonder if he's talking about the climbing or the whole fake dating nightmare.

He's attempting to inch his way back down the wall, but it involves looking down and every time he does, he freaks out. It seems like we're stuck here.

I look back at his parents, then up at the summit above us, at my hands on the handholds. I shake my head, close my eyes, and before I can think about it too much, I let go.

My scream as I drop is completely genuine. But I only fall about two feet before the safety harness catches me, and then I just swing there in open space, pretending to panic.

I heard Mrs. Daly scream, too, but I don't look down. I look up, to where Jude is now hanging on to the rock by one hand, the other one reaching down to me as he shouts, "It's OK! Just reach up to me!"

He's on total autopilot. Not even thinking about the height anymore.

"I can't! It's too high! I don't like heights! I shouldn't be up here!" I wail back, hands over my face like I can't bear to look.

"Regan!" he commands, and I peek out through my fingers. "Stay calm. I'm coming down." He clambers down a couple of rungs and reaches over to help me put my own hands on the rungs beside him.

"I'm sorry. I didn't think it would be this high! I thought I could do it!"

"Just focus," he says, directing me to put one hand in front of the other as we steadily climb back up.

"See, we're doing it!" he says, like he's encouraging a third grader.

"I'm dizzy."

"Just a bit more. Look, all you have to do is touch the top rung and we're done." He reaches up to put his own hand over the top handhold. "Just take my hand," he tells me.

I look up, take a deep, shaky breath, and, straightening one leg, rise a few inches to close my hand over his. Everyone down below cheers, and Jude leans his forehead against the rock face as the safety guys haul me up and over the ridge.

· · ·

When the instructors leave us to get our breath back at the top, I slap Jude on the shoulder, grin at him, and say, "See, I knew you could do it!"

He looks confused for a moment, and then he realizes what just happened.

"You did that on *purpose*?"

"Um . . ."

"What the . . . You are . . . I should have known . . . I can't believe you did that!" He's furious, but I get the feeling he's more annoyed that he fell for it. "Are you ever *not* lying? You're not even afraid of heights, are you?" he says with a huff.

"And *you* would never have gone anywhere near that cliff edge this morning, would you?" I counter. "Speaking of liars. You *are* afraid of heights."

He makes an indignant sound. "I'm not afraid of heights, I'm afraid of *falling* from heights. Which makes complete sense when you're dangling from a thin rope, probably rigged up by some high-school dropout for minimum wage."

"*Nathan* happens to be a very experienced climber. He climbed Everest," I tell him, adding pointedly, "shortly after graduating from high school."

"Everest?"

I spread my hands. "Only the best for Elite Elect!"

I brace myself for his reply, but he just lets out an exhausted breath.

"You could have died," he points out.

"That's a little dramatic," I say. "And I got us up here, didn't I?" I toss him one of the *I Beat the Rock* T-shirts the instructor gave me. "You're welcome."

I wander over to the edge to look out. Far below us, the valley cups the lake in soft green hands and the water holds the sky in turquoise blue ones. The trees sway and the air is alive with birdsong. It's not like I've never seen the place from up here before. I've flown over it in a helicopter *and* a hot-air balloon. But there's something about having climbed to the top under your own steam that always improves the view.

Jude moves a few steps nearer, but doesn't come too close to the edge. The breeze moves his hair and the late afternoon light brings out the red in it.

"How can you be afraid of heights? You must travel on planes all the time."

"I trust aviation engineers. I trust trained airline pilots. I *don't* trust my own fingernails to hold the entire weight of my body. It's not fear, it's logic."

I give him a skeptical look, which he ignores.

He takes another step closer. His parents wave up at us from below.

"Look, I feel like I'm just in the way here," I say, waving back at them. "And you clearly don't want me around, so . . ."

"So?"

"*So why am I here?*" I ask, frustrated. "OK, I owe you for not shooting your mouth off. And I'm happy to repay that debt, but it's hard when I don't know what you actually want."

"It's not fun being kept in the dark, is it?" he says, enjoying my discomfort. "And we're only on day two!"

"Could you be any more annoying?"

He shrugs. "You'll find out. By the way, we're going to a party tonight. At the hotel."

Ugh. I almost groan before a thought occurs to me. "Wait. A party? You mean . . . you don't mean the Midsummer Ball?"

"Yes, that's it. You'll be my plus-one. And my parents would like to invite your . . . *mother.*" He says the word like it tastes bad.

I can hear Naomi in my head. *Are you crazy? Make an excuse and get the hell out of there, Ree!* And I can hear Micah. *The Midsummer Ball? Don't you* dare *turn this down.* Ten-year-old Regan is just screaming.

I try to look unenthusiastic as I say, "Fine. Sure. If you insist. I mean, I hear it's a pretty good party; maybe it'll be fun."

"It'll be excruciating," he says flatly. Then he shrugs. "So you may as well be there. You can't make it any worse."

And then he turns to face the hellish rappel back down the rock. If he wasn't taking me to the Midsummer Ball tonight, I'd consider pushing him off it.

Chapter 8

THE MIDSUMMER BALL HAS BEEN MY FANTASY EVER SINCE I CAN remember. While other little girls draped towels over their heads and had pretend weddings, I turned my mom's dresses into ball gowns and made Micah dance with me to classical music in the living room.

Every year they drown the hotel in flowers and fairy lights, the glass doors are folded back so the dining room merges with the terrace, and the weather's always perfect, like God himself wouldn't dare to disappoint these people. There's an orchestra on the roof garden, a dance floor on the lawn. The sun sets over the lake, and then there's dancing under the stars and fireworks. It's a fairy tale on steroids.

After ten years of daydreaming, I have about an hour to actually get ready, but within minutes of a call to the R&J stylists, a large white box arrives at my door, and Naomi and I carefully remove layers of tissue paper to reveal a dress more perfect than even ten-year-old Regan could have dreamed up.

"Marta, you're the love of my life," I whisper as I hold it up. It's a Jenny Packham—a boned corset finished in tissue-soft tulle, above-the-floor-length full satin skirt with more tulle on top, so fine it's practically mist. The satin is pale green and the tulle a shimmering aqua with fine embroidered vines running from the hem upward. The effect is like seaweed swaying under a tropical sea.

"Oh my God, Ree," Naomi says, snapping pictures as I pose. "It's stunning. Just stunning. I'm going to send these to your mom."

"No, don't," I say quickly. "I mean, send them to me and I'll send them to her." I feel bad enough that I'm going to this thing when I should probably go home and check on her. I've asked Micah to go over instead, and I know that's a cop-out but . . . *But this is work,* I tell myself. And *one* of us has to keep our job.

Naomi's dress is a striking deep blue off-the-shoulder sheath dress with a flare at the hem. Perfect for her figure.

"Do I look like Morticia Adams?" she asks, frowning at her silhouette in the mirror.

"Yes," I tell her, snapping pictures for her husband. "And she was sexy as hell."

The Lakeside dining room has been cleared to create a huge bar area, and plenty of people have arrived already when we come downstairs, the men in black tie, the women in red-carpet creations. The staff glide around like swans with trays of champagne flutes held aloft, uniforms pristine, and there's a string quartet in the corner.

My dress attracts admiring glances as Naomi and I move through the room and out to the terrace, where we can hear the orchestra on the roof garden above. The air has cooled just enough, the sun is sinking into the lake, and the evening light catches every jewel and champagne bubble. Down by the lake, acrobats, aerialists, and fire dancers perform in costumes dusted with glittering stars. After years of fantasizing about this, I wondered if I'd be disappointed, but it's perfect.

"I'm nervous," I admit, fussing with my dress.

"This is just another day at the office," Naomi reminds me, and I appreciate her attempts to steady me when I know she's as uncomfortable with all this as I am.

"It's not, though, is it? I can't keep track of who knows what. What if I say the wrong thing to the wrong person? Oh God, Dr. Lawrence is here! Do you think he's checking up on us?"

"He goes to the ball every year," she reassures me. "Calm down. As far as anyone knows, we're here because Jude is falling madly in . . ."

But I stop paying attention as, out of the mass of men in black dinner jackets, one detaches himself from the crowd and walks up the terrace steps toward us. It's the first time I've seen Jude out of his baggy jeans, but he's obviously used to wearing suits, too, because he moves with ease and confidence, attracting more admiring glances than I did. I have to admit, he looks good in a tux. But everyone looks good in a tux. *I'd* probably look good in a tux.

"Glad you could make it," he says upon reaching us.

"Wouldn't have missed it," I reply. He doesn't need to know how true that is.

We're talking like we're at a business meeting. I suppose we are in a way. But it's a very fancy business meeting and he could at least say he likes my dress.

He doesn't. I can just imagine the scorn Jude would pour all over my princess fantasy. He greets Naomi stiffly, then holds one arm out to me like Midsummer Balls are a chore and sighs. "Shall we?"

But even Prince Charmless is not going to ruin this night for me. I take his arm and step into my fairy tale.

The Dalys are on the terrace, chatting to another couple, but they detach themselves as we approach. Mr. Daly's tux is tailored to perfection and yet he still looks like he's busting out of it. Mrs. Daly is in pink chiffon as delicate as she is.

She throws her arms out to hug me. "Don't you look fabulous! You were born for that dress."

"I like to think so!" I swish my skirt and she laughs. "Your dress is gorgeous, Mrs. Daly."

She flaps a hand. "It's *highly* impractical. And this must be your mother!"

"Naomi. So lovely to meet you." They air-kiss like old friends.

"Isn't everything spectacular!" Mrs. Daly gestures at the lavish floral displays, the delicate paper lanterns starting to glow in the dusk, the ice sculpture of Neptune brandishing his trident and surrounded by ice mermaids. You'd think it would be difficult to impress someone as wealthy as Mrs. Daly, but she's charmingly thrilled with everything she encounters.

Even the makeup can't hide that her eyes are puffy, though, and they grow damp as she beams at Jude. She squeezes his hand and holds it, as though trying to think of a reason not to let go, and says, "Darling, you look so . . ." She laughs and goes with, "handsome!" But that's not what she's thinking. She's thinking *young*. She's thinking *healthy*. *Full of potential*. She's thinking *how can millions of less-worthy people live to old age when my perfect son won't?*

"You both do!" She sighs and waves us away. "Now go! Go and enjoy the party. Just save me a dance!" Jude leads me away, and even though she knows Naomi is some hired nobody, Mrs. Daly takes her arm and says, "Come and see the Ferris wheel!"

And then Jude and I are alone, standing awkwardly at the edge of the dance floor. I grab two glasses of champagne from a waiter and hand one to him. He swirls it absently. Are we just going to ignore each other unless there's someone watching? I'd started to wonder if he *does* want a friend to hang out with and was just too proud to admit it. But he doesn't act like it.

I try to take it all in, in case I never get to do this

again. Every tree surrounding the hotel is like a cloud of fireflies. The fairy-tale couples whirl past us, laughing, gazing into each other's eyes. I notice the family I saw on their clinic tour yesterday. The grandpa has a bowtie tied to his oxygen tank and Cinderella is sitting on the steps, yawning in pink tulle while her teenage brothers are fooling around with one of the paper lanterns on the terrace, tossing it back and forth like a beach ball. I can see Dr. Lawrence sitting at a little table on the other side of the lawn, talking to Dante. Of course Dante's here, sniffing around the richest guests, no doubt.

Jude still hasn't said a word, but we can't stand here like statues; we're supposed to look like we're on some kind of date. *Someone* has to make conversation. And I guess I'm the one being paid, so . . .

"They're a nice couple. Your parents," I try.

"Childhood sweethearts," he says.

"Yeah? You can tell."

But I forgot, Jude doesn't do small talk. "Is that what you're trying to replicate?" he asks, turning to look at me. "Do people really fall for it?"

I bristle. "They want it to be true."

He nods. "OK, I can understand that." Then he frowns. "But I don't understand *you.*"

"What do you mean?"

"I mean, what kind of person casually rents out their heart?"

"Who says I have a heart?" I quip. "I sold that years ago to buy shoes."

He gives me a cut-the-bullshit expression Dr. Burgess would be proud of.

I drain my champagne and place the glass on a passing tray. "What should I be renting out instead, Jude? Trust me, my heart's the most expendable option. We don't all have two college degrees to prop us up."

"You have quite the chip on your shoulder about wealthy people. Don't you think that's a bit of a generalization?"

My reply is interrupted by a commotion from the terrace where the boys with the lantern have knocked a server flat on her back, sending smashed glass and a spray of champagne over a couple of the guests. The boys' mom has a wet stain on her white gown and she starts screaming at the poor girl, who's still on the ground, looking dazed. The boys saunter off, tossing the tattered lantern around, as the mom is ushered away by her husband. The server picks herself up and starts gathering pieces of glass with her bare hands as everyone else just watches.

I turn back to smile at Jude. "No, you people are a *delight.*"

"Obviously, there are exceptions," he mutters.

Cinderella watches the commotion, unconcerned, like this is a normal day in her family. Then she spots us and perks up, waving. I'm about to wave back when Jude raises his glass and winks at her and she giggles delightedly. He notices me watching, colors slightly, and clears his throat. "They're staying in one of the lodges," he says.

"She keeps wandering over with Cinderella books for me to read to her."

I blink at him. "I would pay good money to witness that. I hope you do the voices."

"I point out the gender stereotypes and latent misogyny."

"Swoon," I deadpan.

Another server comes out to help with the broken glass, and the girl on her knees smiles gratefully up at him. Then blushes, because even in his white shirt and black apron with the gold Lakeside logo embroidered on it, he's still the hottest guy at the party.

It's Micah.

I excuse myself and make my way toward him as he drifts through the crowd with his silver tray, nose in the air. I watch him clear a few glasses, then swig a gulp of champagne from one on his way back to the bar.

He sees my dress before he sees me. "Ree!" he whispers delightedly, glancing around and trying to keep his face straight. "You look . . . like an ice queen!"

"Elsa, eat your heart out. *You* look like a waiter," I murmur under my breath, lingering over the canapés on his tray.

He shrugs. "They needed extra staff."

"Why didn't you tell me?"

"I didn't think you'd be here," he says, which isn't really an answer.

"It was last minute. There wasn't time to text you. I didn't think *you'd* be here."

"I needed a job."

"You *have* a job." This is crazy. If the guests see him working here, he won't be able to R&J until Lawrence is sure they've all gone. They wouldn't risk someone remembering he was staff. "Just go and see Dr. Burgess!"

He rolls his eyes. "I will. I did. She didn't have anything. It's hetero week at the clinic, I guess," he quips.

I choose another canapé and pretend I'm watching the dancers. He stands beside me and we talk without moving our lips.

"Anyway, we always wanted to come to this!" he says.

"Yes, but not as *staff*."

"You *are* technically working."

"That's different. You were supposed to check on my mom tonight."

"I did! Well. I went over, but she wasn't home. What happened anyway?"

"Nothing. Doesn't matter."

Someone sweeps past, lifting a canapé from his tray without looking at him.

I sigh. "What's going on, Micah? You're not a waiter."

He shrugs. "Felt like a change. They might even keep me on."

"*What?* But what about . . . What about the permanent R-and-J jobs and living in the resort and . . . and . . . *every day like it's your last?* Don't give up everything you have for—"

"What do I have?" He laughs suddenly, forgetting the crowd, and spreads his arms, embracing nothing but his silver tray.

We glance around and he lowers his voice. "Look, it's OK. Even if I'm working here, we'll still hang out. Same as always."

But it won't be the same. I watch him walk back to the bar, feeling abandoned somehow. R&Jing is fun when he's out here doing it with me. Like we're just partying after school and we happen to get paid for it. The prospect of doing it alone seems different somehow. Seedier. I don't want to wear a ball gown while he's in an apron. It makes them both seem just like uniforms.

I head back to Jude, trying to look more cheerful than I feel, but when I get there, he's dancing with his mom. Apparently he "doesn't dance" but he can *dance*. Actual ballroom. They glide around effortlessly while the sun sets behind them. I've never seen him smile like that.

Mr. Daly is watching from the edge of the dance floor, and Dante has sidled over to talk to him. It makes me uncomfortable and I wish I could warn Mr. Daly. But warn him about what? They own a liquor company; Dante owns several high-end bars. What's wrong with them doing business? I can hardly say, *He fired my mom.*

But I grab Naomi and go over to stand with them, and Mr. Daly immediately extends a hand to her. I don't know if he's grateful for the escape or just too polite to let her stand there like a wallflower.

"I'm not a very good dancer!" she warns him.

"Thank God," he says. "I'm *famously* bad. Jude gets his poise from his mother. Wait till you hear what happened the time I danced with Hillary Clinton."

I glance smugly at Dante, and he scowls as Mr. Daly leads her away, and then they stumble their way around the dance floor, bumping into other couples and laughing. Mrs. Daly is dancing with the hotel owner now, and Jude is with Cinderella, letting her stand on his toes as he whirls her around and she gazes adoringly up at him. At least someone enjoys his company.

Dante grabs two more glasses and hands one to me. "Enjoying the ball?" he says.

I look pointedly at him. "I think they could be a little pickier about who they invite."

He snorts. "The guest list is the main draw. You can make a lot of money at these things." He watches the Dalys on the dance floor, eyes narrowed hungrily. "Nothing like landing a really big fish, is there?"

I stare at him. "You're disgusting, Dante. Do you talk about all the people you work with like that?"

He laughs and shakes his head as he turns to walk away. "Actually, I meant you, Regan. Got yourself a whale, there." He winks at me. "Well done."

I'm still fuming when Jude and his parents get back. I am *nothing* like Dante Colucci. There is no category on earth that includes both me and him.

Jude notices my scowl and asks, "Was that guy bothering you?"

"Stand down, Clark Kent. I can handle him." I'm not about to repeat what Dante said.

"I don't like him," he mutters. "There's something . . . oh, wait. He's not your . . . is he?"

"*No!* God, he's like *forty*!"

"Well, your dating habits aren't exactly normal, so forgive me for wondering."

"I'm exhausted already!" Mrs. Daly says, interrupting us before I can reply. "Be a dear and fetch me some water. Regan, would you like anything?"

"Water would be great, thanks," I say, adding, for Jude's benefit, "I have a nasty taste in my mouth."

They could snap their fingers at any passing waiter, but Jude and Mr. Daly go off to fetch the drinks themselves and Mrs. Daly leads me to a table.

"I don't know about you, but I hate wearing heels," she says, sitting down and kicking her shoes off. She wriggles her toes and sighs with relief.

"These are a little tight," I admit, doing the same. Turns out expensive heels aren't any more comfortable than the cheap ones.

"But if I don't wear them, I'm even shorter!" she complains. "It's a serious problem when your husband is six foot six! It looks ridiculous!"

"I think you're a very cute couple," I assure her.

"Speaking of which," she says coyly. Her face scrunches. "You two are adorable together. How's it going?"

"Great! Really . . . surprisingly well! Yeah, we're having a blast! Getting along great!" God. I really like Mrs.

Daly and I really hate her son. It's annoying that every-thing's reversed and now I'm lying to *her*.

"Really? Jude?" She arches a skeptical eyebrow, and I realize suddenly I'm not fooling anyone. She knows *exactly* what he's like. Of course she does.

"I mean, he's not a pushover or anything."

She laughs at the understatement. "I knew you were perfect for him."

"Me?" I can't imagine anyone worse for him.

"He doesn't open up easily." She sighs. "He needs someone to talk to. Relax with. And you seemed so full of fun and . . . life."

"You think that's enough?" I ask, because being the life and soul of the party really isn't cutting it with Jude.

She shakes her head and gives me a smile that's down-right shrewd. "No. I liked that about you, but I *picked* you because you were obviously smart, persistent, and . . . determined to get what you wanted. I thought you could handle him."

"Oh." I blush. Not *that* smart apparently. Thinking I'd charmed and outwitted everyone at the interview. She saw right through me.

She laughs again. "I'm not naive, Regan." She waves a hand. "The romance doesn't even matter. I don't want you to pretend. Not *really*. I just want him to have a friend. And I was sure you *would* like him, everyone does. When they get to know him. Maybe you'll really . . ." She catches herself and gives a sad little laugh. "I bet every mother says that to you. *If you could just make it real with* my *son*." She rubs her forehead, embarrassed.

Actually, they don't. It's surprising how many of them don't care at all that it's fake. They'd throw a fit if you gave them fake diamonds or fake handbags, but they'll pay extra for fake love.

She sighs and looks out at the party. People laughing, dancing, every one of them trying just for one night not to think about why they or their loved one is here.

"We hoped it wouldn't come to this," she murmurs. "We've poured our *lives* into hoping. Crazy, isn't it?"

"No. I get it." I do. I thought their Death Date research was such arrogance. But there's nothing arrogant about Mrs. Daly. So maybe taking on Fate itself is just what you do for someone you love.

She makes a face. "I don't think he really enjoyed all those activities. Coming here was probably a silly idea." She slumps a little, blaming herself, even though if he didn't enjoy the activities, it was *my* fault. I didn't exactly go out of my way to make his day pleasant. Suddenly the memory of all those barbs stings a little. I tell myself he deserved them. He's an asshole and I was just defending myself. But . . . his parents aren't assholes. And all they want is for Jude to have someone to talk to. Not someone making catty comments and intruding on his last days with his family.

And it's not like I *want* to be like that. Not really. It just comes too easily. And when he's around, I turn into . . . I turn into the person he thinks I am. Just to spite him. Just to prove I don't care what he thinks of me.

What would Mrs. Daly think if she knew how I really treat him?

"Look, maybe it was me. Maybe I'm *not* the perfect girl for him."

She just smiles sadly. "Oh, Regan, if I could give him a marriage, a divorce, three bratty kids, a midlife crisis, and a hip replacement right now, I would. Because that's life. Your Dr. Lawrence was wrong, you know. It's not about perfect. It doesn't have to be perfect."

She sits up and slips her shoes on again as Mr. Daly approaches with our drinks. "This guy, for example." She smiles at him. "Nowhere *near* perfect. I have the toe bruises and ruined shoes to prove it. Did you know he once had to buy Hillary Clinton a new pair of Manolos?"

I laugh.

"But I wouldn't change a thing. Speaking of which," she says, taking his hand and leading him to the dance floor, "I'm going to go risk another pair."

The last of the daylight is gone now, and the stars rival the fairy lights. Fireworks launch from an island in the lake and we gather at the shore to watch. Micah and I used to watch them every year from the beach at Staff Town. The other Staff Town kids will be gathered there now. But their midsummer party won't be until tomorrow night. Too many of them work at the hotels, all of which do some sort of party tonight, though none as lavish as Lakeside's. I wonder if Mom is watching. But she's not, is she? She's holed up in a bar somewhere, trying to forget this morning. I should have found ten minutes to go find her. But today has been so nonstop. And maybe I didn't want to know.

I spot Micah in the crowd. He has a bottle of vodka and a tray of shot glasses and he seems to be teaching a drinking game to a crowd of younger guests, the girls draping themselves over him, center of the party as usual. If management sees him, I won't have to worry about him working here for long.

Stiff fabric grazes my arm and I realize it's Jude, placing his jacket over my bare shoulders. He's a gentleman, he'd do the same for any girl, but I mumble my thanks.

At this point, I know I could coast out this fakery to the end of the week. I'm starting to guess at Jude's reasons for going through with all this, and I know he's not going to rat me out, he never was. In fact he's going to do everything he can to make it look like I'm doing a great job. The permanent contract is in the bag.

But I can't help the annoying sensation that I haven't earned it.

When the fireworks end, the orchestra is replaced by a band called Villain Era, a band with a number one album out at the moment. The younger people crowd back to the dance floor, the older ones to the bar. Jude and I stand awkwardly together and he toys absently with his glass, like he has no idea who Villain Era is and he'd rather be home with a book. Even in a crowd of people, he manages to look like he's all alone.

I feel . . . weird after my conversation with Mrs. Daly.

All the Dalys want is for their dying son to have a friend. And I promised them in my interview that this would be a good thing for him. I told them it would be real. And what am I doing? Using him so I can keep my job. I remember my conversation with Dante and feel a little sick. Mrs. Daly's right. I do know how to manipulate people. *I'm making people happy,* I told Dr. Burgess. It's easy to convince yourself you're a good person if your job is to make people happy. But I guess it also gets me what I want.

Now that he knows the truth, it doesn't matter if I make Jude happy. But if I don't, I'll feel like I've failed anyway. Not as a Juliet but maybe as a human being.

"Are you cold?" I ask.

"I'm fine."

"Hungry?"

"Not really."

The thing is, I can't befriend him if he won't *let* me. Another silence falls, and everything feels more awkward than ever. The air is perfumed with jasmine and I realize all the elaborate planters edging the lawn have been chosen for their night-scented flowers. They don't miss a thing here.

I turn to face him, chewing my lip. "Will you dance with me?" I ask. "And don't say you can't because I saw you out there, Mr. Dancing with the Stars."

"Mr. what?"

I make a face. "I suppose you don't watch TV."

"Not much."

"Come on." I hold a hand out. "I've dreamed my entire life of dancing at this party. Preferably with Timothée Chalamet, but you'll have to do. Please?"

He shrugs and leads me to the dance floor.

The song is a slower one, so I give Jude his jacket back and put my hands on his shoulders. He puts his on my waist and we sway stiffly.

"Where did you learn to dance?" I ask. "I mean real dancing."

"I attend a lot of black-tie charity events. And you can't really say no to old ladies who just donated a ton of money to your charity."

"So you're basically a high-class escort?" I smirk at him. "We should compare notes."

"I'm not sure your methods would go down well at hospital fundraisers."

Beside me I hear someone say "disgraceful," and I realize the couple next to us is looking at one corner of the dance floor where Micah's drinking game is getting a little raucous. One of the guys passes the bottle, Micah takes a shot, stumbles, and almost falls backward, hair disheveled and bow tie askew, and everyone laughs. He's clearly been sneaking more than a little champagne. The couple, a sour-looking pair, make eyes at each other as they spin away, and I wish I could trip them as they pass. It's not like Micah's the only drunk person at this party. On the terrace, the servers are pouring champagne into pyramids of glasses, and some of the younger guests are as drunk in their ball gowns as they would be in their miniskirts at Inferno. I've had too much champagne, too, but I feel strangely sober and deflated.

"Have you enjoyed the party?" Jude asks. I doubt he's interested, but at least he's not being rude.

"Not as much as I thought I would," I admit.

"Oh?"

I'm preoccupied—I keep worrying about Mom, my Prince Charming hates me, I can't help being aware that I don't belong here, and the dress is great but it doesn't make any of that go away. So much for the fairy tale. But I just say, "My feet hurt."

"If you want to go, it's fine. I think we're done here."

But Dr. Lawrence catches my eye then as he sweeps past with a woman I don't know, and I instinctively put my head on Jude's shoulder. I just want it to look romantic, but actually I'm exhausted and it's nice to close my eyes for a moment. We sway as the music swells and the lights twinkle. He smells good. His breath moves the hair at the nape of my neck and his arms feel warm on my bare skin. When I look up, our faces are inches apart and there's a beat, just long enough to become aware of his hands at the small of my back and his chest against mine and to wonder what he's aware of.

I lean in closer and whisper in his ear. "Sorry. My boss just danced past us."

He tuts and relaxes his grip, irritated.

"Well, you wanted it to be convincing."

"A little warning next time?" he complains. "It's hard to

know when you're faking. Or should I just assume that's any time you're being nice?"

So much for friendly. That lasted a whole thirty seconds. "Does this whole Mr.-Darcy-snarky-asshole thing ever work?" I ask wearily.

"I'm sorry?"

"For picking up girls. News flash. Women have moved on since the eighteenth century."

"Nineteenth," he says.

"What?"

"*Pride and Prejudice* was published in the early 1800s. That's the nineteenth century. And for the record, Elizabeth Bennet never really did it for me, either. As far as I could see, all Darcy did wrong was not enjoy parties or dancing and didn't happen to fall instantly in love with her, and she responded by turning the entire village against him. Sounds a little narcissistic, don't you think?"

"Well, he didn't give her a lot to work with," I mutter. God, we just can't stop bickering.

He draws his head back to look down his nose at me. "How are you *supposed* to act with someone who regards you as a paycheck?"

I shake my head. "I'm sick of this. You know, you just assume all kinds of things about me based on my job and then you complain when I assume things about you based on your bank account. You don't know the first thing about me. And I guess I don't know the first thing about you, either, but I know we can't go on like this for the rest of the goddamn week."

He arches an eyebrow. "What do you suggest, then?"

Call it quits and forget we ever met, I want to say. But there's Dr. Lawrence to think about. And Mom. And Mrs. Daly.

I sigh. "What if we start over? Clean slate."

He cocks his head. "Like a truce?"

"Like . . . I don't know. No more rudeness would be a start."

"And no more faking?" he asks skeptically.

I nod. "Fine. No rudeness and total honesty," I agree. "From both of us."

He regards me coolly for a moment. "Interesting. Starting now?"

"Right now."

"OK. I *honestly* hate parties," he says flatly, taking me literally. "Too loud. Too much small talk."

"OK. The first time I tried archery I *honestly* didn't hit the target once," I counter.

"I honestly didn't mean to score that last point at volleyball," he admits. "I was checking my watch."

I laugh. "I honestly didn't mean to collide with you at the clinic."

"Really?" He looks unconvinced.

"Are you kidding? Those cupcakes were too good to waste on you." But I grin and his expression softens.

"I honestly *am* afraid of heights," he admits after a moment. "I have to take a light sedative when I fly."

"So what were you doing up a rock face?"

He shrugs. "I like to push myself."

I roll my eyes. "I honestly don't think I even believe in love. Romance, yes, but love?" I shake my head. "Although I also think I'm in love with your mom."

He laughs and I feel his shoulders relax beneath my hands. "I'm wearing my *I Beat the Rock* T-shirt under my shirt," he says. "I'm honestly pretty proud of it."

"Ha! I *knew* it. I have three of them at home. I wear them in bed." I blush slightly, and there's an awkward beat, because I didn't mean to go straight to nightwear. "Speaking of which . . ." I say quickly, "I'm *honestly* exhausted."

He nods. "Me too. Long day."

"I might . . ." I glance back at the hotel.

"Sure. I'll . . ." He jerks his head toward his parents. We disentangle our arms but stand there awkwardly, an unfinished feeling between us, because how do you finish a date that isn't a date?

"Well. Good night, then."

"Good night."

"OK."

"Right."

As I finally step back, he adds, "Regan?"

"Mmm?"

"You look . . . beautiful tonight," he says, with only the smallest trace of grudging reluctance. "Honestly."

His fancy manners probably just got the best of him, but it's as close to the fairy tale as I'm going to get, and I find myself smiling as I wander back across the dance floor, my skin cooling after the heat from Jude's arms.

Until someone in the crowd grabs my hand and pulls me toward him, and suddenly I'm dancing again. This time with Dante Collucci.

"You two make a cute couple."

"Ugh. Find someone your own age, Dante," I mutter, trying to pull away. But he's got one arm wrapped around me, a hand on my lower back, and his other hand is firmly gripping mine. I can't make a scene with Dr. Lawrence and the Dalys here.

"I have a proposition for you," he says. "You might want to hear it."

"I doubt it."

"I need something from the Dalys, and you can help me get it."

"Dante, let it go. They're here to say goodbye to their son. I'm not going to bother them with stupid business stuff just so you can get some vodka deal for your bars."

His laugh is disdainful. "I don't care about their vodka. What the Dalys have is much more valuable."

I'm confused now. "What are you talking about? All they do is make alcohol and"—my eyes widen as his smile spreads, showing his teeth—"their Death Date research? Are you serious? What do you want with that?"

He looks at me like I'm stupid. "Do you have any concept of how much that kind of information would be worth on the open market?"

"But . . . what information? They haven't found

anything. You know how I know? They're about to let *their son* swallow a dose of *poison*!"

He just exhales slowly and shakes his head at me. "They may not have an answer yet, but that doesn't mean they don't have leads. They've poured billions into it; they must know something."

"You're deluded," I say flatly. "How can that make you money?"

"Don't be such a child, Regan," he says. "When they do come up with an answer, do you think they're going to hand it out free with vodka shots? To people like us? Girls like you?" He looks me up and down scornfully. "It'll be sold to the highest bidder, like everything else. People like us get squat unless we take it for ourselves."

"The Dalys aren't like that," I say.

"Right, that's how they've made their fortune, giving stuff away." He scoffs. "All I'm asking you to do is get in a room with one of their laptops for two minutes. Plug this in and it'll do the rest." He suddenly spins me under his arm, and as he pulls me roughly back in, he pushes a small, hard device, like a flash drive, into my free hand. I glance behind me in panic to see who's watching. Dr. Lawrence is talking to the Lakeside owner. Jude has gone over to say good night to his parents. Naomi is discreetly leading a swaying Micah down to the beach; he looks wasted. Couples dance past, lost in their own conversations.

I close my hand around the device just to make it disappear. "What is that?"

"It attacks their device security. Leaving it hackable. It'll take less than a minute. And I'll make it worth your while."

"Worth going to *prison*?"

"They won't know anything about it. And you'll have earned the easiest money you'll ever make." He leans in closer. "How does a hundred thousand dollars sound?"

Like more money than I can imagine. I blink at him. He must really think this information is worth millions. I don't know if he's drunk or a genius.

I hear Mr. Daly's deep laugh echo across the lawn.

"No. Forget it, this is a *monumentally* bad idea." I tug my hand free of his. "You know what, Dante? Everyone in this resort is terrified of getting on your bad side because they either work for you or they know someone who does. But thanks to you, my mom is no longer one of them. And I'm getting a permanent job with R and J, so I have no intention of ever needing anything from you. You don't own me and I'm not helping you with this."

I try to walk off indignantly, but he just smiles a nasty smile and pulls me back sharply. "Your moral high horse thing is cute," he says, too close to my ear. "It's amusing that you think you have a choice about this. You don't. You're going to help me."

"Or what?"

"Or I have a little chat with Dr. Lawrence about the fact that you and lover boy are faking this whole thing."

I freeze, staring back at Dante's cold gray eyes.

"Wh— How did—?" The penny drops like a boulder.

Apart from Naomi, the only other person who knew about this was . . .

"*What did you give him?*" I demand, furious. Micah wasn't just drunk; he'd taken something. He was obviously high and I was too preoccupied to even notice. I look around for him, but he and Naomi are gone. I want to snap a piece off Neptune's ice trident and stab Dante through the heart with it. If he has one.

"Relax, Regan. He was more than willing. It's a party. You want some, too?"

I grab his lapels and try to push him, but he's got too good a grip on my waist. I glance over at Jude, who notices us and frowns. Now would be a good time for his Clark Kent routine.

"How do you know I won't just tell Jude what you said? He knows everything anyway, I could tell him you're trying to blackmail me. The Dalys would squash you like a cockroach for this." I look back at Jude as he starts toward us.

"Go ahead. Don't leave out the part where you're already involved, though."

"I am not!"

"Hmm. There's a BMW sitting outside your cabin that would suggest otherwise."

"I— That was— That wasn't—" He just looks smugly at me as I go still in his arms. Then I quietly raise a hand at Jude and shake my head. He hesitates but walks back to his parents.

Jude wouldn't understand about the car. He'll just see

another parasite preying on his family and decide he was right about me all along.

"Think about it, Regan," Dante says. "Who are you protecting? Some rich asshole who's going to be dead in a few days? His parents won't remember your name a week from now. You have your mom to think of. Your future. You could move out of that shithole in Staff Town. Get out of the resort altogether. Micah says you like taking photos. You could go to art school. Whatever you want." He looks around at the party and says, with an amused smirk, "You don't even know what money is for, do you? You know what's great about money? It's not cars or parties or clothes. It's that you're bulletproof. No one can fire you, evict you, control you. No one can hurt you. That's a good feeling, Regan. You should give it a try."

I just stare at him, the flash drive still digging into my tightly closed fist.

"You've got three more days to make this happen. Don't let me down." Then he walks away casually, and I trail up the terrace steps in my ball gown, feeling shaky, sick, and most of all, stupid.

Girls like me don't get the fairy tale.

Chapter 9

JUDE: I had a great time last night. You made it very special. Can we meet up again today, I'd love to see you. Is nine a.m. too soon?

I blink at it, wondering if I'm still asleep. Or if his phone's been hacked. I type *I had a great time, too. Thanks for the invite. And the dance. You're a pretty good dancer (honestly).* I hover over send, delete it, type it again, delete it again. Then replace it with,

REGAN: Sure. Bean Street café?

I drag myself out of bed, grab a shower, then open my closet. But nothing could compare to last night's gown, so I don't linger over what to wear. I grab a pair of green shorts, cashmere cardigan, and sandals.

Naomi's stretched out on the sofa in her robe, hair still pinned up and last night's makeup smudged around her eyes. "You look like Cinderella the morning after the ball," I tell her as I wolf down some breakfast.

She shakes her head, then holds it delicately. "Cinderella only lost one shoe. *I* lost the entire goddamn pair."

"What *is* it about shoes?" I sympathize.

"Left them on the beach when I was waiting for Luis to come pick up Micah. Boy, was he mad when he saw the state of him."

"I'll bet," I mutter. For once I managed to come home with my shoes *and* a complete memory of the evening. Too complete. Sobriety is overrated. I haven't told Naomi about Dante's offer. Or *threat*, to be more accurate. It's not that I'm thinking about doing it, but so far I can't think of a way to *not* do it, and I'm ashamed for her to even know about it.

"Worth it." Naomi sighs dramatically. "Next time I'm scrubbing dog poop off my kid's sneakers, I'll close my eyes and remember."

I laugh. "I have to go. Jude wants to see me."

"Wow, he just can't get enough of you!"

"Ha! Believe me, whatever Jude Daly's reasons, they have *nothing* to do with me."

Bean Street is in the Downtown area right on the beach, decorated in a retro 1950s diner style with framed pictures of the original Bergman resort on the walls. There's one of Diana Ross in the 1970s, and if you squint you can see my grandfather, slightly fuzzy, on stage behind her.

The wall art is a big painted quote: *"Live every day like it's your last. One day, you'll be right."*

They're playing a 1950s playlist and the waitresses are doing a choreographed dance routine behind the counter as I arrive. One of them is Kristen, the maid I took a photo of at Lakeside. She must work here, too, and she grimaces at me, embarrassed that I've witnessed the silly routine. I smile sympathetically. If Dante has anything to say about it, I could be working here myself soon. The flash drive is nestled in my bag, because I don't know what to do with it and I don't want to risk anyone finding it in my room. Is it illegal to even have it in your possession? I have no idea, and having it on me gives me a queasy feeling.

As I order, I manage to ask Kristen if she saw my mom at work yesterday.

She shakes her head. "But it was so busy with all the party stuff, maybe her shift got changed. We were cleaning till three a.m. I'm exhausted."

I give her another smile and an extra-big tip.

Jude is in a corner booth, back in jeans and a charcoal sweater, hunched over a book and a coffee. As I sit down with my cappuccino, he sets the book aside and we smile awkwardly at each other. It's weird without the Dalys here. I don't know what we are now. Business partners? Accomplices? Probably not friends.

"Sorry about the text," he says. "I realized if we were actually dating we'd be sending nauseating texts. It'll be more convincing if anyone looks at my phone . . . after."

"Ah. Right. Makes sense." Definitely not friends. I blush at the thought of the reply I almost sent.

"You don't have to stay."

I shrug. "You asked me here. Was there something you wanted to do today?" There are fliers in a plastic stand on the table advertising resort activities. The top one says *Live like a Local! Experience authentic mountain life with a Historical Farm Visit, Maple Syrup Tapping, Log Cabin Building, Wild Camping, and more!* I roll my eyes.

"Not really. I'm supposed to be at a counseling session."

"You skipped another one?"

He waves a hand dismissively. "I don't need them."

"No? You're totally fine about the whole . . ." *imminent death thing*, I don't finish.

He looks surprised by the idea that he wouldn't be. "Counseling at this point is like studying outside the exam room. If you're not ready by now, you never will be."

"To be honest, I did most of my studying outside the exam room," I admit. "But I get it, I don't like counselors, either. If you *do* want to talk, though . . ."

He sighs. "Is that what normally happens at this point? We talk about death so I'll cry on your shoulder or something?"

"Something like that," I admit.

"I'm fine."

I shrug. I tried. And it's not my favorite part, either, so if he wants to skip it, that's fine with me. "OK, well if you don't want to talk, what do you want to do?" I spread out the fliers. "Windsurfing? Forest bathing and meditation? Ooh, let's get piercings!" I honestly think I *would* get something pierced if he'd show some enthusiasm for it.

"You don't have to entertain me anymore," he says, though he looks more amused than annoyed. "Thought we were being honest?"

"Right. Yeah." But what does *honest* look like? I glance around at the 1950s diner, the servers doing the hand jive behind the counter. There's nothing honest about this entire resort. We sit there, him toying listlessly with a sugar packet, me chewing my nails, letting the silence swell into something uncomfortable.

Maybe our truce was a mistake. I'm used to being adaptable; whatever they want—the thrill seeker, the romantic, the nature lover, the wild child—I can be that girl. What I've *never* been with a client is Ree. I feel like an actor without a role. A closet of designer outfits and I'm naked on stage, groping for my next line. I have no idea what comes next. Because there *is* no next line now. No script. No role. No . . . well, no *rules*, I guess.

Which gives me a wild idea.

Impulsively, I push the fliers aside, lean across the table, and say, "Do you want to get out of here?"

He hesitates for only a second before pushing his mug away, too. "Hell, yes. Is there anywhere they're *not* playing Greatest Hits of a Regrettable Decade?"

I grin. "Come with me. I'll give you the Live-like-a-Local experience."

• • •

Taking Jude down Bergman Road, past the entrance to the resort, and onto the road toward Staff Town feels surreal. Forbidden. Impossible. Like stepping through the looking glass. I half expect one of us to burst into flames.

On the way through Staff Town, I point out the "local attractions" like a tour guide.

"And if you look to your left, you'll see our tennis and basketball courts! Special features include rusted shopping carts and trees sprouting from the asphalt to give your sporting experience that extra challenge! Moving on, we have a paddling pool for the little ones, complete with half a fiberglass octopus. Due to our rigorous health and safety policy, the pool leaks, so you can be sure your toddlers are at zero risk of drowning, although poison ivy is always a possibility! And if you'd like to swim, there's always our lakeshore, popular with the younger residents and decorated in a theme of broken glass, needles, and used condoms!"

"I had no idea this place was even here," Jude says. "This was a resort, too?"

"Yep, but it's mostly been abandoned."

"It's like a ghost town."

"It *is* a ghost town. We all died in 1983."

"Where do people live?"

"In the old guest cabins by the lake. And a few of the old buildings have been turned into grocery stores, hair salons, that kind of thing. But the big hotels and entertainment centers farther up the mountain are all derelict now. Good for hiding when you're supposed to be at school."

I hesitate at the path that leads to the cabins, but then take him down it. I can't help seeing them through Jude's eyes, and I stop doing the tour-guide act. I started doing it to make him laugh. But if I keep going, he might actually laugh.

I jam my hands in the pockets of my shorts and scuff my sandals through dead leaves. "We can go back to the resort if you want."

He glances at his watch. "Not yet."

I roll my eyes. "Why are you lying about counseling? Why are you lying about me? Your parents seem pretty easygoing."

"I don't want to talk about it."

He doesn't want to talk about it *with me* he means.

"Right, yeah, I wouldn't understand about parents. I was spontaneously generated from a pile of laundry one day. Look, I may not be university educated but I'm pretty good at reading people, and I get it: Your parents are perfect; I wouldn't want to disappoint them, either. That's why you're doing this, isn't it? That's why you climbed that rock face and went to the Midsummer Ball. Because you want to make them happy."

He sighs. "It's irritating that I have to waste time on this."

"Thanks."

"I mean the whole resort. But you can't pick a fight

with your parents when you're about to die on them. Obviously. I decided to suck it up and convince them I'm having a good time. I didn't mean for anyone else to get involved."

We're approaching my cabin now. Sure enough, there's a shiny black BMW parked outside, looking completely out of place. The offer seemed so ridiculous, I didn't really believe he'd deliver, but now my stomach lurches at the sight of it, because if Dante keeps his promises, then he probably follows through on his threats, too.

"Nice car." Jude nods at it. "True love must be more lucrative than I thought."

"It's . . . a loaner." I hesitate outside. "Wait, I just have to do something."

I don't know who I'm hiding from whom, but I leave him standing on the path and jog up the porch steps. As I twist the door handle, my stomach gives an echoing twist of anxiety about what I'll find inside.

Mom is propped on the sofa with her feet up, watching TV.

"Hey, honey! Thought you were working this week." She reaches into a box of breakfast pastries on her lap.

I put my hands on my hips, incredulous. "I am. Are *you*? I've been calling and calling! I was worried! Where's your phone?"

She makes a face. "Smashed it. Sprained my ankle, too. Those damn porch steps. When they're wet, they're lethal. Luis says he'll get us some rubber mats from the school. He and Elena were over here. And some kid dropped that car off and left the keys. What's going on?"

"Mom, stop." She's rambling and not making eye contact because she's embarrassed about last time I saw her. And I'm worried that what she's *not* saying is how much she'd drunk before she fell. "It's . . . a friend's car. He just needed somewhere to park it while he's away. Never mind the car. What about work?"

"I can barely walk. I called and told them, it's fine. The concierge even sent me a care package, wasn't that nice?" She holds up the pastries.

I perch on the end of the sofa. Her foot does look swollen. But here she is, watching TV like a fully functional human and making me feel like I'm overreacting. Maybe I am. Maybe it was a blip. Or even a wake-up call. I've been worrying about what to say to her, but maybe we don't need to talk about it at all.

"Does it hurt?"

"Like hell."

"I'll be around more," I tell her. "This job has . . . taken a weird turn." I make a face but don't explain. "Do you need anything? Food? Painkillers?"

"Give me those crutches and I'll check."

"Where did you get these?" I hand her the pair of crutches leaning against the coffee table.

"Elena. They're worried about Micah, he came home in a state last night." She struggles up and hops a few steps, wincing. I straighten the couch behind her.

"Micah can take care of himself. He's eighteen."

"Exactly. They don't have to keep him anymore and if

they throw him out, social services won't find him another foster home, he's too old."

"Mom, he's fine."

"I know *he's* fine, it's *you* I worry about. He's a bad influence," she says primly, and I bite my tongue as I follow her to the kitchen. Micah isn't the one with a twisted ankle this morning.

When we've checked the fridge and I've made a list of things to bring her, she follows me to the front door, saying, "So, how's the job?"

Before I can answer, she looks outside, sees Jude standing there, and cocks an eyebrow like *what are you getting yourself into?*

"It's fine. I'm handling it. We're kind of . . . working together."

She gives me a pitying look. "Oh, honey, there's no *together* with people like that. You'll be the one who ends up getting hurt, trust me."

"Mom."

"Look, I'm not judging. I know what it's like. Your father and I used to sneak out to the old resort and have romantic picnics in—"

"In the old roller rink, I know, I know, you told me." I suspect she makes these stories up, because I know the ruins of the old resort inside out and there *is* no roller rink. I was probably the result of a one-night stand in the bathroom of a club and she just doesn't want to tell me. I fold my arms, irritated, though I know she's just looking out for me. Dr. Burgess worries about me getting hurt when these guys die. Mom just knows how much damage they can do while they're alive.

"Mom, don't worry. This isn't like that. It's just work."

"Hmm." She looks out at him, pacing through the leaves. "What's he like? I hear his parents are a big deal."

"He's certainly a big . . . deal." For Mrs. Daly's sake alone, I hold my tongue.

She follows me out onto the porch. Jude looks up and frowns when he sees her, before a flash of recognition crosses his face. I'm surprised he even knew her without her uniform. Mom just lifts her chin and looks coldly down on him from the porch. He's on *her* turf now.

He takes a step forward, but she keeps her nose in the air and hobbles inside without a word.

"I'm sorry. For being rude to your mother yesterday," Jude says, hurrying after me down the Staff Town main street, past the supermarket where Naomi works, and away from the lake.

"Oh, so it would have been OK if she hadn't turned out to be my mom?"

"Of course not. I was just being as obnoxious as possible. I was trying to piss you off."

"Well, you were right, Jude. You really do succeed at everything you set out to achieve."

"I'm not going to apologize for being angry that you were trying to con me. But I *am* sorry about your mum. And . . . for calling you a parasite."

"You are?"

"I didn't mean it in a personal way. This whole place exists to make money off vulnerable people. You're *all* parasites."

"Seriously, you've got to look up the word *apology*."

He jogs to keep up and says, "I just mean . . ." He glances back at the cabin. "It was unfair of me to think I was the only one with good reasons for wanting to go through with this charade. I suppose everyone's looking after someone."

I let my shoulders drop their defensive hunch and slow my pace, but I don't respond and he doesn't push it.

"My parents," he goes on. "They're trying to fit the next fifty years into five days. If it wasn't this, it would be something else. I've never had a girlfriend, so I guess this ridiculous scheme makes sense to them."

"You've never had a girlfriend? Seriously? How come?"

"I can't tell if you're being sarcastic or not."

I laugh. "Let's go with *not*."

"Then . . . because I'm, y'know, dying at eighteen? Who would want that? I mean, unless the pay was pretty good."

It's a joke, but I wonder if the resentment in his tone is more about the fact that I'm just the latest in a long line of girls who were willing to use him for a while. When you're that rich, there must be a lot of them.

"Anyone who could actually be serious about me would only be lining up to have their heart broken," he goes on. "I know you think I'm an arsehole, but I'm not that much of an arsehole. It's bad enough that I have to do this to my parents; I'm not doing it to anyone else."

"What about friends? Didn't you want any friends here with you? Do you *have* any?"

"Of course." He hedges. "A few. But my family have lived all over the world, and I was always younger than the other kids in my class. It was harder to—" He looks around as we turn off Main Street onto another path. "Where are we going anyway?"

"Jamaica."

"Jamaica?"

"You don't own *every* island in the Caribbean, Jude."

The only one of the big Bergman facilities that's been kept in a reasonable state of repair is the entertainment complex. It was the only place big enough for a school for all the Staff Town kids. The old ballroom is now the school gym, which was nice when it came to prom because it still has the fancy moldings, tall windows, and gilded stage. But the high-ceilinged classrooms are hard to heat, and if my school days were anything to go by, *entertainment* is in short supply.

The old swimming pool is still there, too. It used to be an indoor one, but they tore down the building before I was born because it was unsafe. When I started school it was just a big empty hole in the ground, until an enterprising teacher added some picnic benches and planters of fake tropical plants and painted murals of beach scenes with palm trees on the walls so the students could eat lunch there. Everyone started calling it "Little Jamaica."

In the summer, the school is empty, and when Micah is avoiding his foster parents he comes here to hide. Given how mad they must be about last night, I'm unsurprised to find him, halfway through a pack of cigarettes and a six-pack of beer, lying on his back on a picnic table with an open shirt and shades, like he's floating in a pool, sipping cocktails. Jude and I stand on the edge, peering down at him, and he waves a hand and grins.

"It's eleven a.m., Micah." I nod at the beer.

"They'll get warm if I don't drink them now," he says, like that's completely rational. "Come on in, the water's . . . absent."

I sit down at Micah's table, take the latest issue of *Vogue* out of my bag, and prop it on his torso. Jude can't sit still for more than two seconds. He keeps getting up and pacing around Little Jamaica, examining the graffiti while I read bits of celebrity gossip to Micah.

"So, this is your school?" Jude asks. I imagine it's a little different from Oxford.

"It *was*. We just graduated," I tell him. "Ooh, Micah, look at Maggie Gyllenhaal's movie premiere dress!"

"Jesus, was the after-party in a sex dungeon? I basically love it."

"So, is there a . . . summer school or something?" Jude interrupts.

We look up at him. "What do you mean?"

"I mean, why are you here?"

Micah shrugs and lights another cigarette. "Just to hang out."

"Hang out?" Jude says the words like they're in a foreign language.

"Yeah. Hang out. You know? Hang."

"Yes, but doing what?"

Micah looks at me for help.

"Doing this," I tell him. "Like . . . hanging out." I can't think of any other way to say it.

"I understand the words," Jude says, exasperated. "I just don't get it. I mean, what do you *do* all day?"

"This!" Micah spreads his arms to take in the sky and his cigarette and the picnic table.

"I see," Jude says, in a way that suggests he doesn't. Micah offers him the cigarette, and he says, "Smoking is horrendous for your health."

"Yeah, but if you share them, then you're only smoking half." Micah passes the cigarette to me and Jude shakes his head. I don't smoke much, but I take it to annoy him.

"Dude, you need to loosen up," Micah says. "Live a little. I mean, given . . . y'know. I'd be up for anything. Why not let rip?"

"I could've been saying that for the last eighteen years. Where would that have gotten me? Why waste time when there's so little left? Some people have a bucket list. I have a list of things I consider a waste of time. This"—Jude gestures around—"would be right at the top of it."

"Aw, thanks!" Micah says, like it was a compliment. "What else is on it?"

"Breakfast," he says.

"Breakfast?" The two of us spit the word back at him.

"Also more than two courses at dinner, dancing, hair-cuts, sleep, social media, TV, movies, Christmas, small talk, magazines, alcohol—"

"Fuck, I love his accent," Micah says.

"Haircuts are a waste of time but books aren't?" I ask.

"Books are a great use of your time because you can live an entire life in a few hours by reading a novel. A haircut wastes an hour of your life just to achieve something that will last three weeks."

Micah laughs. "I love it. Jude's Bucket List of Time Wasting. We should make him do every single thing on the list." He hops off the table and pats it. "Here, start with this." He grabs a bottle and shifts over to sit down on the other bench.

Jude sighs and shuffles his butt onto the end of the table. "Anything once," he says as he lies down between us and slides on a pair of shades. Above us the sky is a warm blue, punctuated by clouds drifting like the conversation.

"Well?" Micah says after a while.

"Well what?" Jude answers.

"Are you relaxed?"

"I'm listing state capitals alphabetically."

"Jesus, you're my foster parents' wet dream."

"I'm surprised they let you out of the house today," I mutter. I don't blame Micah for last night, but my life would definitely be less complicated if he wasn't so *up for anything*. He probably doesn't even remember what he told Dante.

"They didn't. Window. I'm supposed to be in my room applying for jobs." He makes a face.

"You *have* a job," I say again. "And what about Lakeside?"

He laughs. "Yeah, I don't think I'm welcome back there."

"Ah."

"I regret nothing," he says dramatically, passing the bottle across Jude's body. "The job sucked anyway."

I take a swig. It *is* warm. "I did tell you."

"You know Luis wants me to work with him? Can you imagine? Going back to your high school as the janitor? Not *even* the janitor. The janitor's *assistant*. That is very much"—he takes a long drag and blows the smoke up in a long plume—"*not* me."

"Luis?" Jude asks.

"Micah's foster dad," I tell him.

"It's temporary," Micah says firmly, though he's been there two years already. "I'm eighteen now, I'm going to get my own place as soon as I've saved enough." Micah spends his money faster than he makes it, so I'm not expecting this to happen anytime soon.

"What's wrong with them wanting you to work for a living?" Jude says.

Micah looks across Jude at me to say, "Is he for real?"

"Incredible, isn't it," I say, reaching for the cigarette. "You'd think he knew something about working for a living."

"You think *I* don't work?" Jude says.

"I think you don't *have* to work," I say. "There's a difference."

"There is, yes. Working when you don't have to work requires self-discipline, maturity, a sense of purpose, and some ambition. Don't you ever want to aim higher than . . ." He glances around. "Well. The bottom of the pool."

"Kind of a bitch, isn't he?" Micah muses.

"He's an asshole."

"It's sort of hot."

"Jesus, Micah, you have the worst taste in men."

"I'm right here, you know," Jude says, sitting up and passing the bottle of beer back from me to Micah.

Micah takes a drag on the cigarette. "Anyway, we do have ambition. We even tried to get into the vodka business once! I mean, it wasn't quite on the Daly scale—"

"He doesn't need to hear about that."

Micah ignores me. "It was so funny. We were eight, and we collected all these empty vodka bottles, filled them with water, and took them to school to sell."

"It was dumb," I mutter.

"We thought vodka was just expensive water. Like Evian or something. Anyway, the older kids at school were weirdly excited to buy them and we came home with our pockets stuffed with cash. Until we got hauled into the principal's office. It was brief but beautiful." Micah shakes his head sadly.

I reach for the cigarette. What *I* remember about that incident is that when I got to the principal's office, I expected to be yelled at. Which wouldn't have bothered me. Micah and I were used to being yelled at. But what actually happened was that the principal and his secretary started gently grilling me about how I had access to that many empty bottles of vodka. I lied. I said we'd taken them from a dumpster behind one of the resort clubs. It was the first big lie I'd ever told, and at the time, I didn't even know *why* I lied. It was just the way they were looking at me. Like I was in some sort of trouble, but not the kind you get yelled at for.

The way Jude's looking at me now.

"I'm bored." I flick ash on the ground. "And hungry. Let's go to the beach. Or back to the resort. We could have lunch at the top of the Imperial. There's a sky garden."

But Micah's phone pings and a sloppy grin spreads over his face. "Carlos is coming to the party tonight," he says smugly.

"Who's Carlos?"

"What do you mean who's Carlos?" He's indignant. "He's the love of my life, thank you very much."

"Wait. That guy from Inferno?"

"I think it's serious."

"It's been two days!"

"What can I say? It was love at first sight. He said I have a beautiful soul." He sighs, and I know he's sunk.

Micah will fall in love with someone who compliments his *hair*, never mind someone who seems to actually like him.

Jude snorts. "No one really believes in love at first sight," he says.

"No, it's a real thing!" Micah says earnestly. "I've done it *tons* of times."

"I think your job might have given you a warped idea of what love is."

"Nuh-uh," Micah says. "We have actual training in it."

Jude laughs. "You realize, *Romeo and Juliet* isn't even a romance," he says, passing the bottle. This time he takes a sip from it and makes a disgusted face. "It's a tragedy. Juliet didn't die to be with Romeo; she did it to escape her insane family and a forced marriage she didn't want. If she'd had school and a job, she'd have thought twice. You don't decide you can't live without someone you met a few days ago. People just don't fall in love that fast."

"I think the plot is completely reasonable," I say, flicking through my magazine.

"You do?" He looks half irritated, half amused.

"I did that play in school, too, you know," I say smugly. "Well. The first half. Then Micah broke up with Aaron Arnott and . . . it was a whole thing. Anyway." I wave a hand at him. "Did you know the original *Romeo and Juliet* stories took place over several months?"

Jude says nothing, so I assume he didn't.

"Shakespeare changed it so the whole play happens in the space of five days. And *that's* why it works. Five days in, *he's* still perfect, *she's* still flawless, the romance is next level. If the story had lasted five months, they'd have walked away from the suicide option, if they hadn't already gotten bored of each other and broken up. The ending of *Romeo and Juliet* could *only* have happened within five days or after fifty years. Anything in between is ridiculous." I reach across Jude for the forgotten cigarette dangling from Micah's fingers as he scrolls on his phone.

Jude lies back on the table, hands behind his head, and after a moment he says, "The way I see it? *Romeo and Juliet* isn't about love at all, it's about death." He squints at the cloud formations making short-lived pictures above us. "These two kids grow up surrounded by death, in a world where petty arguments are solved with swords, their friends end up killed, and the reason they're racing down the aisle at the age of thirteen is because this is the fourteenth century and even if they survive the murderous feud, the plague will get them by the time they're twenty-five. So, what do you do if life is short and perilous? You fall in love with a complete stranger at a party, marry him the next day, and when the shit hits the fan, as it tends to do when you marry complete strangers you met at a party, you run away from home, fake your own death, and then make a melodramatic leap for the kitchen knife because, y'know, you're thirteen and these seem like reasonable options."

Micah frowns at his phone. "How romantic. Have you considered a career in writing Hallmark cards?"

"I'm just saying, you can't fall in love in five days. But you *can* make some very stupid decisions."

Micah looks at me and I shrug. "You see what I'm working with here?"

He grins. "You've had worse. Remember TikTok guy?"

"Oh my God."

"What guy?" Jude says.

"He was a film student," I tell him. "He had cancer and I think he started out documenting his treatment on TikTok. But then it turned into this documentary of his own death."

"He was creepsville," Micah says.

"It was morbid. He insisted on interviewing everyone about how they felt about him dying and shit. He had everyone in pieces all the fucking time. I think his parents got him a Juliet just to get rid of him for a while."

Micah laughs. "Didn't he plan his whole funeral in a TikTok post?"

"He wrote the eulogy! And then, and this is the creepiest part, instead of me dying with him, he had me film *him* dying. I'm, like, lying in the bed next to him, pointing a camera at him, and he's telling me everything he's feeling and how we're going to be together forever and ever, et cetera, et cetera."

"Weird." Micah shudders.

"Yeah, but the creepy thing is, he's not even talking to me, he's talking *to the fucking camera*. I swear."

"Sick."

"He wasn't as bad as Crying Boy, though." I grin.

"Crying boy?" Jude asks.

"Cried every time we had sex," Micah says. "Like, every time. For the whole time."

"Tell him *why* he cried, Micah."

"Because he was weird!"

"That's not what *he* said. Wasn't it because you were *so beautiful*? And sex was *so beautiful*. And the world and the sky and bunny rabbits were *so beautiful*."

"Fuck off. He was a messy crier, too."

"Well, you didn't *have* to sleep with him."

He shrugs. "He was also kind of hot."

"At least he did all the crying. He didn't insist that *you* cry, at the drop of a hat, *on camera*. And I'm not a crier!"

"She's not," Micah affirms.

"I don't cry! I had to pull out tufts of my own hair to make my eyes water."

"God, we've had every flavor," Micah muses. "And you have to pretend to like them all."

"Bad musicians."

"Worse poets."

"Jocks."

"Jerks."

"Racists."

"Republicans."

"Trustifarians."

"Philosophers," Jude says quietly.

The echo of our laughter rings out from the old pool

tiles for a moment, sounding suddenly harsh. Fuck. We forgot. Because he's here, in Staff Town, muddying the waters, we forgot.

"Shit, Jude, that's— We're sorry," I say.

"Sorry, Jude."

"We didn't mean *you*. We were just—"

Jude snorts as he sits up. "You think I'm that sensitive? Come on, that's why people go to counseling, isn't it? To talk about their imminent demise with people who don't give a fuck about their imminent demise. You two should charge— Oh, wait, you do."

"Jude. It's not that we don't—"

"Seriously, it's fine. I'm not exactly known for my tact, either." He hops off the table. "I should go. I'm spending the afternoon with my parents."

"Right, yeah. OK." Jesus, what have we done? I'm supposed to be getting him to open up, and the first time he voluntarily brings up the subject of death, what do I do? I make jokes. Dick move.

I don't want him to just walk off like this, but I don't know how to fix it. I look helplessly at Micah, who looks helplessly back and then calls, "Jude!" as he turns to go. "Um . . . Hey, why don't you come to the Staff Town party tonight? It's way up in the ruins, it's going to be amazing."

"Party?"

"Jude hates parties," I say quickly. I can't imagine Jude at the Staff Town party. It's really not his scene.

"Aw, come on, it'll be fun! Music, dancing, drinking,

girls. You can tick a whole bunch of stuff off your bucket list of time wasting."

That earns him a small twitch of Jude's lips. I wait for him to say he'd rather die, but his eyes flicker to me, as if for permission.

"You should come. I'd like you to come," I say too quickly to be convincing.

He considers for a moment, kicking at a stone as if he's reluctant to leave. I can't imagine why. Though suddenly it occurs to me that when we "hang out," we don't do nothing. We talk. We've been talking for a solid hour, even if most of it was rambling nonsense. Probably not the kind of talking Mrs. Daly meant, but if Jude never just hangs out with anyone, who does he talk rambling nonsense to?

Finally he plucks the cigarette from Micah's hand and takes a drag. He coughs. "That's disgusting," he says, handing it back. He turns to go, waving over his shoulder. "See you tonight, then."

Chapter 10

AS SOON AS JUDE IS SAFELY OUT OF EARSHOT, I TELL MICAH ABOUT
Dante's threat and show him the device I'm carrying around
in my bag.

"Fucking hell," he whispers when I'm done. He winces
at me across the picnic table. "I'm sorry, Ree. I don't even
remember talking to him. He was handing out pills at the
bar like they were candy. I was bored."

I sigh. "It doesn't matter now. So, what do I *do*?"

He chews his lip. "Where would they keep their laptops?"

"I meant how do I get out of it!"

"I know but . . ." He glances around, as if there might
be someone listening. "If you don't have a choice . . . And
that's a lot of money, Ree."

"It'll be a lot of jail time, too, if I'm caught."

He thinks about it. "Well, maybe you don't have to
hack anything. Maybe if you just asked some questions? I
mean, it's your job to get him to open up and talk about his

feelings, right? He must have feelings about his parents' research. If you can find out enough info to keep Dante happy, maybe he'll leave you alone. Just talk to Jude."

"Talk to Jude? You just *met* Jude, right? Ugh." I slump with my forehead on the table, tired suddenly. "Wasn't this job supposed to be *fun*?" I mutter.

Micah strokes my head. "You can handle him."

But it's not that. It's not like I'm ever honest with clients, but somehow my skin crawls at the idea of mining Jude for information for Dante. *Parasite.* I can almost hear him spit the word at me. But I can hear Dante's words, too. *Who are you protecting?* Jude doesn't care about me. He doesn't even like me. And his parents are nice, but I'm just someone they hired. I have my own family to think of.

I glance at my watch and curse. "I have to go. Burgess. Because this day wasn't bad enough."

Micah grimaces in sympathy as I get up. I have a headache already, but unlike Jude, I don't get to skip counseling.

"OK, so where are we at, day three?" Dr. Burgess asks. "You've been spending a lot of time together. How's that going?"

Hmm. Should I start with the fact that he hates me? That I've put her job and Dr. Lawrence's business at risk? That I'm being blackmailed by someone who wants me to spy on their most important clients?

"It's fine. Good. We've been . . . talking mostly. He's

definitely the deep and meaningful type." I can't keep the wry twist off my lips.

"And is that raising difficult issues for you?"

Talking to Burgess might be more stressful than talking to Jude. They'd probably hit it off.

"Not really." She gives me one of her interminable silences and I find myself adding, "The opposite, if anything."

"Oh?"

I shrug. "He's so . . . together. About everything. His mom thinks he needs someone to talk to, but from what I can see, he's totally fine about the fact that he's on his way out. He doesn't even need counseling."

"Well, a lot of people think they don't need counseling." Burgess's face is carefully neutral. I ignore it.

"Maybe he doesn't, though." I look up at her. "You're a doctor. Do you know much about his parents' research institute?" I ask casually. Micah's right, I need something to feed back to Dante, but maybe Jude isn't the only person who knows stuff.

"I've read a few articles about them. Why?"

"It's just . . . Eighteen years and billions of dollars? They can't have found *nothing*, right?" I give her a skeptical look. Still casual.

She only tilts her head a fraction. "What are you saying, Regan?"

"I'm just . . . It's interesting. I mean, maybe they *do* know something. Maybe they have a plan. Maybe *that's* why Jude is so chill about all this. Maybe his death *isn't* inevitable. Camus said people don't kill themselves because hope gets in the way."

She arches an eyebrow. "Camus?"

"Saw it on a social media post. I'm just saying, maybe there's hope for Jude. It's possible, right?"

She exhales slowly. "Regan, you remember the training session on the grieving process? And acceptance? And how we talked about denial and bargaining with reality?"

"I'm not—! I'm just . . . It's just a fact; they *could* be working on something. It would explain why Jude's so calm about it all."

"Regan," she presses gently. "It's normal human psychology to see evidence everywhere for things we want to be true. It's called confirmation bias. But ask yourself *why* you want this to be true. Have your feelings—"

"No!" She's twisting everything as usual. What I *want* is information, not the third degree. "Look, forget it. It's just a theory. I was making conversation. I don't care if . . . I don't even like him."

"You don't?"

I snort. "*No.* He's super irritating. Arrogant. Entitled. Rude. Smug. Condescending. Judgmental. Take your pick." Somehow I'm hunched in one corner of my chair, arms and legs folded and my jaw set, glaring at the carpet. So much for casual.

"You feel he's judging you?"

"He judges everyone."

"In what way?"

For a wild moment, I imagine telling her about the

hiking expedition. *Parasite. What's the going rate for someone's dignity?* Is it *normal human psychology* for completely unfair insults to burn themselves onto your brain?

Instead I shrug. "Just the usual rich asshole stuff," I mutter. "Nothing is good enough."

"Remember, he's only judging the facade. You're playing a role, Regan. He hasn't even met the real you, right?"

I swallow and force a smile onto my face. "Right."

"So his opinion of you doesn't matter."

"I guess not."

"Anything else you want to discuss?"

I glare at the carpet, my head only full of things I *can't* discuss. I shake them away. "No. I'm fine."

She glances at the clock. "OK. We'll have another session before Jude's procedure. But if you want to talk about anything in the meantime, you know where I am."

"Right, yeah. Thanks." *But no thanks.* Why do I always come out of this room feeling worse than when I arrived?

I unfold myself from the chair and make my way out of the clinic, past the maintenance teams carefully removing any wall art with the color purple in it.

The sun is low in the sky as Micah and I make our way out of Staff Town and up to the Bergman ruins for the party. They're farther up the mountain than the cabins, and if Jude thought Staff Town was a ghost town, the ruins are like a time-slip. Several acres of old hotels, swimming pools, a bowling alley, ice rink, recreation centers, bars, tennis and racquetball courts built in every decade from the 1930s to the 1980s. The guests at Elite Elect would call them vacant, abandoned, or disused because they're not used by *them* anymore. But this place is used every day by campers, squatters, graffiti artists, skateboarders, loners. People come to party, couples come to get some privacy, scrappers come searching for metal and whatever they can sell. Animals have moved into the lobbies, birds nest in the high-ceilinged dining rooms, ivy creeps up the thickly carpeted stairs. Some places are falling into rubble already, others are surprisingly intact with bedrooms that still have mattresses, even sheets, blooming mushrooms and mold. Tables, chairs, and chests of drawers sitting around in such an ordinary way, you barely notice that the people are missing.

We grab two old sun loungers in the Sheherazade Room of the Moroccan Lodge, a bar draped in red velvet swagged curtains and strewn with low couches upholstered in gold, where everyone goes to smoke whatever they're smoking. Micah's lounger is missing an armrest and the plastic slats of mine sag beneath me like molten candy. Above us, the chandeliers, missing half their glass, creak on rusted chains, catching the last of the sun and illuminating the flaking gilded paintwork in beams of stuttering light. I lift my phone to take a picture of one, a tiny bird's nest tucked inside it, but it's far away and the light's too low for a good shot.

The Staff Town kids always have parties here because the tennis courts out front make a clear space for the bonfire, and there's a stream that runs from higher up the mountain, over a little waterfall, and into a natural plunge pool just beside the hotel, before continuing down to the lake. Inside, the rooms are dry enough for couples to sneak off to, and the paneled walls of the huge dining room are rapidly becoming an unofficial graffiti art gallery.

I didn't know whether to dress for Jude or for Staff Town, so I went with a sundress of my own and added a sweater for later. It's not even dark yet, but most of the Staff Town kids are here already. Dancing, smoking, dragging chairs and mattresses out of the hotel. Jodie is perched on the bar top in the center of a crowd of guys with a beer bong. Micah and I would usually be several drinks deep by now, but instead we're sitting stiffly on our loungers. He's just finishing his first beer, and I haven't had anything yet.

"He must be running late," Micah says.

"I sent him directions, but he didn't say what time he'd come," I remind him. But he's frowning at his phone and I realize he wasn't talking about Jude.

I hand him another beer. "It's still early."

"He'll be here, he promised. He said he wants to see where I live. And he wants to meet you." He goes to check his phone again, but I nudge him, nodding at the figure who's just appeared in the doorway.

Same shirt and jeans, but Jude's wearing a black wool coat this time, and he's made an endearing attempt to neaten his hair, as if tonight *he's* the one going to a fancy party where he doesn't belong. He stands at the edge of the room for a moment, looking for me, then weaves his way across the cracks in the ornately tiled floor, through the detritus of broken chairs, sticky tables, and already drunk dancers. I leave Micah to go and meet him, and he holds out a bottle of wine shyly. I didn't think Jude Daly did shy. For a moment he looks like the teenage boy he is and not the college graduate he sounds like.

"I wasn't sure what the etiquette was." *Aaand* there he is.

There's a scream from outside the windows, and then laughter as someone gets thrown in the pool by half the school's football team. They won't be the last.

"It's pretty laid-back," I reassure him, nodding toward the beer coolers. "You can help yourself."

We each grab a bottle, and he leaves the wine in one of the coolers. Someone will drink it—and throw it back up by midnight.

We hover at the edge of the crowd as I ask stilted questions about his afternoon and wonder if the whole night is going to be this awkward. He tells me they had a family picnic on Bergman Island.

"It was nice, actually. Just spending some time together. Laughing at old stories." His lip twitches as he adds. "Y'know. *Hanging out.*"

I nudge him with my elbow. "Look at you," I tease. "Down with the kids." We both relax our stances slightly. He's wearing aftershave, and I'm touched that he made an effort for this.

He looks out over the room, taking in the faded grandeur, the weird mix of retro elegance and modern high-school blowout. The Staff Town midsummer party used to be the highlight of our year. But when you've been to the Midsummer Ball, it looks lackluster, and I can't help seeing things through Jude's eyes. The cheap red plastic cups and beer coolers. The rotting velvet of the Sheherazade Room. There's no power, no running water, no working facilities. When it gets dark, the only light will be from the bonfire, and the speakers blaring Marshmello outside right now are battery powered. This is no Midsummer Ball.

"You don't have to stay," I tell him, leaning in and shouting so he can hear me over the noise. "It was nice of you to come, but I know you hate this stuff."

"No, I want to stay," he says, leaning in, too. "Look, I'm not . . ." He picks at the label on his untouched beer bottle, takes a breath, and says, "I promise I'm not usually such an arsehole."

I laugh, taken aback by the directness of the word *arsehole* yelled in my ear in an English accent.

"I hope I didn't insult your friend. About the job and everything." He nods at Micah, who's now chugging a beer at the bar while the crowd chants his name.

"It's OK, 'arseholes' are Micah's favorite kind of people." We watch him sink to his knees as the beer bong drains, before falling over, skinny arms raised in triumph. Even Jude can't help but smile.

The smoke in here is getting ridiculous so I lead him

outside, where the bonfire is piled up and they're building a trampoline stack of mattresses near it. The hotel veranda is full of people already and more are dancing on the buckled, weedy asphalt of the old tennis courts. The sun dips below the horizon, the music pumps up, and the bonfire is ceremoniously lit by someone tossing a Molotov cocktail onto it while the crowd roars their approval.

"Look, I'm not, either," I say. "Usually such a bitch, I mean. I'm sorry about this afternoon. That was insensitive."

He waves it away.

"No, really," I say. "I've been feeling shitty about it all day and I want to explain." Except I'm not sure I know how to. "You keep asking how I can do this job. Today . . . That's how. I guess it's just how we think about things. Keeping it light, I mean. Making jokes. You have to, otherwise . . ." I shrug. "That's why people hire us, right? Because no one wants to think about *otherwise*. We're here to distract them from *otherwise*. So, it just gets to be a habit, I guess."

"Don't worry, I'm fine about all that," he says, like it's a dentist appointment he's here for. "It's just this place." He kicks at the weeds. "It brings out the worst in me. But you have been . . . distracting. In a useful way," he clarifies. "And I'm grateful that you've gone along with this whole thing. I know it's crazy. I thought the least I could do was come up here and reciprocate."

"Reciprocate? Is that what they call partying in Oxford?"

"Yes. That's why parties in Oxford are bloody awful."

I look him over appraisingly. "I think this is probably your best apology yet."

"I'm always up for learning new skills. So, I'm forgiven?"

I consider, then roll my eyes with a grin. "Have a drink, Jude. It's a party."

He grins back at me and clinks his beer bottle against mine.

Two hours later, Jude Daly is drunk.

I mean, he's not chugging beers and throwing girls in the pool, but he's had five beers, lost his coat, taken his shoes off, and I definitely heard him slur the word *conflagration* when he stumbled close to the bonfire.

Several girls ask him to dance, and after beer number three he started saying, "Why not?" and then there was no stopping him. Micah and I stared in disbelief for a moment before running to join him.

It's weird, the three of us crashing around as the music pumps up, yelling lyrics, laughing, stumbling, bouncing dance moves off one another. Having fun. *With Jude Daly.* It's strange how quickly all the hostility of the past few days just gets dumped at the edge of the dance floor when a good song comes on. I keep forgetting who he is for a moment, finding myself relaxing, back in a *much* more familiar groove. Maybe he's forgotten, too, because he looks like he's actually enjoying himself.

And Jude said he *didn't* dance. He never said he *couldn't*. Maybe the alcohol just brings it out, but if anything, he's even better-looking on the dance floor, and the girls are hanging off him.

"How is this guy still single?" Micah yells in my ear as Jude finishes another beer.

"He works hard at it," I yell back, though I can't help laughing as he tosses the bottle behind him straight into the pile of empties without looking. Then I mutter, "Jesus, give him a lap dance, why don't you!" and fire Jodie a disgusted look as she grinds against Jude in a Lycra jumpsuit.

Micah just laughs. "Since when do you care?"

"I don't! But he's drunk; she's taking advantage."

"I don't think he minds."

Jodie sticks her hands under his shirt, and I push Micah at them. He grabs Jude's arm, dislodging her. Jude twirls him like they're on a ballroom dance floor and the crowd cheers.

I stagger away to collapse on the veranda steps, panting and watching the dancers—black contorted shadows, flames licking at the night air. I lift my phone automatically.

But parties look different when you're sober. And when you point a camera at something, you can't help seeing every little detail. The people vomiting at the edges of the stream while others wade through it to swim. Plastic bags and beer cans floating in the water. Disheveled couples stumbling out of the hotel missing items of clothing. The fug of acrid pot smoke and pale moonlight hanging over everything. Someone tosses more wood on the bonfire and sparks hiss violently into the sky.

I find Micah—backlit as he detaches himself from the dancers and saunters toward me, shirt unbuttoned, hands in his pockets—and press the shutter. It doesn't matter where Micah is, he looks like he's on a catwalk. He sits on the step behind me, wrapping his arms and legs around me and leaning his cheek on my shoulder. The boards beneath us creak ominously as I lean back against him.

"What a total waste of an evening," he mumbles contentedly into my neck.

I laugh.

"Have another drink, you're too sober," he complains.

"Technically, I'm working."

He lifts his head. "But he *knows* everything."

"Yeah, but his parents don't. It's still a job. I'm supposed to be looking after— Oh my God, is he smoking? What is he smoking, Micah?"

"Oh, let him live a little. It's his last summer. And possibly his first."

"His parents are trusting me with him."

"He's eighteen, not eight."

The dancers are falling over and laughing, makeup sweated off and hair sticky, probably thinking they look like something in a music video. I wonder if that's what we looked like to Jude the night he came to Inferno.

It's like we've switched places. Me, sober at the edge of the dance floor, judging everyone, while Jude swigs from every bottle that's handed to him and girls grope him and blow smoke into his mouth. I don't know what

I was worried about; he fits in here better than I fit in at the Midsummer Ball.

His whole body moves differently when he's relaxed. His jawline, posture, the way he moves his limbs, and the shape of his shadow on the asphalt behind him. Normally I'd itch for my phone, but the moment is so unlikely, so miraculous, a photo would dilute it somehow.

It's after midnight already. How did that happen? But time doesn't obey the normal rules at Elite Elect. School semesters drag; summers fly. Guests and clients and weekends vanish in a blur while it feels like we never get any older. Didn't we graduate just a minute ago? And here we are at midsummer. Jude's last summer. I watch as he dances, eyes closed, bottle held aloft, completely in the moment, and wonder how time passes for him.

I hug my sweater to me, chilly now. The bonfire has settled into a heap just low enough for people to start fire jumping. They take a run up and leap over the flames, howling, while the crowd eggs them on, landing on the pile of mattresses on the other side. They do it every year. No one's been seriously injured yet, but let's just say it's lucky the stream is so close. Only the most experienced jumpers are game at this point. The others wait until later in the night when the fire is smaller. Normally Micah and I would join them, but he's too drunk and I'm not drunk enough.

Jude has moved, and when I spot him again, someone is yelling something in his ear and he laughs. Then he turns and walks away. I think he's coming to find us, but after a dozen steps he turns again, pauses, leans into a crouch. The crowd parts to make a path.

"Oh *shit*. Micah, he's . . . he's not . . ."

But he is. He's barreling full tilt, howling, toward the fire while the crowd chants, *"Jude, Jude, Jude, Jude!"*

Micah and I grip each other in panic, too late to get up, too late to even shout. Our hands go automatically to our heads, our inhales fail to exhale as he takes off in an unsteady leap, legs drawn up, bare feet brushing the flames. He comes down heavily on the other side, completely missing the mattresses and rolling in a ball of dust, weeds, and broken glass.

There's a beat of total silence. Then, "He's OK!" someone yells, and the crowd releases a roar.

"Fuuuuck!" I breathe, and I hear Micah exhale behind me as his forehead hits my shoulder blade. He starts to laugh, and soon both our bodies are shaking with it.

"Mother of fuck. That was—"

"Fucking dangerous!"

"Impressive," Micah concedes.

I'm still trying to breathe normally.

"It's no fun if you're not doing *something* stupid, right?" Micah says what he always says. But it's different when you're watching someone else do it. I'm imagining explaining third-degree burns to Mr. and Mrs. Daly as I watch Jude brush himself off while people slap his back and girls hug him.

"He doesn't do anything by halves, does he? You have to give him that." I laugh incredulously, then mutter,

"Jesus, Jodie, he can brush the dust off his own ass."

He scrubs dirt out of his hair, and I can't help laughing at the way it sticks up at every angle when he's done.

Micah watches me watching him, and says, "Ree."

"Hmm?"

"You don't *have* to spend all this time with him, you know. It's not a real R and J anymore."

"I know. It's for his parents. And Dr. Lawrence. And if I'm going to keep Dante from—"

"Right, right, but . . ."

"What?"

He tightens his arms around me a little. "It's just." He sighs close to my ear. "We know how this ends. Right?"

I sit up sharply. "Of course." I tut.

"OK, just—"

I twist around. "*You're* lecturing *me* about guys, Micah? Seriously? Carlos is where exactly?"

"Ouch," he says with a huff.

I turn back and mutter, "Well, I'm hardly new at this. I can handle it."

"Sure. Right. I know."

"I think it's time to get him out of here." I disentangle myself from Micah's arms. "Before they start diving off the hotel roof."

"But it's still early!" Jude protests as Micah and I drag him away from the crowd. He has no idea what time it is. "We haven't even gone swimming!" People are stripping now and splashing into the pool, squealing at the cold.

"I'm not delivering you back to your mom with pneumonia. Where's your coat?"

"Um . . ."

"Where are your shoes?"

"Ah . . ."

He sways, giggling like a schoolboy at his bare feet, which sets Micah off, and soon they're holding each other up, laughing about nothing. Jude's shirt is filthy, one knee of his jeans is torn, and there's a smear of blood on his palm.

"Jesus, are drunk people always this irritating?"

"I don't wanna go yet," Jude declares.

"He doesn't wanna go yet," Micah relays, though I'm standing right there.

"Let's go to that club!"

"No," I say firmly before Micah can leap on the idea. I'm not taking him anywhere near Dante. "They wouldn't even let you in in this state."

"Let's go back to Regan's place!" Micah says. "Her mom will have—"

"*Definitely* no."

"Or Lakeside! She has a suite!"

"Naomi will be asleep."

They keep coming up with ridiculous suggestions to keep the party going—*Let's steal a speedboat! Let's go cliff diving! Let's break into a hotel kitchen!*—until I say, "Ugh! OK, fine. Come with me."

We hunt up Jude's coat and shoes, grab a couple of blankets and a cooler of beer, and I lead them farther up the mountain, following the stream while they stumble behind, tripping over tree roots and rocks in the dark, singing tunelessly and laughing like idiots.

But the laughter is infectious. By the time we reach a place where the ground levels out and the stream is wider and deeper, we're all giggling. The music from the party is muted here, and the only light is from the moon. There's a clear view, and we can see the lights of the resort far below, the black humps of islands breaching the lake, and the wall of mountains on the other side. There's no broken glass, no litter. And Jude and Micah singing Villain Era tracks at the top of their lungs won't bother anyone.

Micah hits a random playlist on his phone and they dance unsteadily, splashing in and out of the edge of the stream and spilling their beer while I sit on the grass, laughing at them.

"I'm getting the hang of this!" Jude yells.

"Of what?" I yell back.

"Staying upright!" he says, almost toppling over as he stops watching his feet to look at me.

Micah applauds. "Fuck me, I love drunk Jude," he says.

"I'm hungry. Does anyone want pizza? We should swim! Let's swim!" He's halfway into the stream and pulling his coat off when we catch him. It takes both of us to drag him back.

"It's freezing, you nightmare!" I laugh as he pouts at me.

"I'm not cold!"

"That's because you're wasted."

He swings me into his arms to dance me around in an

unstable waltz that doesn't at all match the beat thumping from Micah's phone. I squeal, because staying upright *is* hard, especially when you're going backward. Jude straightens his spine and sticks his nose in the air and Micah conducts us with an invisible baton. As the song comes to an end, Jude swoops dramatically to one side, dipping me over the edge of the water, and I scream and grab his lapels. But his arm is firm at my back as he bends over me, his face so close to mine I smell cigarette smoke and aftershave while Micah whoops in the background. There's a beat where I'm suspended over the water, blinking up at him, but before I can even process it, he swings me up again, spins me away, grabs Micah in his arms, and dips him, too, planting a loud smack of a kiss on his lips as he does it.

Micah laughs so hard he can hardly stand while Jude dances on with an invisible partner and I just shake my head, still breathless.

"Jesus, did he take something?" Micah says, wiping his eyes.

"Look at the stars!" Jude throws his arms out and his head back and tries to turn in a circle to take in the dusting of glittering constellations above us. But that upsets his balance finally and he topples, landing flat on his back on the scorched summer grass.

Micah and I bend over him, offering hands to pull him up, though we're no steadier ourselves, but he just lies there, grinning, eyes unfocused. "Ursa Major," he says, shooting a hand up to point at the sky between our heads.

"*Asshat* Major," I say as Micah and I give up and collapse on either side of him. At least if he's lying down, he's manageable. We catch our breaths for a few moments. The sheer size of the sky is sobering.

"I think you can tear up that bucket list now," Micah pants, turning the music off.

Jude chuckles. "This," he says, gesturing vaguely at the world, "was not in the plan."

"Plan schman." Micah waves a hand dismissively. "I never plan. Why would you want to know how life turns out in advance? *Spoiler alert!*"

"But you *do* know," Jude says, shrugging. "We all know."

There's a beat as we absorb that. It's the second time Jude has brought up the subject himself, and if he wants to talk about it, I should encourage him and do a better job than I did this morning. But when I open my mouth, nothing comes out.

"Not necessarily!" Micah rolls over and props his head on one arm to look down at us. "What about people who have no Date?"

It's true, there are a rare few. No one's born without one, but sometimes there are birth defects that make them hard or impossible to read.

"Those people are seriously fucked up," I say.

"Imagine not having a Date, though," Micah goes on, eyes shining like he's telling us a ghost story. "Having *no idea*. Like, it could happen at *any moment*."

"Sounds awful," Jude says.

"No way. It's the ultimate thrill ride. It'd be like living your whole life in free fall. Every day would be so intense! I mean, you'd have to really *live*."

"My parents met a couple who gave their baby a skin graft to cover his Date so he'd never know it," Jude says.

"Shit, that's got to be illegal!" Micah says, shocked.

"And abusive," I point out.

"Well, yeah, social services took the kid away. There was also a guy who got his surgically erased."

"What's the point of that? Doesn't change anything."

"But he also got himself hypnotized so the date was erased from his memory, too."

We're silent for a moment, taking that in.

"I'm gonna get that done," Micah declares, and I snort.

"You are not!"

"I am!"

"You'd never have the nerve." He's just trying to look edgy in front of Jude.

"You don't need to get it done. You could die at any moment anyway," Jude says.

"Yeah, but it's unlikely. Nearly everyone dies on their Date. I've decided I'm going out the way I came in," Micah says, lying back on the grass again. "Kicking and screaming. I'm hoping for a heart attack while screwing a Hollywood actor, but I'll also settle for a tragic plane crash involving drugs, rock stars, and a private jet. Just make sure Dante names a cocktail after me."

"You're going to be eighty-four," I remind him.

"And forty-three days," he says.

"You're going to trip over your walker and be found three weeks later half eaten by your cats."

"I'll take that bet." He narrows his eyes and lights a cigarette.

"Camus died in a car crash," Jude says, settling himself more comfortably with an arm behind his head. "After saying that a car crash would be the most absurd way to die." He grins at me. "Death by irony."

"That would be an awesome name for a cocktail," Micah says, and the two of them giggle.

The grass is starting to feel cold beneath me. I'm a little too sober for this conversation. And it's too quiet now that the music has stopped.

"The ancient Greeks thought that people who died young were beloved by the gods," Jude muses, staring up at the stars.

I squint into the blackness above and imagine a host of beautiful people in togas, reaching down into the bowl of humanity like they're selecting a grape. Choosing Jude because of course they'd choose Jude. They read *Zeitgeist*.

"And they thought the entrance to the underworld was across a stretch of water called the River Styx," he adds. "You had to be taken there by the ferryman of Hades."

"You're giving me a nerd-on," Micah says. "Do you have to be super intelligent *in an English accent*?"

Jude huffs a soft laugh. "When I was a kid, I thought it was an actual journey and I used to plan what I'd pack."

"What did you decide to take?" Micah asks.

"Footwear. And a hat. Loo roll."

Micah chokes on his cigarette smoke.

"Would *you* want to be without loo roll in an emergency?" Jude says. "It's the frigging underworld, there could very well be some brown-trousers moments. What's so funny?" But he's giggling, too.

"It's just, you never know what's going to come out of your mouth next," Micah says. "One minute it's fucking ancient Greece and the next it's getting the runs in the afterlife."

People come at death from every direction. Some people make jokes, some are super practical, some get weepy. If this is how Jude wants to talk about it, I should let him. I should join in. But so far, Micah's doing a much better job of that than me. For once, the jokes won't come and I only lie there feeling awkward. It's just that . . . for someone who insists death is no big deal, Jude knows a hell of a lot of random facts about it, and now that he's started talking about it, he can't seem to stop. And talking about it is one thing. Talking about it *while drunk* is another. Things you do *while drunk* have a tendency to end badly; I should know.

The laughter is subdued now, the conversation a little morbid, and I'm starting to worry I've made yet another mistake. Because maybe he *was* fine. Maybe he *didn't* need to talk about it, maybe we don't need to do this. We were having fun, and now . . . I kind of want to change the subject. But there's no natural segue from *diarrhea in hell.*

"Did you know, in ancient Greek mythology, Sisyphus

was punished for wrapping Death up in chains so no one on earth could die?"

"He got punished for that?" Micah says. "They should have given him a medal."

"People kept aging. But no one could die."

"Oh." Micah shakes his head and lies down again. "The Greeks were fucked up, man." He passes the cigarette and we all take a drag. His phone pings and he snatches it up before exhaling audibly. "Luis," he mutters, embarrassed because it's obvious who he's waiting to hear from. He pushes his hair back casually, like it's no big deal.

Jude sits up to toss the cigarette butt into the stream and says, "There were some parties at the hotels tonight. Maybe he couldn't get away."

"Yeah. He didn't say he'd *definitely* make it, so."

I impulsively want to hug Jude. For outright lying when I know he hates being dishonest. For being kinder than I was.

Micah puts the phone away. "So, have your parents experimented on people?" he asks. "Like, do they find people who are about to die and do tests on them? Or do people volunteer?"

"It's more about understanding how Death Dates work," Jude says, still sitting up, staring out at the black expanse of the mountains. "Finding patterns. Using Death Date algorithms to predict national disasters, pandemics, that kind of thing."

"And have they found any answers?"

This must be the kind of stuff reporters hack Jude's

phone for, but he doesn't seem to mind Micah asking questions. Probably because no one could suspect Micah of having ulterior motives.

But he does. He's asking for my sake. Searching for something that will get Dante off my back. And I feel sick suddenly. Jude is drunk, and we're no better than Jodie taking advantage of him on the dance floor. I have an urge to tell them to stop talking, put the music on again, have a drink, and stop bumming everyone out; it's a fucking party. Instead I find myself listening. Holding my breath.

Jude says quietly, "No. No answers," and the air rushes out of me.

"It *might* be possible, though, right?" Micah presses. "There are lots of stories."

"No," Jude says firmly. "There are myths, and there are legends. You might as well be hunting for vampires or fairies. Did you know Saint Jude is the patron saint of lost causes?" He grins. "My parents thought that was worth a shot when they chose my name."

"If you don't believe it's possible, why do you let them do it? Why do you let them waste their time and money?" I ask, sounding irritated suddenly.

He turns back to look at me, surprised by my tone. He shrugs and says, "It makes them feel better. Like they're doing something about it."

He looks out into the dark for another long moment, then grabs a blanket and lies down again, spreading it over the three of us. We shuffle closer beneath it, and I listen to both of them drift off, my cheek resting lightly on

Jude's shoulder. But sleep eludes me for a long time. The music from the party has stopped now. The moonlight is bone-cold, the sky heavy, and the stream mutters anxiously to itself. The sick feeling in my stomach is worse, but for once it's not the beer or the cigarettes. And it's not Dante's offers or his threats.

No. No answers.

It's just . . . having it confirmed like that. So flatly. I mean, I *knew*, of course I knew, but . . . I knew it about the Jude Daly from yesterday. Not the Jude Daly from today.

Chapter 11

IT'S BARELY DAWN WHEN I WAKE, STIFF AND SHIVERING, BUT JUDE is already standing by the edge of the stream, hands in his pockets, bare feet in the water. The sky is a cold silver, and my mouth tastes disgusting. God knows what I look like.

Micah has rolled over so his arm is flung across me. I remove it gently and pull the blanket over him as I get up.

Jude's clothes are torn and grass stained, his skin grubby. And he can't be feeling great. Guilt washes over me like a wave of nausea. Wednesday. Friday is his procedure day, Saturday is his Death Date, and I just let him waste a whole night fooling around with a bunch of strangers and left him with a hangover.

"Not sure you're meeting the Lakeside dress code." I try a tentative joke as I join him, expecting anger, or at the very least sarcasm.

But he grins and says, "*Now* can we swim?"

I look at the ice-cold water, then down at my own filthy outfit. "God, yes."

We laugh, strip to our underwear, and wade in, squealing and gasping as the water seizes us with freezing fingers, squeaking and yelping as we dunk our heads and bounce around in agony. Even my internal organs are screaming. But we scrub at our hair and skin, and after a few minutes I feel human again. We yell for Micah to join us, but he just groans and rolls over.

Jude floats on his back, eyes closed against the light as the sun rises higher, water droplets freckling his pale skin. I float beside him, watching the blue of the sky deepen and warm, and for a while there's nothing but trickling water, birdsong, and the tug of the river current beneath us. When our outstretched fingers bump, we link fingers so we're tethered.

"I've swam in every ocean in the world," he murmurs.

"How does the Bergman River compare?"

He pretends to think about it. "It's a solid three stars," he says.

I flick my wrist, splashing him, and he rolls away laughing and already splashing me back, and soon we're competing to see who can splash more water and squeal the loudest about it.

"OK, OK, five stars, five stars!" he protests as I send a whole wave over his head.

"That's better," I say, pushing my dripping hair back, my nose in the air.

"The Pacific's overrated."

"I've heard that."

We grin at each other, bobbing lazily, getting our breath back. I don't want to get out, but eventually our feet and hands start to go numb and we wade reluctantly back to shore.

We have no towels or fresh clothes so there's no choice but to shiver in our underwear as we put on last night's outfits. I silently thank Marta because at least my underwear is pretty, though Jude is gentleman enough to turn his back. We dress over damp skin and drink ice water from the cooler and nothing's ever tasted so good.

"So, what are your plans for the day?" I ask as I wring out my hair.

"I have a fundraiser for my Make a Difference foundation at the hotel this afternoon."

"You're still working?"

"It's a good opportunity. Lots of rich people keen to improve their karma." He grins. "But I'm going on a lake cruise with my parents first. Would you like to come?"

I almost say yes, but I shake my head. "Your parents will want to have you to themselves." He nods. He knows it's true, but he's polite enough to seem disappointed.

"But . . ." I chew my lip, thinking. "It's still early. Do you have some time this morning?"

Most of the trails in the old Bergman resort have become overgrown, some consumed altogether by undergrowth, so you can emerge from clumps of trees to suddenly find

yourself standing in front of an old diner or the remains
of a hotel, saplings unfurling from a lone chimney stack,
snakes of ivy climbing stairs to nowhere.

Micah was in no state for hiking so he went home,
and I lead Jude farther up the mountain myself, relaying
the history of the place and how my grandparents met
here.

"It's eerie," Jude says, examining a metal sign rust-
ing outside a hotel. THE FUN NEVER STOPS AT THE PARA-
DISE ROOMS! "It's like everyone just vanished all at once.
Or abandoned the place because something terrible
happened."

We peer through the broken windows. There's a
broom propped against the wall in a litter of dry leaves.
An open guest book on the reception desk, the writing
blurred by damp. The silence is loud, and I feel like if we
turned around quickly enough, we'd catch a glimpse of
the band, or people dressed for dinner.

"Sorry, this probably *isn't* what your parents had in
mind when they hired me. I don't know why I brought
you here really."

"Why do *you* come here?" he asks as we walk on,
skirting the edge of an empty swimming pool. The diving
board stretches into the arms of a pine tree and loungers
rust in a few inches of mud at the bottom.

I shrug and mumble something about taking photos.

"Photos?"

"There's some cool old architecture and stuff." That's
not what I photograph, but he wouldn't understand. It's

the stuff left behind that interests me. Couches vomiting stuffing and skunk cabbage. Chests of drawers bloated with damp. Heart-shaped baths foaming with ceiling insulation. Sometimes you find personal things—a hairbrush, reading glasses, a pair of monogrammed ice skates. I like finding evidence of the staff. The ones who don't feature in the millions of vacation photos of this place.

"Can I see?" he asks.

I reluctantly hand him my phone, and he starts swiping through the photos. A perfume bottle still half full. A tree winding its trunk through the slats of an old wooden bench. A game of shuffleboard with the disks laid out. A Beatles record still on the turntable of a dance hall.

"They're stupid," I mutter, watching his face, his expression giving nothing away.

"They're not stupid," he says. He looks at me thoughtfully. "They're just . . . unexpected. I like them. They're about . . . abandonment maybe? Loss. What we value and discard or—"

"Yeah, you don't have to make fun of me." I snatch the phone back. "I know they're not art or anything." I walk on and he follows.

"Art is just a way of expressing ideas," he says. "Why can't they be art?"

I scoff. "Because no one wants to listen to my ideas. Does everyone who went to Oxford talk like you? Or just the child prodigies?"

"It's called getting an education. I believe they have those in America, too, though I can't vouch for the quality."

We're only teasing, smiles behind the barbs, but it's irritating that he thinks he can explain my photographs better than I can. They're *my* photographs! Do rich people have to own everything?

I shrug. "It's just a hobby. They're hardly *Zeitgeist* material."

We pass a bowling alley. There was a fire inside and everything's charred. Electrical wiring dangles from the ceiling like chandeliers. Something scampers out of the undergrowth in front of us and Jude yelps.

"It's just a chipmunk." I smirk.

He makes a show of regaining his composure. "I knew that. I knew that. Plus, I'm really brave and manly, so . . ."

I laugh.

"Well, this isn't London. You have actual deadly creatures in this country."

"I *have* seen rattlesnakes up here," I admit. "And there are black bears, bobcats, coyotes."

"You're telling me this *after* we slept out all night?"

"We might see baby deer at this time of year, too. They'll eat what's left after the chipmunks are done with you."

He stops dead behind me, and I turn to tell him I'm kidding. But he's peering into the trees.

"What's up there?" he asks.

"Up where?" I squint into the dim light, my eyes too dazzled by sunlight.

"I think I see something."

"There's nothing up there. There's no path."

He gives me a disappointed look and says, *"The path is made by walking,"* then takes off into the trees, leaving me to scramble after him. "It's from a poem," he calls over his shoulder.

"Of course it is." I sigh, pushing branches aside and watching out for poison ivy. Then I yell, *"Was it a poem about rattlesnakes?"*

I lose sight of him but follow the trail of flattened undergrowth, and when I finally emerge, about a hundred yards farther on, he's standing in the middle of a huge low building overhung with half a glass ceiling above a skeleton of metal girders. My mouth falls open.

"What is this place?" he calls as I descend a little set of steps into the large hall he's standing in.

"I have no idea! I didn't know it was here." I thought I knew the ruins inside out. My fingers are reaching for my phone already, but I force myself to look around first. One wall is gone and there's practically no furniture, just a large flat space littered with broken glass, tumbled metal lockers, and buckled floorboards.

In one corner there's a pile of leather and rubber wheels.

"Oh my God." I put a hand to my mouth. "It's the roller rink."

Mom didn't make it up. There *was* a roller rink. She came here with my dad.

"You want to skate?" Jude asks, coming to join me.

"No," I snap too quickly. "I mean, no thanks." I cross my arms over my chest. My underwear is still damp and I feel cold suddenly. Sneaking out to the roller rink with a guest from the resort? I have the unsettling feeling that I'm walking in my mom's footsteps, and it sends an unpleasant shiver up my spine as I wander around.

Some of the glass ceiling is intact, and vegetation noses through the broken windows. I can hear pigeons in the rafters. The place smells damp, earthy, and everything is washed in a dim green light from the encroaching woods outside. In one corner of the rink, a wild rose has bloomed into dozens of small pink flowers, engulfing a leaning stack of plastic chairs, and I raise my phone, ducking down to get the right angle. I never move anything when I photograph it; where it ended up seems important. I take the photo and lower the phone to find Jude watching.

"You never told me you were into photography."

"It's just something to do. It's nothing." Our voices echo on the remaining glass.

"Is it?" he asks, kicking at another pile of skates.

I think about times I've sat up in the ruins for an hour waiting for the light to be right. And how, when things seem like a whirlwind, I take out my phone just for the steady feeling you get from freezing a little bit of the world in a frame. "I don't know. I guess it's not *nothing*," I admit.

"So why aren't you pursuing it?" He lifts out a skate to examine it.

"Pursuing it where?" I ask, confused.

"If this is your passion, don't you want to take it further?"

I scoff at him. "You're such an overachiever. Come on. No one wants to see this stuff." I gesture at the skates and chairs. "They're . . ." They're ugly and broken and worthless and this is silly and I can't explain it. But Jude continues to watch me, head cocked to the side, like there might be more.

"People don't see this stuff," I finally say. "I don't mean because no one comes out here. Even if they did, they wouldn't see this stuff. You know? I mean, they'd *see* it, but . . ." I throw my hands up. "I don't know. I told you it was stupid."

"It's not stupid. And if you want out of this fake romance job, then—"

I bristle at that. "I never said I wanted out."

"Don't you? I find it strange that someone who makes her living by lying is sneaking up here to take such brutally honest photos." He bends to pick up more skates, tossing others back.

"Being a Juliet is a great opportunity. Every girl in school wanted this job."

"Maybe they did, but *you* didn't."

I make an outraged sound. "You barely know me. How do you know what I want?"

"You told me. You want your photographs in *Zeitgeist*." He doesn't even look up from his roller skate sorting, while I stand there, trying to look indignant rather than stunned. Exposed. Emotionally hijacked. "You need to get out of this place," he says. "It's not good for you. I get that it's scary to go after what you want, but—"

I interrupt him with a snort. "Jesus, is this the part where you pin a yellow ribbon on me and tell me to *follow my dreams*?" I shove my hands in my pockets and kick shards of glass out of my way as I wander around.

"What's wrong with following dreams?"

I shake my head. "Nothing. If you can do it in a private jet," I mutter. "You know, my grandpa dreamed of being a singer? He ended up a blur in the background of a photo of someone else. And *he's* the family success story. My grandma wanted to be an actress. She ended up being sawed in half at birthday parties. My mom got pregnant by someone whose dreams didn't include her, and here we are." I stop in front of him and gesture at the ruins of the building. "This is where dreams get you."

He endures this tirade with an amused expression. "So instead, your plan is to live a fake life fake dating fake boyfriends?"

"Yeah, but in a nice hotel suite," I quip.

He hitches an eyebrow, and I roll my eyes.

"What? It's better than *really* dating some *real* asshole who's going to leave you and your *real* kids high and dry in your *real* cabin with your *real* leaking roof."

He has the decency to drop the amused smile. "Your dad?" he asks.

I shrug. "He was a resort guest. It lasted five minutes." I look out at the rink. Maybe there was even a whole roof back then. Maybe the floor was intact and the disco ball still spinning. But look at it now.

"Did he know about—?"

"Yep."

"Oh." He nods, cradling a three-wheeled roller skate. "Starting to see why you might have a thing about rich arseholes," he says, and I huff a laugh.

"It's great to know your entire existence is basically a cliché," I say wryly, pushing over one of the skates with my shoe. Exposed spiders race for the shadows. "It must happen in vacation resorts all over the world. Summer flings."

"Has it . . . ever happened to you?" he asks. He fusses over a boot, not looking at me, and adds, "Besides with me, obviously."

"*Obviously.*" We grin sidelong at each other. "Nah, that's Micah's department."

It's true. I'm all for a summer romance, but I'm not deluded enough to think it's more than temporary. I never go beyond kissing, beyond the surface, beyond the end of the week. The girl I'm playing doesn't *exist* beyond the end of the week. It's like having a safety harness. I can only fall so far.

"Maybe *that's* what your photos are about," Jude muses.

"Ugh. They're not *about* anything!"

"Well, your dad left. You must feel rejected. Abandoned. Maybe you avoid following your dreams because you feel unworthy and—"

I interrupt him with a laugh he's clearly not expecting.

"OK, Dr. Freud, spare me the analysis." I kneel to take some shots of the roller skates.

"You don't think that's affected you?" he asks.

"I never even met him!" I look up at Jude. "You know, I once found this shoebox in my mom's closet. Like a memory box or something? All her most treasured possessions." I go back to my photo. "It was pathetic, actually. Her old report cards and prizes. School play programs. Yearbooks. Her homecoming queen tiara. A college prospectus." I make a face. "And then there's a picture of my dad, an ultrasound, and my birth certificate."

When I look up, he's frowning, confused.

"And that's it." I lift my empty palms. "The box stopped there. *Nothing good* has happened to her since."

I give him a pitying look. "I know you think I have, like, abandonment issues or some shit. I'm broken. I'm scared of not being good enough and blah, blah, blah. *Bullshit.* Someone wanted me enough that she gave up on every dream she ever had to raise me. *That's* love. But look where it got her. Look where it gets everyone in Staff Town." I take a shot of the heap of old leather on the floor.

"It doesn't have to be that way."

"You're not exactly qualified to comment on how normal people live. We're like"—I look around us, searching for the words—"like pieces of furniture. We're here to be used and then tossed away when we're worn out. The people I grew up with exist to help rich people make *their* dreams come true, not follow their own." I lower the phone and sigh. "I love my mom, but . . . I decided when I saw that box that I wasn't going to be like her. I hate to tell you this, Jude, but I'm not some worthy case you can rescue with one of your charities. I don't *want* a shoebox of impossible things to dream about. Life's too short. I want to enjoy *right now*. I want to have fun *right now*. I want to be happy *right now*. Sorry, but you were right, I *am* that shallow."

He nods down at me, sitting on the floor, my scowl daring him to judge me. "Yeah, you *look* happy," he says.

I throw my hands up. "This from Mr. Denial."

"Meaning?"

I scrabble to my feet, tap my foot for a second, but the words won't be held back. "Meaning no one could possibly be as *fine* as you're pretending to be about all this," I challenge him. "Just because your bucket list is full of degrees and awards instead of skydiving and swimming with dolphins doesn't mean it's not a bucket list. It's all just a way of not thinking about it."

I know I'm only lashing out because he touched a nerve and I expect him to retaliate, but he just continues to look irritatingly amused. "I'm fine about dying *because* I've thought about it," he says. "I've spent my entire life trying to achieve things that are meaningful so that when I go, I'll have no regrets. I *am* fine."

"Guess we're both fine, then."

He shakes his head wearily. "You know, you have this idea that I live in some artificial reality of wealth while you live in the real world. This isn't the real world, Regan." He spreads his arms to take in the whole resort. His hands are still clutching random roller skates. "This is a theme park. There's nothing real about it. Do you ever wonder how it might warp someone to play in Death's doorway but never actually cross over? You live as though you're going to either live forever or die tonight. Neither of which is true." He drops the skates, folds his arms, and looks at me. "You think all this *live every day like it's your last* crap is about defying death, like you're some kind of rebel. Like that's brave." He shakes his head. "That's not brave. You need to stop living like today is your last and start living like it *isn't*."

There's a momentary standoff. A silence we can't break because neither of us is any good at backing down. Finally he bends, lifts a pair of roller skates, and holds them out to me.

"No way," I say.

"Put the skates on, Regan."

"No!"

"It'll be fun. You said you wanted to have fun." The amused smirk is tugging at the corner of his lips again.

"I'm not putting those on."

"Yes, you are."

"No, I'm not."

"Are so."

"Am not!"

"Don't make me come over there."

But I'm starting to laugh already as we argue like little kids. He's kicking off his shoes and pulling on a pair.

"We have deadly spiders here, too, you know."

"Well, like you said, life is short." His lace snaps and he leaves it undone.

"Jude, these things are rusty. And gross. And the floor's uneven. And there's glass everywhere." He waits patiently until I run out of excuses. Then he holds up the pair of skates and I roll my eyes and take them.

"These aren't even the same size!" I complain as I lace them up.

"Oh, you think that'll affect your double axel?"

"Has anyone ever mentioned you're an asshole?"

We totter gingerly to the end of the rink that still has a roof, where the floor is clearer and the floorboards aren't quite so buckled, and try to skate, yelling and shrieking when the rusty wheels jam, tripping over debris and holes in the boards. We reach automatically for each other's hands, pull each other along, hold each other upright.

"Can you go backward?" he says.

"I can't go forward!"

"Here." I scream as he takes my hands and pulls me against him, so he's going forward and I'm going backward, my feet barely on the floor, gripping his jacket and protesting.

"I've never done this before!" he says, delighted with himself.

"You're kidding," I deadpan. Then I shriek and bury my head in his shoulder as we careen too close to what's left of the guardrail.

But I'm not really afraid. I have to admit, even at his most infuriating, there's something about Jude that makes you feel safe. Even when he's being reckless, he's somehow looking out for everyone around him. His arms are like a safety cage at my back and he's watching the floor over my shoulder.

"Whoa!" He swerves us sideways suddenly and we spin in a circle for a moment, clutching each other, braced for impact. But we manage to stay upright and come to rest. I can feel his whole body shaking with laughter and I wish Mrs. Daly could see him. Out of control, eyes damp with mirth on Day Four. The feeling that I had anything to do with that gives me an unexpected rush and I grin up at him. He's got two days left and I'm aware of how generous it is of him to give me a minute of it. He could be doing *anything*, and here he is in a derelict skating rink arguing about someone else's future.

Suddenly I want to apologize. For being so defensive, so prickly.

"Jude, I . . ." But when he looks down at me, nothing comes out. Instead, my eyes notice yesterday's stubble, and the faint outline of childhood freckles across the uneven bridge of his nose. I wonder what I look like to him, standing here bedraggled and confused in the Bergman roller rink. Just another feature of the resort? Something left behind in the ruins? A vacation snapshot stuck in the only frame I've ever known?

"Ree," he says quietly, but his words are abruptly cut off as a huge sheet of glass from the ceiling gives way, plummets thirty feet, and hits the ground in an earsplitting, heart-stopping smash of razor shards.

Jude's body is wrapped around me before I've even realized what's happened, the two of us crouched on the ground, his arm over my head. But the glass came down at the back of the room, far from us.

"Are you OK?" he breathes.

I raise my head and we blink at each other in shock. When I've caught my breath, I exhale a laugh. "Yeah. I think."

"You like to live dangerously, huh?" he says, glancing up at the rest of the glass above us, his body tensed like it might follow at any moment. Which I guess is possible.

"It's no fun if you're not doing *something* stupid, right?" But my voice is weak and shaking as we stand and I step awkwardly out of his arms. It was *incredibly* stupid to bring him here. The whole place is a death trap. The thought of what could have happened makes me feel ill. "I'm fine," I say. "Come on, we should get back."

We leave the rink and make our way to the path and I try to shake off the jittery feeling left by the falling glass. And more than the glass. The skating, the whole morning, and last night, too. I have the disorienting feeling that something has shifted, like an unstable building. I don't trust the ground I'm standing on and I just want to get back to the resort, back to normality. I shouldn't have brought him up here; I don't know what I was thinking.

Someone who makes as many bad decisions as I do shouldn't be chasing any dreams.

On the way down, we keep the conversation to neutral subjects. The lake cruise he's going on, the talk he's giving at the fundraiser. But we walk slowly, and at some point he takes my hand to help me over a fallen tree and somehow we just never let go. When we finally arrive at Lakeside and spot his parents finishing brunch on the terrace, we must look like the perfect couple, strolling up the steps hand in hand. I don't know anymore if it's for show or for real.

He lets go to embrace his mom, and then she hugs me, too, asking about the party and looking us over with a frown. I'd forgotten what a state we must be in; I haven't even showered.

Jude spares her the details and she seems thrilled that he had fun. She's polite enough to invite me out on the cruise with them, but they need their alone time.

"I'm hanging out with my mom today. We're getting *all* the spa treatments!" I say, slipping into a character everyone knows is fake. The words feel flat and ridiculous in my mouth, but I promised Jude I'd keep up the act.

Mr. and Mrs. Daly gather their bags and head down to the pier. Jude waits until they're gone before turning to me to say goodbye. For the first time, I feel a twinge of regret that he's leaving, and he lingers, like he's not ready to go, either.

"So am I officially a local now? Do I get a certificate? T-shirt?"

"You get ripped jeans and dirt on your face. Congrats."

He looks down at himself and laughs, rubbing the back of his neck. "These were my favorite pair."

The sunlight brings out the red in his hair and the freckles on his cheekbones. I feel like every time I look at him, I see something new. Right now it's a softness in the jaw he usually holds so tensed. I lift my phone between us while he's distracted with brushing off his clothes, choosing my settings so the view behind him is a blur of green.

The *snap* jerks his attention back to me, and he instantly looks uncomfortable. But I keep shooting while he unfolds and refolds his arms, looks down, looks up, looks embarrassed. He crosses his arms awkwardly, like he hasn't had them long enough to learn what to do with them.

"You *told* me to take photos," I say innocently.

"Touché." His lip quirks up at one corner. *Snap.*

"You'd think someone who'd been in *Zeitgeist* would be comfortable in front of a camera."

His head tilts. *Snap.* "Why would you think that?"

I shrug. "You looked comfortable."

The eyebrow hitches. *Snap.* "Spent a lot of time studying it, did you?"

"Don't flatter yourself. It was by Yvette Scholes. I like her work."

He grins. *Snap.* "She was very good. And very *quick.* Are you done?"

Snap.

"Yeah. Thanks."

His face relaxes. *Snap.*

When I've put the phone away, he looks out at the lake, the cruise vessel waiting for him, and says, "Is it strange that I preferred Staff Town to the resort?"

"Yes. Extremely," I tell him. "But I'm glad you had fun. Sorry about the hangover. And the weird tour."

He laughs. "You're an excellent tour guide. And hangovers aren't as bad as people say."

"Well, you *are* very brave and manly."

"Exactly."

"So."

"Yeah."

He clears his throat, I shuffle my feet, unable to meet his eye suddenly because when I do, I feel unsteady, like we're still spinning. It feels like there must be more to say, but I don't know what and if I open my mouth I have a horrible feeling something giddy will come out.

"See you later, then," he says, grinning a downright silly grin, and I marvel at the idea of a giddy Jude Daly.

"Um . . . yeah. Yeah, later." We're both giggling now. "I'll be around so . . . yeah."

We're interrupted by a small commotion as a group of people bustle out of the glass doors and down the steps toward a waiting limo. Jude takes my elbow to lead me out of their way before I'm mown down. It's the family from the clinic, here for their grandpa's procedure. A gaggle of bellhops hurry after them, carrying matching luggage. The mom has her huge sunglasses on and the boys are subdued now, the dad walking between them with a hand on each shoulder.

And then the grandpa comes out behind them. Still dragging his oxygen tank, without the bowtie now, walking slower than ever.

I frown at Jude. "That's weird, it looks like they're leaving. Did he cancel his—"

He frowns. "I don't know, I assumed—"

And then it hits me. Cinderella. She's missing.

Jude's noticed, too. We stare wordlessly at each other for a moment as the family climbs into their limo and reality lands a gut punch. All this scampering around ruins and dancing and flirting and philosophizing like life is just a big hypothetical argument. What an absolute fucking idiot I am. The impact of it crumples me like paper, and my own helpless expression is echoed in Jude's flattened eyes.

I know what's coming before he even says it.

"Actually, Regan . . ."

I nod quickly.

"It's just, I should spend some more time with—"

"Of course. Yeah. Absolutely."

"And it's probably not . . ." He rubs his eyes as he exhales slowly. "This isn't smart," he says quietly, more to himself than to me.

He lowers his head and walks off to join his parents, his tread heavy on the steps. I watch until he's all the way down on the jetty, as if he'll change his mind and come back.

But I know he won't. I know he's right; neither of us needs complications like this. The Dalys wave and call their goodbyes to me, but all I hear is Micah's voice. *We know how this ends. Right?*

Chapter 12

A SHOWER. A LONG, STEAMING, SCALDING HOT SHOWER POUNDING my skin so hard I can't hear myself think. That will fix everything.

It doesn't, but at least by the end of it, I no longer smell like stale beer and cigarettes. By the time I'm dressed, Naomi has left a note to say she's having lunch in the roof garden restaurant. The suite is too quiet, so I go to join her. She's at a little table for two at the far edge, looking out over the lawn, sun hat on, reading a novel.

She beams at me. "How was the party? Did you stay at your mom's?"

"Uh, yeah. It was good. We had fun."

"Great! Have you eaten? You want something?"

I don't, but I take a leftover slice of bread from her plate to please her.

"So, Jude wasn't *too* annoying?" she asks, watching me reduce the bread to crumbs on a napkin.

"Annoying is his default setting." But I only say it because it's easier to bitch about him than to think about him being nice to me.

"What did he do now?"

I wave a hand. "Nothing. He just likes to tell everyone else how to live their lives. Unless you're going to Harvard, you're a waste of space apparently." I shake my head. "Like people from around here just waltz off to Harvard," I mutter.

But Naomi folds her arms and says, "*My* kids will."

"What?"

"Well. Not Harvard. But why do you think I do this job? It's because my kids are going to college if I have to sell a kidney to get them there." She makes a face. "I might have to sell two. But a little ambition never hurt anyone."

"I can't believe you're siding with him!"

"I'm not siding with anyone. I get it, you're still young, you don't want to think about the future, but—"

"But I *am* thinking about it! I'm doing all this so I can get a permanent contract."

She frowns, opens her mouth, hesitates, then says it anyway. "Ree. You can't do this job forever. What happens when you're twenty-three, twenty-four, and there are no more clients?"

I shrug and play with my bread. "Something will turn up. I'll think about that when it happens. And when I'm old, I can be an R-and-J mom like you." I look up quickly. "I mean, not *old*, but . . ."

She just laughs. But then she studies me for a moment,

leans across the table, and says, "Ree. Pretend boyfriends? Pretend kids? Even if you *could* do this job forever . . . you don't want to. Don't you want something real?"

My mouth falls open. She's sitting here in her designer maxi dress talking about *real*?

"I mean, it's fun right now," she says. "But it's not good for you."

"Why does everyone keep saying that? I'm fine."

"Are you? Is Micah? I worry about him. Boyfriend after boyfriend. He needs some . . . permanence in his life."

I laugh at that. "That's the *last* thing Micah needs." It's true. Micah likes the drama. He can't help it; the more disastrous a relationship, the more he's into it. The worse the guy, the harder he falls. "Micah doesn't *want* things to last," I tell her. "He'd get bored. That's why he goes for the guys who are on their way out, or the guys who are only here as guests. The guys with a boyfriend back home, the guys who are straight, the guys who are married, the guys whose families would disapprove, the guys who teach at our high school, the guys—"

"The guys who have a cast-iron reason for leaving him that he doesn't have to take personally," Naomi says.

I glower at the breadcrumbs. I don't need this right now. Why is everyone so set on finding problems where there aren't any? I know Micah better than anyone. He's fine and so am I.

"I just mean—" Naomi starts.

"It doesn't matter. Whatever. I have to go anyway," I say, aware that I sound like a sulky child.

"You haven't eaten anything."

"I'm not hungry. And I have to check on my *actual* mom." A sulky, *bratty* child.

Before I can get up, the server comes to clear away the bread evisceration on the table.

"Hey, Kristen!" Naomi greets her. I think Kristen's mom works at the supermarket with her.

"Hi, guys. How was lunch?"

"Well, I didn't have to cook it so I gave it five stars before I even sat down. Did you cook it?"

Kristen laughs. "Nooo! I don't cook; I just bake. I can barely boil an egg."

"Have you tried Kristen's cakes, Ree? She has a stall at the artisan market on Saturdays."

"Oh. No, I didn't know."

"It's going great! I'm supplying a couple of the cafés now, too."

"Good for you! The carrot cake is to *die* for. We'll miss it when you go."

"You're leaving?" I ask as she piles plates on her tray.

"Yeah, I finally signed the lease on a little place in Brooklyn. I'm so excited!"

"An apartment?" I ask.

"Oh, no, it's going to be a bakery!" She blushes happily. "Can't afford an apartment. I've got a room in a shared place with no kitchen, but I guess I can live on carrot cake, right?"

"That's amazing, Kristen."

"I mean it's going to be *so* expensive to set up. But I've

been doing an online business class and working every shift I could get my hands on since school." She shrugs. "It'll be worth it."

I feel foolish suddenly. Because all the time she was cleaning my room and serving me drinks and I was feeling bad for her, she was probably pitying me because she'll be leaving soon, along with Naomi's kids apparently, while I'm still here, maybe taking over her job someday when I'm too old to be a Juliet.

"It sounds fantastic. Good luck," I tell her.

"Thanks, Ree." She hesitates before turning away, and says, "Hey, I'm sorry about your mom. I thought it was harsh."

My empty stomach twists. "Mom? What about her?"

"Oh!" Her face blanches. "I thought— Ree, I'm so sorry, I thought you knew. I shouldn't have said—"

"What happened? Tell me." Did she have another accident? Is she in the hospital having her stomach pumped? Did the leaking ceiling collapse on her? My mind races with the possibilities. It's a shock to realize just how many bad things you're living on the edge of.

She looks deeply uncomfortable. "Well. They fired her this morning."

"*What?* No, she . . . she sprained her ankle, she can't walk, she only missed a couple shifts, she's—"

"No, it was . . ." Kristen lowers her voice, embarrassed. "They found some stuff in her locker. A couple of bottles from the bar. The bar supervisor reported her. He's a jerk." She grimaces. "I mean, everyone gets a free drink from the bar now and then, everyone takes the shampoos and stuff. But management . . . Well, I thought it was harsh. Everyone liked Cath. I'm sorry." She gives Naomi a helpless look and scurries away with her tray.

Today is just proof of why you shouldn't let yourself get carried away by the kind of garbage Jude Daly goes around spouting. The universe puts you right back in your place.

Naomi tries to get me to come back to our room, but I can't sit there stewing about everything, so instead I roam the resort, searching for a distraction, for the thing that will make it all go away. That's what this place exists for, right? Distraction. But the clubs aren't open yet, I've done all the activities before, I've lost my appetite, and nothing my R&J credit card can buy will change anything.

I know I should check on Mom, but I can't face it. She's probably drowning her sorrows already. And I don't want to see Micah because I'll end up telling him about our walk in the ruins and he won't *say* "I told you so" but we'll both know he did. I even think about talking to Dr. Burgess, but I'd only have to lie to her.

I grab a coffee instead and find a lounger on the beach, and I sit there glaring at all the couples splashing in and out of the water, the Jet Skis blaring by. I don't know how I got here. A week ago I was on top of things, I was having a great summer. Why is everything suddenly such a mess? Because people keep complicating everything, that's why—Dr. Burgess, Jude, Naomi. Everyone's happy to tell me what's wrong with my life, but no one has any alternatives to offer, do they? *Aim higher. Think about your future.* Yeah? And what about Mom? What about Micah? There are people here who need me. And what does Jude want me to do, hack his mom's laptop so I can pay for art school? Would he still be telling me to *follow my dreams* if he knew *that* was my ticket?

Think carefully about your options. What options, Dr. B? Cyber theft? Waiting tables? Leaving town to fail at becoming a photographer? Staying to look after my unemployable mother? They're all so fucking appealing.

Don't you want something real? I grimace. *Well, Naomi,* I silently tell her as I email Dr. Burgess to beg for an advance on my salary, *I think we can assume shit just got "real."*

I give my lounger and umbrella up to a girl turning lobster pink in the sun and walk back up the beach. The annoying thing is, of all the words swirling in my brain, the only ones that seem appealing right now are Dante's. *You know what's great about money? It's that you're bulletproof.*

I walk for another hour, but my traitorous feet keep carrying me back toward Lakeside, my eyes scanning the lake. By late afternoon, the cruise boat has docked and I wander across the lawn, squinting up at the big dining room doors, which they've left open to the terrace. The room is full of people sipping champagne, and at the front, Jude is standing with a microphone giving his fundraising speech. He's changed into a white shirt and tie and I can hear his voice from halfway down the lawn. Behind him a huge screen shows pictures of smiling young people, presumably the ones Make a Difference has helped. I see Mr. Daly's silhouette beside Mrs. Daly's tiny one at a table just inside the doors. All the resort big cheeses are there, too. The hotel owners, Dante, Dr. Lawrence, plus a couple of famous actors, probably patrons of the charity.

I should just go up to my room, leave the Dalys alone. They've got two days left and the last thing they need is my drama. Jude made it clear he doesn't want to see me. I turn around. What am I even doing here?

"Following your dreams is easy if you can do it in a private jet."

I startle, turning back as I hear my own words booming across the lawn in Jude's accent.

"You know, I started this foundation with the assumption that every life can be made meaningful. But actually . . ." He lowers the notecards he's holding and looks up at the audience. *"Every life already is meaningful. No matter how difficult or small or short. Everyone's life is valuable. Everyone has something to contribute."*

I drift a little closer. It's like that first video of him we watched. Confident, assured. Though his voice seems warmer now, less aloof.

"But some people don't get the chance. And it's not just about dying young. Some people don't get the time, sure. But others don't get the opportunities. And some people think no one is interested in what they have to say."

He glances outside, sees me on the lawn. There's a long pause before he continues, still looking at me.

"Some people have no idea how special they are."

He turns back to the audience.

"That's not fair. That's not OK. I didn't get much time to make a difference in the world, but I've made peace with my death because through this foundation, I'm going to go on contributing long after I'm gone. And you can, too. You can donate by . . ."

He gives them the details of the foundation before being replaced at the mic by one of the Hollywood actors.

I shouldn't have come here. But I shouldn't be doing a lot of things. I shouldn't be bothering him with my problems, I shouldn't be showing him the places that matter to me, I shouldn't be thinking about him when he's not there.

And he shouldn't be walking across the terrace toward me right now. I shouldn't be walking up the lawn, walking faster, breaking into a run.

I'm halfway there before I register I'm moving, and when I reach him, our arms, bodies, lips meet like something locking into place. I feel him hesitate for just a fraction of a second as some internal argument plays out, and then his indecision melts into urgency, the kiss deepens, and all I'm aware of is his aftershave, the firmness of his chest, his hands at the small of my back. There's something about kissing that dictates its own path. You're not really in charge of it. You stop being you. You're just a person being kissed.

When he finally draws his head back to look down at me, his dark eyes contain every emotion. Confusion, longing, resignation. But most of all, concern.

"What's happened?" he asks.

I burst into tears.

I lay my head on his chest and he strokes my hair as I listen to the thud of his heart beneath the crisp cotton of his shirt.

"Breathe, Ree," he whispers. "Just breathe." So I do. On the back of every sob, I allow myself, against all good sense, to breathe him in. Aftershave and soap and something warm and deep that's just him. He wraps himself around me, murmuring, "It's OK, it'll all be OK," when we both know that can't possibly be true.

He strokes my back and rocks me gently, like a child, and it gradually turns into a sway, almost a slow dance on the lawn. No fireworks this time. No music or lights or ball gowns. Real-life fairy tales are much darker things.

I lift my face to smile bleakly up at him.

"Thought you didn't dance," I tease.

"Thought you didn't cry," he says softly, wiping the tears away with his thumb.

"We shouldn't—"

"No, we shouldn't."

He leans down as I stretch up, his arms pulling me in, everything pulling us in. But our lips have barely brushed when there's the sound of breaking glass and an incredulous shout from the dining room.

"Oh my God, someone did it!"

We jerk apart to look toward the terrace, where a man is standing by one of the dining tables, broken wineglasses on the floor, staring wildly at his phone. He brandishes it at the room. "He did it! Someone did it! Turn on the news! There's a survivor!"

PART III

Thus
with a
Kiss

Chapter 13

THE COMMOTION HAS ALREADY SPREAD FROM THE DINING ROOM to the lobby by the time we get up the terrace steps, and people are pouring in from other rooms, everyone checking their phones, talking excitedly. I'm holding Jude's hand as I pull him inside. A waiter switches the TV on the wall to CNN and turns the sound up over the hubbub. BREAKING NEWS flashes across the screen and the room falls quiet to hear the news anchor.

"Reports are just reaching us that an as-yet-unidentified man, believed to be in Venezuela, has outlived his Death Date. If true, this would be the first case in recorded history. Rumors began last night, but skeptics dismissed the claims. This afternoon, however, several independent doctors have gone on record to verify the account. The man's name has not been released to protect his identity, but Dr. Eamon Mallon, a leading dermatologist, has examined his Date and says he believes the reports are true. Dr. Nina Nowak has also . . ."

The clamor rises again as people murmur to one another, some looking skeptical, some tentatively hopeful, most just confused. There have been reports before. But they tend to appear on social media and turn out to be hoaxes or exaggerated rumors. I've never seen one on CNN. I've never seen one involving actual doctors. It's like David Attenborough just went on the news to say he's met Bigfoot.

More people crowd in. I notice they're all furtively glancing in one direction, and I suddenly realize why everyone's congregating in the dining room. It's not because the TV is in here. It's because the Dalys are. Everyone knows who they are, and everyone wants to see how they'll react. Because if they take this seriously, then . . .

Jude and I are still by the doors and I find myself watching, too, as Mr. and Mrs. Daly take in the news and turn slowly to look at each other. The room holds its breath. Then the Dalys each reach for their phones in unison, stand, and walk quickly outside, already dialing.

That's when the commotion turns to chaos.

"Try NBC, what are they saying on NBC?"

"It can't be true; it's just not possible."

"Call Isaac, ask if he's heard anything."

"I'm canceling. I'm canceling right now."

Jude just looks apologetically at me and then runs after his parents, leaving me standing in the dining room with a dozen conversations swirling around me, trying to hear the news anchor. Trying to hear my own thoughts. The waiter flicks between channels and it's on every single one. *The Survivor*, they're calling him. Like he's been pulled from the wreckage of a disaster.

There's a collective *ping* as everyone's phone receives an email from the clinic, inviting us all to talk to the counselors if we feel we need to. I get those emails, too, because I'm supposed to be a resort guest. I see Dr. Lawrence hurrying out.

People are talking about canceling their procedures. Waiting it out. Just in case. Others are throwing their hands up and complaining about how ridiculous it is. The name Daly is everywhere.

"Honestly, people will believe anything!" I recognize the couple who tutted at Micah at the ball, skepticism screwing their snooty faces into creases. A week ago, I'd have been agreeing with them, but now I surprise myself by snapping, "Did anyone ask you?" They blink in indignation and I push my way through the crowd to get closer to the TV.

"A video has gone viral on social media, believed to be from the man himself . . ."

Dante is already up front, straining to hear. "Now *there's* a development," he says as I push my way in beside him.

The picture cuts to an amateur video of a guy recorded

against a bright window, his face in shadow. Then a close-up of a hairy forearm where a Date, two days ago, is clearly displayed. He speaks in Spanish, and an English translator talks over it.

"I never even really believed in my Date. You know? Even when I was a kid. I can't explain it, but I just couldn't imagine it really happening. I'm only forty-three, but I didn't book an end-of-life procedure and everyone said I was crazy. But I just had this feeling . . ."

"Now would be a good time for you to hold up your end of our little bargain," Dante murmurs.

"Bargain? You mean that time you *threatened* me?" I say without taking my eyes off the screen.

"And then on the day, I didn't do anything special, I wanted it to be normal. I had dinner with my family, and then I got up to go to the deli on the corner, they do the best espressos and I know the owner. I wanted to say goodbye, and, I don't know, I just suddenly decided, totally out of the blue, to go to the gas station first and pick up some cigarettes. I mean, the thing is, I don't even smoke! You have a Date like mine, you don't risk lung cancer. But I thought, well, I'm either going today or I'm not and I feel like having a cigarette, so I walked to the gas station and . . ."

"Fair's fair, Regan." Dante turns his body toward me as I strain to hear the TV. "The value of the goods just went up." He juts his chin at the screen. "So I'm prepared to raise the offer."

"When I got back, my whole family is crying in the

garden and fire trucks are screaming down the road. There's been a gas explosion at the deli. When they saw me coming up the street with a cigarette in my mouth . . . Man, they thought they'd seen a ghost! By then it was ten p.m., and so we waited and midnight came and . . . noth- ing. And here I am . . ."

"Leave me alone, Dante." I edge away from him, closer to the TV. But he follows.

"I'm afraid that's not one of your options. But get me what I want and I'll sign over a ten percent share of the profits of Inferno to you. For life."

I turn to stare at him. I've seen how much money crosses that bar every night. Mom and I could live on it forever.

"I'm not fucking around here, Regan. I'm making you a good offer, but don't cross me." He leans in closer. "You'll regret it." Then he walks away.

The room filters back into my awareness, like some- one turning the volume back up.

"I mean, it was so random, so close. I don't under- stand it; I'm not a doctor. I don't know what I did right. I just . . . did something different. Maybe that's all it takes, right? Just one thing to be different."

The room falls silent as the video ends, but our thoughts are almost as loud as the uproar was. My own are a tangle. You can't cure death, right? But then, they used to think you couldn't cure lots of things that are now curable. So what does this mean? What does it mean for the resort? What does it mean for the world? I don't know.

And it only takes me a second to realize I don't care.

I only care what it means for Jude Daly.

When I reach the Hermitage, Jude is sitting on the veranda steps with his head in his hands. The doors are open and I can see Mr. and Mrs. Daly inside, pacing in opposite directions, talking urgently on their phones. I make out snippets as I mount the steps.

"*. . . need to send someone immediately . . .*"

"*. . . can't possibly leave now so . . .*"

"*. . . get Sanders on the call and tell him to . . .*"

"*. . . the exact sequence of events that . . .*"

They sound frantic.

Jude lifts his head at my footsteps and gives me a baleful smile. "Sorry for running out on you," he says.

I sit beside him, neither of us saying anything, still in shock.

"*. . . I've called CNN, they don't . . .*"

"*. . . speak to Eamon Mallon, please, it's urgent . . .*"

"*. . . copy of the confirmation of that . . .*"

"*. . . any firsthand testimony would . . .*"

Jude stands and motions me to follow. He leads me around the building to another entrance, into a hallway, and up a set of stairs to a loft bedroom beneath the apex of the roof. It's simple but warm and comfortable, just a bed and an arched window overlooking the lake, exposed beams beneath huge skylights. It's very Jude. Plain and honest. We can't hear his parents from up here.

He sits on the end of the bed and I join him.

"What are they going to do?" I ask quietly.

"What they're good at," he says. "Research."

"But . . . there's no . . ."

"No time. I know. They know." He scrubs his face with his palms. "But they'll do what they can. They're desperate. They want to chase this up, but they don't want to leave me and they don't want to give me false hope." He makes a helpless gesture.

I slide my hand between his and he holds it on his lap, studying it, tracing freckles like we have all the time in the world. He seems calmer than his parents, but surely he can't be. My own heart is fluttering like a trapped bird, but panic isn't going to help him, so I'm trying to be steady.

"And what . . . what do you want to do?"

"Well, I think I should stay with them tonight; they're upset."

"No, I mean . . ." Typical Jude, only thinking about how this affects his parents. "What do you want to *do*. About . . . your procedure?"

He frowns at me, confused. "What do you mean?"

"Well, people are canceling already." I can hear Dr. Burgess in my head. We're *never* supposed to influence a client on their procedure. But Jude's not just a client.

"Why would I do that?"

"Because—"

"Regan, I've seen rumors before. They never come to anything. I'm not going to risk a horrible death for such a slim hope."

"But that's just it!" I grasp both his hands. "*Hope*. You

said even miserable people don't end their lives because one thing gets in the way. Hope. You said we didn't have any. But we do now."

He angles himself toward me, speaking like he's explaining something upsetting to a small child. "Even if this guy is legit, it's the biggest lottery win ever and it's not going to happen twice. Why would I assume it could happen to me?"

"Because . . . " I want to say, *Because of us. Because life couldn't be that cruel.* Instead I say, "Because nothing's impossible for people like you! If there's a chance, just *one*, if just *one* person is going to get this, it'll be someone like you!"

"Regan, that's not—"

"I don't mean the money. I mean . . . Nothing stops you," I go on. "If there's no path, you just go right ahead and make one. You can do anything! You keep telling me I can do anything I want with my life, so why is this any different? Why can't you decide your own fate?"

He makes an incredulous sound. "The difference is this is actual capital-F *Fate*." He exhales deeply. "I've made my decision. I made it years ago."

"So, you're going to die *on principle*? You can change your mind, you know. I change mine ten times a day!"

"Well, I don't." He stands and starts pacing, an echo of his parents downstairs. "And I don't make impulse decisions based on zero evidence. That's not smart."

I stand up, too, watching him. "It's not about *smart*. It's . . ." I frown. "You're just scared."

He blinks at me. "Scared? You think I'm choosing *death* because I'm *scared?*"

"Yes! You told me I was scared to take a risk on my photography. Wanting something you might not get is scary."

"This is *very* different." He stops pacing, but he looks exhausted, defeated, staring at the floor. I've never seen defeat on his face before. I don't like it.

"I know, but"—I go to him, take his hands—"you don't have to do it alone."

"What?"

I swallow, duck my head so he has to look me in the eye. "Cancel. Leave town. And . . . and I'll go with you. I'll walk away from all of this—the resort, my job. All of it. Like you said I should. What if we were *both* brave, Jude? What if we *both* just decide how it's going to go? Fuck Fate. What if we do something different? Something no one, not even Fate, expected of either of us. What if that's all it takes? Just one thing to be different. Isn't it worth a shot?" I squeeze his hands, my voice insistent, expectant, *hopeful*. If hope's all we need, I have enough for both of us. If all we need is *one thing* Fate wasn't expecting, I can be that thing for Jude. I fall silent, waiting for his answer.

But he closes his eyes, lowers his head, pulls his hands away.

"Jude?"

"Ree, I—"

"No. Just . . . *no.*"

"Ree."

"You're just going to quit?" He takes my shoulders in his hands, but I push against him, angry suddenly. "No! You can't just give up! It's not . . . You don't do that. Not when people . . . not when there are people who . . . when there are people who . . ." My jaw works soundlessly for a moment. "Jude, I—"

His face falls. "Oh, don't," he begs. "Don't, Ree."

"But I—"

He shakes his head, pulling me close, muffling my words against his chest. "I'm sorry. I'm so sorry. I never meant . . ."

His words rain down on me like shards of glass. I can still feel the ghost of his lips on mine, and now they're saying, *"I'm sorry. I shouldn't have. This was a mistake."*

I push him away. "A mistake?"

"I knew it was a bad idea, I just—"

But I stop him with a raised palm. "Right. I get it."

"Regan."

"No, I get it. I'm being ridiculous. I forgot for a second." I wipe my eyes roughly. "This is just business, right? You're a guest. And I'm"—I shrug—"a tourist attraction. An activity. A checkmark on a bucket list."

"Regan, you know that's not true." He moves closer, tries to put his hands on my arms again, but I step away.

"No. I don't. Fuck this. Fuck *all* of this. And fuck you, Jude." I back toward the door, then turn and walk blindly down the hall. He doesn't even try to follow as I run downstairs and outside, berating myself for being so stupid. So weak. Because I was right, wasn't I? About dreams.

About girls like me and guys like him. I was right about everything. Most of all, I was right about love.

The cabin is empty when I get home. I should go looking for Mom, but the thought of searching every bar in the resort is too humiliating. I slump in front of the TV instead, but the only channel not talking about the Survivor is a crappy rom-com. I mute it, but you can still figure out exactly what's going on because it's so fucking predictable.

On the coffee table, there's a huge bunch of flowers.

To Ms. Cath Blythe. Apparently I am terrible at apologies, but I hope you like these flowers. They are sincerely meant. Jude Daly.

She's arranged them in a vase. She never could hold a grudge. In fact, she's a giant pushover. So maybe she's forgiven him. Or maybe it's just been a long time since anyone gave her flowers.

In the movie, the hero makes his grand gesture to the heroine, the bravest thing he's ever done, and she dutifully rewards him by falling into his arms. I turn it off, throw on a sweater that smells damp, and crawl into bed, wishing I could delete every scene from my brain like photos from my phone.

I'm woken at three a.m. by a crash out on the porch.

"Goddammit!"

She's knocked over the bag of glass recycling I left there. I shut my eyes tight, willing myself to go to sleep again. I'm *not* getting up. I'm not going out there to help her as she fumbles with the door key and the neighbors peer through their windows. I'm not going to check that she locked the door or shut the refrigerator. I'm not going to go get her water or take her shoes off or put her to bed.

Another crash, louder this time, and a yelp. I throw my sheets back with a growl and stomp out there.

"Mom? Mom, are you OK?"

She's in the kitchen, sucking her finger, the vase of flowers smashed on the floor around her feet, her ankle bandage soaked.

"I was jus' gettin' a snack, hun. You wanna snack?" Her voice is slurred, eyes unfocused, one hand gripping the counter for balance as she stands there pretending this is all normal and there isn't a pool of water and broken glass around her feet.

I stand in the doorway. "Mom, I don't have shoes on. Come out of there."

"Lemme make you a snack! Hey, le's make popcorn an' watch a movie! You wanna watch a movie?"

"No."

"Aw, come on! It'll be fun! You never wanna watch movies with me anymore!" She pouts.

"It's late."

"Ugh, don't be so *boring*! You're so *boring*! You know your problem?" She points a finger at me and I feel my stomach clench. "You're *uptight*."

"I don't need this right now, Mom."

"No, really. Is-s still early!" She starts opening cabinet doors searching for popcorn.

"It's three a.m.! You need to go to bed."

"I mean, aren't you s'posed to be young?"

"Aren't *you* supposed to be an adult?" I can't help snapping, though I know I shouldn't encourage her.

"Ooh! So fucking judgy!" She cackles.

I fold my arms, braced for it.

She waves her arm at me, snapping her fingers. "Judge, judge, judge. Jus' like those *assholes* at Lakeside."

"Mom."

"I know you think you're better'n me. Better'n everyone. With your *fancy* job and your *fancy* promotion." She knocks a box of crackers off the shelf and it spills on the counter. "You're not like them, y'know. Never will be. Not really. They string you along when it suits them and then *bam*!" She claps her hands together. "Fired for, like, *no reason*."

"Mom, stop it."

"No, *you* stop. Like, you don't even have to *be* here, y'know?" I roll my eyes. It's nothing I haven't heard before. "Go find one of your rich boyfriends, yeah?"

I bite my tongue. I've heard way worse.

"Go live with your *other mother*, Miss Coraline." She puts on a simpering voice. "Fucking perfect fucking Naomi."

Ignore it, don't take it personally. She doesn't mean it. It's my own fault for getting in her way.

She's still opening cabinet doors. "Go pay your own

fucking rent 'stead of judging me all fucking . . ." Her face goes pale and she puts a hand to her mouth.

"Mom?" She stumbles past me, out of the room and down the hall to the bathroom, and I hear retching.

I stand there for a moment, reminding myself I'm not a crier. Then I slip on some shoes, clean up the broken glass and spilled water, put the flowers in the sink and the crackers back in the box. When I go to the bathroom, she's huddled on the floor, skinny fingers clutching the toilet bowl, face sweaty, and her hair coming undone.

I could yell at her. Stand over her and make her feel guilty for being an irresponsible parent when everyone else manages to hold down a job. But what's the point; she won't remember it tomorrow.

And I don't even care about the job. If it was just a job, just money, just sprained ankles and broken phones and empty promises, I could live with it. It's *this* I can't stand. It's this we don't talk about. Don't think about. The meanness. The way she turns into someone I don't recognize.

"I'm sorry, honey. I'm sorry, I'm sorry," she moans before retching over the bowl again, and I almost wish she'd go back to yelling at me.

I can't do this. I can't *see* this. It's too fucking sad, and if I start crying now, I'm never going to stop. I leave her robe and a jug of water on the bathroom floor without even looking at her and go back to bed.

I don't get up for most of the next day, just lie in bed watching TV, disgusted at myself for hoping that every knock at the door is Jude. The mail person delivers some bills. Luis brings the rubber mats he promised for our slippery porch. Mom gets up around noon, then goes back to bed again. But Jude doesn't come.

I feel like I'm being eaten alive in slow bites by every tick of the clock. Thursday. Day Five. Tomorrow is Jude's procedure. The day after that is the Date marked on his arm. And the day after *that* is the day I'm supposed to just get on with my life like nothing happened. Figure out how to pay the rent now that Mom's unemployed and Dante is gunning for me. Figure out how to get out of this bed.

I want to turn the TV off, but I'm listening for *Breaking news, the Daly Research Institute has just announced . . .* But there's nothing but the same interviews with the same doctors, the same amateur video played over and over until I know it by heart. *"I don't understand it; I'm not a doctor. I don't know what I did right. I just . . . did something different. Maybe that's all it takes, right? Just one thing to be different."*

People are canceling their procedures all over the world now. And dying in terrible accidents instead—a falling cable car in the French Alps, a sinkhole in Texas, a freak insect bite in Melbourne. So far, no one else has made it past their Date. I have no idea if Jude is even still at the resort. His parents could have convinced him to cancel and taken him home already. Would he come to say goodbye? Probably not.

They start talking about the Daly Research Institute and there's a clip of Jude at fifteen, laughing with a group of teenagers they've helped. I tell myself I haven't lost anything. Because even if he survived, he'd go home and find someone like him. Someone selfless and good and serious about their life. Someone nothing like me.

By dusk, the cabin is too dark, too quiet, too full of my own thoughts. My phone pings and my heart stutters. But it's just an email from Dr. Burgess. The advance on my paycheck has gone through.

I heard your mom isn't working at the moment, but I hope it will help to know that we've decided to offer you the permanent contract. You can come in anytime to sign it. We've been busy dealing with panicking people all day, but Jude seems to be coping well; he doesn't want to cancel. You've obviously done a good job of helping him face things and accept the inevitable. Well done, Regan.

I stare at the message before swiping it off my screen. Then I throw on a short dress and heels, and grab the keys to Dante's BMW.

Chapter 14

I KNEW I'D FIND MICAH AT INFERNO. AND I DON'T SEE DANTE ANY-where, so I go to join him where he's leaning on the bar, peeling the label off his beer bottle, not even looking up when the bartenders blow fireballs. I don't see Carlos any-where, either.

I lean beside him and blurt out, "So I kissed Jude Daly, almost told him I'm in love with him, and begged him to cancel his procedure."

He turns slowly to stare at me. Then silently passes me his beer. I take a deep swig as he crooks a finger at the bar-tender to keep them coming.

"He won't even *try*?"

"Nope."

We've found a table on the second-floor balcony and moved on to cocktails. It's easier to talk like this. It's easier to breathe in and out. Maybe Mom's got the right idea. If you can't beat 'em, drink until you forget they exist.

Below us, the place is packed with people dancing, lights strobing over skin, shadows leaping on the walls. Maybe it's the news of the Survivor, but there's a tension to the place tonight. An extra energy, like everyone's putting on a front to cover the fact that no one knows what to think anymore.

"Even after you said—"

"I didn't say it," I correct him quickly, toying with the chunk of pineapple perched on the rim of my glass. "Not exactly. Anyway, you can't fall in love in five days, right?" Jude's own words on the subject.

Micah makes a face. "Right, yeah," he mutters.

Oh. I wrench my mind from my own problems for a second. "Carlos left already?"

"Nope. Just found something better to do."

"I'm sorry, Micah."

He grimaces. "They're all just passing through, right? One way or another." It's what I said to him a few days ago, but the words sound harsher now.

"At least you didn't tell everyone he said you had a *beautiful soul*," he adds. "*That* would be embarrassing." He makes a joke of it, but his laugh is hollow.

I cringe as I remember promising to leave town with Jude if he canceled. As if that would be an incentive for him. I have no place in his real life—I'm a beach sarong, a Hawaiian shirt. Fine for a vacation but not for everyday use.

I finish my drink and push it away. "We need another round."

"I might just have a Coke. Luis and Elena will lose their shit if I'm out late again."

"Since when do you care what Luis and Elena say? You're going to let me get shit-faced and weepy alone?"

He sighs and waves at a passing server.

When the drinks arrive, I hold mine up to clink and say, "Fuck it. This isn't me. I've been acting crazy for days. I need to get back to normal. I got my permanent contract, we should be celebrating, right?"

He doesn't clink back. "Are you going to take it?" he asks.

"Oh, don't *you* start! Why wouldn't I take it?" My voice sounds angrier than I mean it to.

"What about Dante? You could still get fired if he tells—"

"It's his word against mine." I set my jaw. "And *I* just did a great job with their most important clients. Apparently, Jude's fine about going ahead with his procedure because of *me*. Totally up for kicking the bucket, thanks to *me*." I hold up my glass. "I'm employee of the fucking month."

Micah watches this show of bravado as I chug back my drink, then slam it on the table.

"Fuck Dante. I'll take my chances. And fuck all this moping around. *I'm* going to sign my contract and *you're* going to go see Burgess and this time next week things will be back to fucking normal. Right?"

There's no answer.

"Right?"

When he looks up from the table, he says, "I can't do it anymore, Ree."

"What?"

He sets his drink down. "It's just . . . too much. Too many. And every time, it's worse. It's like being kicked over and over in a bruised place."

"Are you serious?"

But he is. He leans his elbows on the table and puts his face in his hands, rubbing his eyes wearily. "I'm a fucking mess."

"You never said . . . You didn't tell me . . ." But I know that's irrelevant. He shouldn't have had to.

"I can't do it," he says again. Then he looks searchingly at me and adds, "Can you? Honestly?"

"I . . ." I swallow. *Honestly?* I want to tell him he can't do this to me, I *need* him, we're a team. But he's staring at the table, his gaze far away. He looks simultaneously like a little boy and an old man. And the truth is he *is* a mess. He's a mess and everyone knows it. Dr. Burgess knows it. Luis and Elena know it. Naomi knows it. They all tried to warn me. And what did *I* do? Hand him another drink and push him in the direction of the next guy, the next client. I thought if he was drunk enough, if the music was loud enough, if the guy was hot enough, if he was having enough fun, he'd be OK. I remember Dr. Lawrence's question about whether people really die for love. Micah has been self-destructing for years because he's so desperate to be loved. And not just as a Romeo, but in every relationship he's ever had, every foster family placement he's ever messed up. And I've let him. Over and over and over again. Because *honestly*, it suited me to have a wingman. Because *honestly*, if I admitted he was struggling, then maybe I'd have to admit I was, too.

"What choice do I have?" I spread my hands helplessly.

He glances around the club, and up at the floors above, where the offices are. "There's still . . . Dante?"

I stare into my empty glass. It feels like staring over the edge of the rock face Jude and I climbed. A long way down and no soft landing. Mom wasn't much older than me when she started working for Dante. If I help him do this, he'll own me. Forever. But maybe there's no other way. Mom was right; I'm not one of them and I never will be. Jude thinks I'm just scared to try, but it's a fact—a statistical, actual *fact*—that it almost never works out for people like me. We don't go to college. We don't have the money to become artists. We don't marry princes and we don't escape the lives we were born into. That's only in fairy tales. *That's* why people love fairy tales. It has nothing to do with romance; it's about seeing a broke girl get a happy ending for once. Maybe *that's* why Mom watches them.

As I reach for Micah's drink, he nudges my knee with his and when I look up, Jude is standing at our table, his black coat out of place alongside the scantily clad, sweating clientele at Inferno.

"What are you doing here?" I growl at him. It's only when I stand up that I realize how unsteady I am. I leave

Micah at the table and start walking toward the stairs, and Jude trails after me.

"Regan. Can we talk? I want to apologize."

"I have literally lost count of your apologies, Jude."

"You have to understand—"

"I do! Seriously, don't sweat it. You think you're the first client I've had? I'm a good actress." He keeps glancing at the balcony rail, and I notice he's staying away from it. A cruel impulse seizes me and I stop to lean over.

"What are you doing?" he shouts over the music as I take out my phone.

"It's called art, darling." I put on a snooty accent. "I'm expressing myself." Because *this* is me. The club, the dancers, the strobe lights. The flirting and laughing and casual hookups. The music pounding every thought out of your head. Jude has no idea who I am.

"You're going to drop that," he says, moving a step closer as I try to get directly above the hot bartender with the tight leather pants.

"Stop being such a fucking downer, Jude!" I get up on tiptoes and reach out farther. Farther still, anger fueling my determination to get the shot. I lift one foot off the floor. The bartender is about to light the alcohol on the bar beneath me.

My foot slips and my ribs hit the balcony rail hard, just as a hand grabs my upper arm and yanks me back. I barely hold on to my phone.

"Are you OK?"

"I'm fine," I mutter, regaining my balance and clutching

my bruised ribs. I snatch my arm back and he steps gratefully away from the rail, then follows me down the spiral staircase.

When we reach the dance floor, I notice Dante behind the bar. He sees me and puts down the bottle he's holding. I push deeper into the crowd and Jude struggles to follow. There's a group of frat boys drinking like they're at a bachelor party instead of here to say goodbye to a friend, and I start to dance with them. They immediately surround me, roaring their approval, crowding Jude out as he tries to push through.

But Dante reaches me first, seizing my elbow from behind. "You'd better have something for me, Regan."

"I've got nothing." I turn and spread my empty hands as if to show him a magic trick. "There *is* nothing." I laugh suddenly, as if it's funny, then glance back at Jude making his way toward us with polite apologies. "They've got *nothing*," I say again, laughing helplessly now, unable to stop, even though nothing about this is funny.

"*Not* good enough." Dante yanks my arm so hard the laughter stops abruptly.

"Well, what do you want me to do? Figure out how to cheat Death myself? Here." I fish the car keys out of my bag and thrust them at him. "I shouldn't have taken them; I can't help you. And you can tell Dr. Lawrence whatever you want, I don't care. I'm quitting anyway." I realize it's true as I say it. Because *honestly*, the thought of showing up to work next week to another client on the archery range, another guy at Inferno, dancing with him, smiling at him, flirting with him . . . it makes me want to vomit.

Dante's expression darkens as he says, "You'll regret this, Regan." But Jude reaches us then, and Dante immediately turns on the charm, shaking his hand, asking if he wants a drink. Jude barely acknowledges him.

"Regan, please. It's not personal, it's not about you," he's saying.

"Clearly."

The music gets louder and Jude raises his voice even more. "Canceling would be irrational. It makes no sense."

Dante shouts something about the VIP balcony, but Jude ignores him, which I can see irritates him.

"There's always an explanation with you, isn't there? You have to turn everything into a logical argument." I wince as one of the frat boys elbows me in the ribs and Jude draws me away from them.

"I've handled everything so badly," he says. "I just never thought someone like you would—"

"Someone like me?" I snap as the crowd starts singing along to the music. "Oh right, because I'm just a parasite, I don't feel things. Because God forbid anyone should *feel* anything! That's right at the top of your time-wasting bucket list, isn't it, Jude?"

"I didn't mean . . . It's just better if I stick to the plan. For everyone."

"Spare me the noble self-sacrifice bullshit. Just go, Jude. Forget it."

"No, I—"

"What? What could possibly fix this? Where do we go from here?"

He opens his mouth, but nothing comes out because there's no answer. No solution. No compromise we can make.

Dante takes advantage of the pause to sidle back and throw an arm around Jude's shoulders. "Not worth it, buddy, trust me," he says conspiratorially. "Come and have a drink upstairs."

"What?" Jude shrugs Dante's arm off, still looking at me, but Dante doesn't move away.

"I'm telling you, she's not worth it."

Jude finally turns to look at him. "Excuse me?"

And then, even though there's nothing in it for him anymore except being vindictive, Dante gives Jude a knowing look and says, "Well, we both know what she is, right?" He tosses the car keys in one hand and says, "It'll only cost you a BMW for a favor, but you have to pay extra for nice manners."

Jude freezes, staring at the car keys, then at me.

I want to explain. And I want to tell him I don't have to explain myself to *anyone*. But all I do is stand there wordlessly, braced for the disapproval. Disappointment. Judgment. Or worse, maybe he'll just walk away because I'm not worth his time.

Instead, his hand makes a fist at his side and without warning, he swings it straight into Dante's smug jaw.

Dante goes down hard, clutching his bloody lip, while

the crowd draws back. He kicks out at Jude, but Jude hauls him up by the lapels and punches him again before people start pulling them apart. Two bartenders are heading toward us, and two bouncers from the other direction, tearing through the crowd that's crushing in now to get a look. Drinks spill in the commotion and an argument breaks out next to us. The frat boys decide getting in a fight is *exactly* what's been missing from their bucket lists and they pile in, punching indiscriminately. By the time the bouncers get there, it's a mess. Someone grabs me roughly and I lose sight of Jude, and then I'm being manhandled through the crowd. I feel one heel snap beneath me before I'm pushed out the doors into the street with the frat boys, who barely pause before heading off to look for somewhere else to drink.

A moment later, Jude is thrown out, too. Dante appears behind him, yelling that we're not welcome in any of his clubs again.

The two of us are left in the street, panting and adjusting to the dark, the quiet, as onlookers wander away and the doors to Inferno slam shut.

"What did you do that for?" My first reaction is to yell at the guy who just stood up for me. But Dante is going to take his fury out on someone, and it's not going to be Jude, is it?

He looks incredulous. "Are you kidding? What are you doing working for a guy like that?" He winces and rubs his shin. Dante must have gotten at least one good kick in.

I hold my bruised ribs. "That's none of your business."

"You're better than this, Regan."

"Oh, shut up! Shut up, *shut up*! Stop telling me how to live my life just because you're too scared to live your own!"

"Me?"

"You! You're the coward! That's why you've never had a girlfriend, isn't it? It wasn't to protect them; it was to protect *you*. You called *me* dishonest. You can't even be honest with yourself!"

"That's not fair."

"*Nothing* about this is fair!" I scream at him. "It's not fair that I have to do this job! It's not fair that I have to look after my mom! It's not fair that she's on her own! It's not fair that *nothing* about you and me matches. Not our parents, not our schools, not our houses, not our personalities. Not our Dates—" My voice cracks and I gasp for breath as he steps closer, drops his shoulders, and tries to put his arms around me.

His voice reverberates through me as he says, "It'll be OK. You'll be OK."

But I push him away roughly. "How would you know? Fuck it. Leave, then. Go!"

"Ree."

He tries to step closer again, but I batter my fists against his chest, propelling him backward, and yell, "Just *go*! Don't pretend to care; you don't care about me! You won't even try! People love you and you won't even *try*!"

He tries to restrain me, but I wrestle harder, screaming the words in his face, louder and louder, as we struggle. "So, go ahead and leave! Why not? Everyone else does! You're just like everyone else! You're just like the rest of them! You're just another dead boy! *You're just another dead boy! YOU'RE JUST ANOTHER DEAD BOY!*"

The fight goes out of both of us like a spent firework. I drop my hands, Jude staggers backward, and I hold my breath as the words land around us. If I move, the whole world will shatter.

"Jude, I—"

"You think I *want* this?" he says quietly, with an edge I've never heard to his voice. His body is shaking. "You think this is my choice?" he says louder. "You think I'm *happy* about it?"

"Jude—" I whisper.

"I'm fucking *furious*!" There's a breath of almost hysterical laughter beneath the words. "I'm fucking . . . I'm fucking terrified!" I take a step back and close my eyes.

"You think I wouldn't love to hang around and watch you waste your time?" he says. "You think I wouldn't *love* to stick around and watch you kick your life and your choices and your heart around the streets of this godforsaken place like they're garbage?" The laugh turns bitter. "Talk about *privileged*. I'd fucking *kill* for that!" he roars.

"Jude, please—"

"But *I* don't have a choice! *I'm* the one who doesn't have a choice, do you get that?"

I told him to feel something, but I didn't want this. Not this. I want him to be cold, arrogant, untouchable

Jude Daly again. I want him to tell me he's fine, he's got it all figured out. I can't bear this. I can't bear his fear.

"I don't have a choice," he says helplessly, his voice breaking and his shoulders beginning to shudder as he buries his head in his arms and my heart shatters on the sidewalk. "I don't have a choice."

I stumble toward him, pulling at his rigid, shaking arms until I'm inside them, wrapping everything I can around him, making a cage of my body. I want to tell him he's not alone, he'll never be alone, I'll never let anything happen to him. I'd say anything, do anything, defy *anything* to make it better. But I can't promise any of that. So I just hold him while he buries his head in my shoulder and sobs.

The moon lights our way to the ruins, and the twigs and rocks beneath the soles of my bare feet are satisfying, grounding, stop me from thinking about anything but the next step.

We pass the Moroccan Lodge and continue uphill, creatures rustling in the undergrowth as we pass. We head for the stream without discussing it. When we get there, Jude puts his coat around my shoulders and we huddle together on the bank, the spot we slept in after the party. The lake far below is the same expanse of black against the same wall of mountains. But everything else is different now.

"Have I messed up your life?" he asks. Even now he's thinking about me.

"No. I don't need your help with that," I say with a wry smile. I reach for his hand. The knuckles must be bruised, but it's hard to see in the dark.

"What about your parents?" I ask.

"I texted to say I'm OK. They'll probably be on the phone all night."

"Have they found anything?" I ask, trying to keep my voice steady.

"They're interviewing the Survivor guy. But there's nothing concrete yet. It could just be a genetic mutation. A once-in-a-lifetime fluke."

I nod, because if I try to speak I'll fall apart.

I get up and walk to the edge of the water, inhaling deep breaths of cold air and hugging Jude's coat to me. It smells like him.

He follows, and after a moment, he fishes some pebbles out of the stream and starts skipping them across the surface of the water. He's monochrome in the darkness and my brain is snapping mental pictures. I wish we could stay in the ruins forever. I wish this place would work its spell—stop time, turn us into ghosts or people in a photograph, never getting older.

"You need to flick your wrist more," I tell him.

"I suppose you're an expert in pebble skimming as well as archery?"

I take a pebble and send it bouncing far beyond his.

"And you thought I'd been wasting my time all these years." I dust my hands off.

"I take it all back."

We grin at each other. But he's run out of pebbles, and he shoves his empty hands in his pockets and asks, "Would you really have left with me?"

"Yes."

"Maybe you'll still go someday. Do something amazing," he says.

I smile at him, but the whole idea seems impossible now. Mom needs me here. Micah needs me here. Jude keeps telling me this isn't the real world, but it's the only world I know.

We walk back up the bank and Jude sits behind me, his coat and his arms and legs wrapped around me. His head fits in the hollow of my neck like it's meant to be there.

I sink back against him. His skin is cool and I can feel his chest rise and fall with each breath. I realize I'm studying it. Trying to learn every movement.

"Are you OK?" he asks.

I almost laugh. "No. Are you OK?"

He almost laughs. "No." He inhales deeply, slowly, pulling me closer. "But this helps," he says. "I get it now. The R-and-J thing. It's just . . . this. Someone to hold you. Isn't it?"

I nod. "I think so."

I twist my body toward his so I can slip my arms around him and lean my forehead against his. His face is a dark blur, his breath warm on my lips.

"That part's not fake, Jude." I draw back a little so I can focus on him. It's important suddenly that he knows this. "No matter what the guy's like, no matter how we feel about each other. When it gets to that part, when the family all piles on the bed and surrounds us and everyone's holding everyone else? There's nothing but love in the room. *Nothing.* I know because I feel it, too. In that moment, I've loved every single one of them." My voice cracks and my body starts to shake, and he leans his forehead on mine, listening. I think his eyes are closed. I can feel tears landing on my hands where they're laid on his chest and I don't know if they're mine or his.

"Every single one. And it's . . . it's beautiful. Everyone gets so quiet. Everyone just . . . lets go. Of all the stuff that doesn't matter. For those moments, they're still together and they don't waste them. They're grateful. And the thing is, you can't be sad when you're grateful. So, there's nothing to be afraid of, there's just . . . love."

He lets his head fall onto my shoulder and I push my hands into the tangle of his hair.

I still want him to change his mind. I want him to fight. I want him to stay. I want him.

But I whisper, "If it's what you want, Jude, I'll be there."

And he pulls me close and whispers, "Thank you."

We're quiet for a long time after that. Breathing in time with the ripples of water breaking over the rocks in the stream. Watching the stars inch across the sky. I remember Mrs. Daly asking, *What do you do with the last few days?*

You wind yourselves around each other, until you don't know where he ends and you begin.

You stay in the present, realizing it's a strange place you've never been before.

You talk about nothing. You talk about everything.

"I think it's all in the shape of the stones," he says. "The wrist flick is just for show."

"I think you're full of it, city boy."

"I'll have you know I am a fire-jumping woodsman. I did the Live-like-a-Local experience and everything. Still haven't gotten my T-shirt by the way."

"You have to master the beer bong before you get the T-shirt. This isn't Oxford, we don't dole out certificates to just anyone."

"Fair enough." I'm leaning back against his chest and he wraps his arms tighter around me. After a long pause, he says, "What's your happiest memory?"

"Singing 'Let It Go' with Micah at our fifth-grade talent show."

"Did you win?"

"We were awful. Like, shockingly bad. But we had so much fun. What are you most proud of? Apart from your *I Beat the Rock* T-shirt."

"I once built a robot that would pet your dog when you were away from home. I thought that was pretty cool. Until the dog ate the motor. What's your favorite food?"

"Chocolate."

"Not that nasty American muck."

"You Brits and your chocolate snobbery. Favorite way to relax?"

He hesitates and then admits, reluctantly, "I've watched *The Lion King* a few times. Like . . . a few *hundred* times."

I mock gasp. "A *movie*! Thought those were on your Bucket List of Time Wasting? You *hypocrite*!"

"I know," he moans in shame. "But it's comforting."

"Riiiight." I muse. "So, your favorite movie is about a kid with massive responsibilities who runs away to have fun with two slackers? Hmm."

He laughs.

"Not sure how I feel about that." I pout. "I mean, I guess it depends on whether I'm the meerkat or the warthog. Neither is really flattering."

"Hey, Pumbaa is adorable." He shrugs. "Maybe I just like a happy ending. First crush?"

"Micah. Obviously. Did you really enjoy the Staff Town party?"

"So much it kind of frightened me."

"Frightened you?" I laugh. "Why?"

He thinks for a moment. "It's stupid but, you know the saying, 'Time flies when you're having fun'?"

"Yeah— Oh."

"Exactly. I've always had this feeling like, if I let go, time will just slip away, and another day will be gone."

I lean my cheek against his and count the seconds as they pass in silence, making sure to notice each one.

"Why photography?" he asks. "Why the ruins?"

I shrug. "I honestly don't know. But it's like everyone decided they weren't important. And every time I take a photo, it's like saying *fuck you, everyone.*" He laughs. "Why did you tell me you knew I'd been hired?"

I can hear the smile in his voice. "The real you seemed more interesting?"

"You couldn't stand me!"

"I couldn't stand that you were interesting. Why don't you believe in love?"

"I do. I just don't want to. Someone always gets hurt. Do you believe in God?"

"I don't really think about it. It's eternity I wonder about. The idea that you go"—he spreads his hands—"wherever. And it's for always." We think about that for a moment. *Wherever. Always.* Words that are going to swallow Jude up. Swallow us all up. Words I've never really thought about before, but suddenly they make the whole sky and all its constellations look small.

"Do you think we would've lasted?" He asks the question I know I'll be asking myself for the rest of my life.

"I don't know." And my question in reply is "Does it matter?"

"No." It doesn't. We barely know each other. We can't possibly know what might have been. And all we've lost is the chance to find out. But that feels like such a lot.

He's quiet for so long I nudge him. "Your turn."

"OK." But he's quiet for another few moments before he says, "What's your Date?"

I turn to look at him. His eyes are completely black in this light, the sunny gold flecks replaced by pinpricks of moonlight.

I sit up to shrug off his coat and stretch a hand around to the area below my shoulder blade. He gently pulls the strap of my dress over my arm, tugs the zipper at the back down a few inches, unhooks my bra strap.

"They put a fake skin patch over it."

His fingertips graze the skin, searching for it, and I shiver. He peels it off carefully so it doesn't hurt. I bend forward over my knees so he can see. He runs his thumb over it.

"You'll be . . ." He silently calculates. "Ninety-two?"

"And one hundred fourteen days."

The exhalation he lets out makes me think of all the times I've stood outside fancy hotels or lusted over brochures. I wouldn't blame him for being bitter. But he bends his head and I feel his hair on my skin and then his lips as he presses them to each number in turn.

And then to my shoulder blade. Then my shoulder. The top of my spine. The back of my neck, the base of my hairline, and I'm raising my body up to meet him, offering my throat, reaching my arms back for him. I'm turning so his lips can find my jaw, my ear, my eyelid, my cheek, and finally my mouth. He spreads his coat beneath us as I draw him down on top of me, and we pull each other out of our clothes for the same reason we've been asking each other questions all night. Because nothing less than everything is enough now.

• • •

Afterward, wrapped in Jude's coat, he falls asleep and I try not to. I've spent my life hurtling toward the next party, the next dance, the next drink, the bigger, brighter, better thing that's just around the corner. Tonight, nothing is better than *here* and *now*. I'm in love with every rock digging into my skin. I make myself aware of every inch of my body where it touches his body, clinging to the present like it's a cliff face.

But maybe the present can last forever, if you go slowly enough. So I stay awake and I tell myself he's here *now*. And *now*, and *now*, and *now*, and I try to hold on to all the nows, but every one of them slips through my clenched fists like grains of sand. And then it's morning, and the sky is pale, cold, empty.

When I stir, Jude is sitting beside me, arms wrapped around his knees, looking out at the view across the mountains. He turns to smile and helps me sit up, wrapping an arm around me, and I snuggle against his side, telling myself it's so early, it's still practically last night. That the day doesn't really begin until someone breaks the silence.

"I've made some decisions," he says into my hair, and I close my eyes, bracing myself. *Not yet. Not yet.* This is where he tells me how it's going to go today. He can go to the clinic anytime, it just has to be done today, before the clinic closes. If it's not, he'll be escorted off the resort grounds by midnight because no one's allowed to be here on their actual Date.

He'll want to spend time with his parents, of course. I'll have to show up with Naomi and let Mr. and Mrs. Daly think I'm just a really good actress when I say goodbye to him. How do you say goodbye when you've barely said hello? How do you say goodbye when you can't even breathe? How do you say goodbye when all you want to say is *Not yet. Not yet. Please not yet.*

"Are you sure?" he says.

"About what?" I lift my face to look at him, confused. There's dirt on his cheek, thickening the stubble.

"About leaving town with me. If I decided to . . ."

My eyes widen. *"Jude,"* I breathe. I don't dare even process what I think he's saying.

"It's just . . ." He shrugs. "Where there's life, there's hope, right?"

I sit up straighter, as if that will make this conversation make sense. Make it go the way I want it to. "But do you really believe that?"

"Yes."

"Do you really believe the Survivor could be real?"

He smiles. "No. But . . ." He pushes my hair back, brushes dirt gently off my forehead. "This way, we get more time together."

My mouth works soundlessly for a moment as what I *want* to say and what I *should* say battle for control.

"Jude," I finally manage. "I meant everything I said,

but . . . don't do this for me. Don't do it for your parents and don't do it for me. Today is about you." Dreading the answer, after this moment of hope, I ask, "What do *you* want? Honestly."

He thinks for a moment, while my heart stops entirely.

"I want what I've always wanted," he says finally. "I want to have no regrets." He pulls me closer and says, "I would regret giving up a minute I could have spent with you."

"But you really think it could work? It's worth trying?" I'm clinging to fistfuls of his sweater, fistfuls of hope.

He grins. Then laughs. "I think it's absurd. Not to mention irrational, reckless, and irresponsible." He leans his forehead against mine and says, "Fuck it. Let's do it."

Chapter 15

THE DALYS SWING INTO ACTION IMMEDIATELY. WHEN WE GET TO THE
Hermitage, they're on the veranda, still on their laptops.
I doubt they've slept. Mrs. Daly's eyes are raw, and when
Jude tells them he's canceling, she throws her arms around
him like a drowning woman, only letting go long enough to
hold one hand out behind him, to silently take mine.

It's a reprieve. A last-minute, last-chance, last-ditch effort
and the odds are *massively* against us. We all know all of
this. But we also know we don't have to say goodbye to him
today, and everyone's refusing to look beyond that.

Of course the Dalys have had plans drawn up for years,
covering every eventuality. They tell me they've been testing
safe houses all over the world. Everything from bombproof
shelters to caves in the desert.

"It's too late to go to the island in the Caribbean. We
can't risk flying on your Date, for obvious reasons. We'll
have to get there before midnight tonight. But there's an

underground bunker not far from here," Mr. Daly says. "We can have the team set everything up today, and we can be safely locked down there by this evening. Bombproof, virus proof, radiation proof, you name it. It has a hospital-grade operating room. There'll be a full medical team, trained staff, risk assessment experts, everyone screened for contagious diseases, any supplies you could ever need. If we can get through twenty-four hours there, then . . ." He and Mrs. Daly share a wordless, agonized glance.

"It sounds perfect," I say.

Jude makes a face. "Except everyone they've tried it on so far has died."

"Oh. How?"

"Undetected embolisms, strokes, massive heart attacks. One guy had a stress-related allergic reaction to the catheter they were putting in so he wouldn't have to risk falling in the bathroom."

I sag. He takes my hands. "Look, it's a long shot. But it's our best option."

"Right," Mrs. Daly says, gathering herself. "Get Carla on the phone—I want an armored jeep to pick us up, just in case. Contact the medical team, tell Graham to . . ." She disappears inside, followed by Mr. Daly.

"Um, Mum?" Jude calls after her.

"Yes, sweetheart?" She ducks her head back out.

"Is it OK if Regan and I slip out for a few hours while you organize things? I'll be back this afternoon."

She looks reluctant to part with him, but she says, "Of course, darling. What are you going to do?"

"Nothing really." He grins at me. "Hang out."

She smiles and squeezes his hand. "OK, have fun. They can have the bunker ready for us by eleven p.m. We'll arrange for the car to pick us up by ten and we'll be out of harm's way before midnight."

"Sure. Oh, and Regan and her mom are coming with us."

We both blink at him in surprise, but she only misses a beat before saying, "Of course they are!" like she'd be appalled by any other possibility, and dashes back inside.

"Jude," I whisper. "I have to talk to Naomi about that, she can't just—"

"It's OK, she won't have to come," he whispers. "I'm going to come clean before we leave. Tell them I know everything."

"You are? I thought you didn't want them to know that you knew about the R and J."

He shrugs. "I wanted to make them happy. I think we've just done that." He glances at the house. "I'll explain everything to them on the way to the bunker, but I don't want to get into it now, there isn't time." He smiles at me. "I have plans for today."

I smile back.

"Mum, one more thing," he calls into the house.

"Yes?" She comes out, already dialing on her phone.

"I'll need a car."

What *would* you do if today was your last?

Turns out all my answers to that question have been

wrong. Turns out the *question* is wrong. Because it's not about what you do. It's about who you do it with.

I run back to my room at Lakeside to shower and grab my things while Jude does the same. Naomi has to stand outside the bathroom while I fill her in on everything that's happened over the roar of running water because I'm not wasting a minute on explanations.

"What do you mean you're not coming back?" she frets, following me around as I dress, grabbing my own denim skirt and a sweater from the closet.

"Come back for what? You're the one who told me I don't want to do this job forever!" I yank a brush through my hair, already looking around for my sneakers.

"I know, but this is extreme! You're only eighteen, there's plenty of time, couldn't you just—"

"There's *no* time! Jude is . . . I can't think beyond today, I just can't."

"Look, I know you want to help him, but . . . is this really what you want?"

"It doesn't matter what I want. This is his *life* we're talking about."

I grab my bag. All that's in it is my phone and the few personal things I brought with me.

"And what about *your* life? That matters, too."

I hesitate for a moment at the door, looking around at the beautiful suite, but there's nothing here I'll miss. Except Naomi.

"This is what I want," I tell her.

"What about Micah?" she says. "And your mom?"

I study the veins in the marble floor for a moment, but I don't take my hand off the door handle. I can't think about Mom. Or Micah. Or Dante and what he might do to them when he hears I've skipped town. Or what I'll do if this crazy plan doesn't work. Because none of it is worse than what'll happen to Jude if we stay.

"We're leaving at ten," I finally say. "I'll text Micah to meet me at Jude's place to say goodbye. And I'll talk to Mom before I go. I don't know what else I can do." I give her a helpless look. She sighs and comes to hug me.

"I'll look out for them," she says, and I hug her back.

"Thanks, Naomi," I whisper. "For everything. You're . . . you're a really good mom."

As I step out onto the terrace, a vintage red Ferrari convertible is gliding up the drive, Jude grinning at the wheel in a pair of Ray-Bans, his hair already windblown. I take one look at the ridiculous Italian sports car and burst out laughing.

"It was this or a Bentley," Jude says, leaning over to push my door open. "Apparently the hotel doesn't lend out Toyotas."

"Of course they don't," I say, jumping in.

"I had to promise my parents we'd drive like we're transporting eggs," he says.

"You drive like that anyway; you were terrible at dirt track racing."

He revs the engine in response, looking dangerously at me from over the rims of his sunglasses. I laugh, but it turns into a squeal as he suddenly releases the brake and I'm thrown back in my seat. We screech off down the hotel drive, down Bergman Road, and leave the resort behind.

Of course, Jude Daly is an excellent driver. We take the twisty mountain roads at an entirely reasonable pace, but any speed in a Ferrari feels exhilarating.

"Aren't the views bothering you?" I ask as we take a hairpin onto yet another road with a steep drop to one side.

"Yep!" he calls back cheerily. "Fucking terrified! That's why we're going downhill."

"Where *are* we going?" I ask, because he hasn't told me yet.

"You showed me your favorite place, now I'm going to show you mine. I'm taking you for lunch at my favorite deli in Manhattan."

"Manhattan! We're going all the way to the city? For a *deli*?"

"It's only a two-hour drive. Maybe less in this thing. Haven't you been to the city before?"

"Sure, all the time. Well. Twice. On school trips. And the second time, the bus broke down and we arrived thirty minutes before MoMA closed, so . . . "

He laughs. "It'll be worth it, I promise. It's a *really* good deli."

I shrug. "Guess we're going to the city, then." If Jude told me he wanted to spend today swimming in radioactive waste, I'd agree. So I put on my sunglasses and start a playlist, and we cruise down the mountain, singing along to the cheesiest songs, telling stories, asking questions, letting our hands swim in the air currents as if we're aimless, free, just two teenagers in a red convertible.

"It looks . . . nice!" I say, standing on a random street on the Lower East Side, staring at the most nondescript, generic, slightly grungy, if I'm honest, deli in the history of delis. There are neon coffee cups dancing in the window. I walk the length of the front window, examining the pastries and pastrami sandwiches wilting on trays. Maybe it's one of those secret places only locals know about. Maybe their coffee is miraculous. Maybe they have some family recipe for cheesecake that will blow your tiny . . . I reach the end of the window and stop, my mouth falling open. Then I spin around to look at Jude, who's leaning against the doorframe, almost bursting with suppressed laughter. I look back at the huge, glass-fronted building next to the deli.

International Center of Photography.

Jude comes up behind me, slipping his arms around my waist. "OK, I've never actually been to this deli. I just saw it on the map when I was looking up how to get here."

I turn in his arms, trying to find words. "I . . . but . . . this is your day, Jude."

"It's our day." He takes my hand and leads me toward the doors. "Come on."

• • •

Stillness. The vast, white, airy gallery rooms of the museum are lined with framed images—vibrant street scenes, monochrome portraits, abstract fragments, harrowing war photography, scathing photojournalism—but what I find in each room, no matter the color, energy, anger, humor splashed across the walls, is stillness. Your own thoughts, suddenly audible. After the chaos of the past few days, it's strangely peaceful to wander around these almost empty rooms, aware of our footsteps on the floors, our breathing as we stand before each photograph.

At first, I feel out of place, and I cling to Jude's hand, letting him lead me to each gallery, watching other people to see what they make of the pictures. But before long, I get sucked into an exhibit about climate change by young photographers. And then one about animals in cities. Then one about wealth and consumerism. Then one that's just selfies of teenagers in iconic locations.

In a city where people live in shoeboxes, I'm astonished by the space given to each image. The respect. We watch video clips of the artists describing their work and what it means. Talking confidently about it, as if it's serious. Powerful. As if it matters.

I start tentatively pointing out which ones I like to Jude, then getting excited about the colors in a shot of street kids in India, the facial expressions on a group of soldiers beneath a dead tree in Afghanistan. "Look! Look at this one. You see the shallow depth of field here? And the way the lines of the building are directing you right to her eyes? You see how intense that is?"

Jude is just watching me, smiling contentedly. But I feel guilty suddenly. Getting carried away by flat images when he's standing right there.

"Come here." I pull him in and try to take a cheesy selfie of us with the photographs behind, but Jude is too busy kissing my neck and making me giggle to pose and I willingly give in.

"Maybe your photos will be on these walls someday," he says.

I turn and say, "Maybe they will," punctuating my words with kisses. "Maybe we'll live in New York and I'll study here and you'll . . . I don't know, probably do something epic like play piano at Carnegie Hall."

He laughs. "I'm not actually that good at piano. I hear Carnegie Hall is fussy."

I shrug. "You can practice. If we can find time between, y'know"—I kiss him again—"'hanging out.'"

"If I'd known hanging out involved so much kissing, I'd have done a lot more of it." He kisses me again, then murmurs, "What else? What else are we going to do? Tell me."

"Well, kissing was, like, ninety percent of my plan, but if you insist . . . we're going to live in Paris for a year."

"Paris!"

"Yep. I'll be a street photographer and you'll play piano in bars for free meals."

"I do have a trust fund, you know."

I hush him. "Trust funds are not romantic. You keeping me warm in a freezing French garret is."

"That does sound appealing," he concedes. *"Je trouverai un grenier extraordinairement froid."*

"Oh, for God's sake, your French accent is even better than your English one. No fair." I huff and pull away, and he laughs and pulls me back again.

"More. What else will we do?"

"We will . . . hitchhike to London and you'll show me around. Then we'll go to Rome on a train." He closes his eyes, listening, smiling as though he's seeing every detail. "And sail to Greece and swim in the Mediterranean."

"It's not the Bergman River, but it'll do."

"And then I'll get a job photographing rock bands and we'll tour with Taylor Swift and she'll be totally into you but you'll barely notice her."

"Taylor who?" I have a feeling he's not even kidding.

"Then we'll settle in California for a while. But not too long because I don't want to lose my natural pale skin and cynicism."

"Six months, tops."

"And your parents can come and stay for Christmas."

"They go to Bali at Christmas."

"Not after they taste my instant mashed potatoes."

I lay my forehead on his chest, inhaling the scent at his throat as the photographs look on and envy us.

"And we'll never argue," I add.

"Never."

"Or break up."

"Course not."

"We'll just get old and slow and take ten minutes to order coffee at Starbucks."

"On purpose. Just to annoy everyone."

"And live every day just exactly like this."

"Like it's our last."

It's late afternoon when we get back. Jude stops the car at the turnoff for Staff Town so I can go home and pack while he returns the car and has dinner with his parents.

"I'll see you tonight, then." I'm reluctant to leave him, even for a few hours. I'm even more reluctant to explain this to Mom.

I guess he's reluctant, too, because when I reach for the car door, he says, "Regan, wait."

"You OK?"

"It's just . . ." He rakes a hand through his hair and looks out at the road. I wish we were still out there. Still in the ruins this morning. Still swimming yesterday. The fact that time only goes in one direction is cruel. "The rest of today is going to be chaotic," he says. "And tomorrow will be worse. Can we just . . ."

He stretches an arm out for me, and I slide over to rest my head on his shoulder and wrap my arms around him. We allow ourselves a few more moments of *now*.

"I shouldn't have gotten you involved in all this," he says quietly. "It was selfish."

"You just wanted to make your parents happy."

"I did. But . . . I liked you, too."

"Since when?" I laugh, looking up at him. I can't think of a single moment when I wasn't being an asshole to him, so how on earth did we get here?

He smiles without opening his eyes. "First time I saw you."

"At the *clinic*?" I'm incredulous, remembering what a dick I was that day.

He smiles a softer smile, pulls me back in. "You had frosting on your nose."

I inhale sharply. Of course. He was there, on the floor above when I was waiting to see Dr. Burgess. He told me. It feels like a lifetime ago. And it feels like no time at all.

I lift my head to kiss him, and when the kiss ends, our lips barely part, so they brush as he murmurs, "It's been a good day."

"Perfect day," I agree.

"No regrets."

"Not one."

His lips find mine and linger there. The kiss deepens and his fingers press into my back, pulling me closer for a moment. Then he lets go, and I get out of the car. He watches until I've started down the sidewalk and turned the corner, and then I hear the engine as he drives away.

"What do you mean you're going with Jude?" Mom says, hobbling around behind me, bewildered, as I pack a bag.

"I'm sorry, I know it's last minute, but it's just how it worked out. I have to go."

"You're not going anywhere!"

I almost laugh. Sternness has never come naturally to her. "You can't stop me, Mom. I'm eighteen." I say it gently, but she just plants her hands on her hips, balancing on her crutches in the doorway to my room.

"What about your job?"

I shake my head and start pulling things out of drawers. "I'm not doing that anymore. I can't. I thought you'd be happy."

"But . . . Ree, I can't even walk properly yet. I need you here."

"Naomi will check in on you and—"

"Naomi knows about this? Who else? Was there an ad in the paper? How long have you been planning this?"

"I haven't! It just happened! Mom, please. Don't take it personally. I'm not leaving *you*."

"No? It sure looks like it."

"It's not about you. This is a good thing for me. Can't you be happy for me?"

She drops her hands, and her voice is more confused than angry. "Happy? Honey, you barely know this guy. And he's about to—"

"It's not about him! It's about taking control of my own future." It sounds ridiculous even to me, but I try to inject some firmness into the words as I throw my ID into my bag.

"But . . . you're still a kid. What are you going to *do*?" She looks at me like I've suggested going to the moon.

"I don't know. I'll think about that later. There isn't time now. Jude thinks I could be a photographer."

"Oh, *Jude* thinks. Well, if *Jude* thinks. What would Jude know about us?"

I sweep my photos into a pile and stuff them into a folder, irritated. "*He* believes in me. He thinks I can do more than spend my life cleaning hotel rooms."

"Thanks a lot."

"You know what I mean."

"I do, yes," she snaps. "And it's easy for him to say. You think this is what I wanted in life?" She gestures at our cabin. "I had a kid to raise, in case you hadn't noticed. Not that you get any thanks for that apparently. Not that you get an ounce of gratitude. No, after everything you do for them, they just up and leave with the first rich kid passing through!"

"I'm not! Mom, this is different."

She looks pityingly at me. "Oh, it always is, honey." She shrugs. "Maybe he is different. But *you're* not. You're doing exactly what a million girls have done before you. *Taking control of your future.*" She scoffs. "You're not taking control of your future. You're handing it to some guy who can do whatever the hell he likes with it. I should know. I thought *I* was an idiot. At least I was never fool enough to follow the asshole out of town."

I set my jaw and stuff more clothes into the bag. They smell damp and I can barely see what I'm packing through the tears threatening. "I am *nothing* like you." I say. "This *is* different."

"Yeah, it's different. *You* want an actual goddamn miracle."

"Mom, stop." I don't want this to turn into an argument. I don't want to leave on bad terms. "What's so wrong with having some ambition for myself?"

She looks indignant. "Are you kidding me!" she snaps. "Who was the one who spent the last eighteen years telling you to work harder in school? Who told you to stop fooling around with Micah and do your homework a million times? When you were skipping class to smoke pot in the ruins at *twelve*, who begged the principal not to kick you two out? Everything I've done has been so that you could get an education, get a job, have a life—"

"What life?" I explode, turning on her and throwing the jacket I'm holding onto the bed. "A life like yours? Why would I want to be *anything* like you? You're so miserable you can't get through the day sober! Forgive me for wanting more than the leftovers from their fucking minibars!"

And there it is. We look at each other across the words spilled like a pile of clothes on the bed, across ten years of silence. The mixture of anger and shame on her face is a mirror image of what's on mine. I should apologize. I open my mouth to do it. But nothing comes out. And when she draws herself up, all innocent, her lips trembling, and says, "What do you mean?" I throw my bag down in fury, march to the kitchen, and open the trash can, rooting through it while she tries to physically pull me away. I throw her off and produce a beer bottle, slamming it on the counter. Another. *Slam.* Two more. *Slam. Slam.*

"It's only beer! And I didn't have anything until six! I've been sitting around here all day, I can't walk, I was bored, I needed—"

"Stop it! Stop it! There's always an excuse! I can't do this anymore! I can't pretend anymore! I can't cover for you and lie for you anymore!"

"No one asked you to! I'm *fine*!"

"No, you're not!" I plead with her, my voice cracking. "You're not fine, Mom. You need help, you need—"

"Whatever. Go. Go, then." She puts her hands up between us. "There's no talking to you. Go and you'll see. See for yourself." She grabs her coat and keys and hobbles out, slamming the front door.

I stand alone in the kitchen for a moment. Then I wipe my face, leave the bottles on the counter, and walk slowly back to my room where my bag sits open on the bed. This is crazy. What state will she be in by morning? And what about the day after that and the day after that?

But I'm not thinking beyond tomorrow, I remind myself. I can't. I zip the bag and leave.

I texted Micah to explain the situation and ask him to come see us off, and on the way back to the Hermitage I spot him—a shadow in the gathering dusk up ahead on the path.

"You came," I say, falling into step beside him.

"You know me," he says, taking my bag for me. "Always here for the crazy. Not sure I can make you look like the responsible one this time, though."

"Yeah, that's basically what Mom said." I grimace. "You think it's the worst idea ever?"

"Yep."

"But you know I have to try."

He smiles sadly. "Yep."

We walk in silence for a few moments, crickets chirping around us like this is any other night.

"Micah, I'm sorry. About . . . everything. I should have noticed you weren't happy. I *did* notice, I just . . . I didn't want to see it, I guess."

"It's OK, Ree."

"No, it's really not. And I hate leaving you like this."

"I'm fine. I'll be fine."

I sigh. "You know, I'm starting to think the word *fine* doesn't mean what anyone thinks it means." He laughs.

There's a black car parked outside the Hermitage with a driver waiting for us. No turning back now. The clinic will be closed already and the Dalys will have to be off the resort grounds before midnight. Jude can't change his mind even if he wanted to, and I admit feeling relieved about that.

A bellhop on his way out with a suitcase tells us the Dalys are upstairs packing the last of their things. We perch on a couch to wait. A laptop sits open on the coffee table, new email notifications pinging every few seconds. I see Micah notice it and glance at me.

I wonder what I would have done in this position a week ago. I certainly wouldn't have been betting on the minuscule chance that the Dalys' plan could work.

Or my equally small chance of making a new life for myself. Regan from a week ago—a more sensible Regan—is screaming in my head, telling me to be smart, to not waste this opportunity, to take the safe bet and solve all my problems in one shot.

I take the flash drive out of my bag, and Micah watches as I set it on the floor, stamp on it, then toss the pieces and all my metaphorical eggs into one Jude-shaped wastebasket.

Micah grins at me. "Well, it's no fun if you're not doing *something* stupid."

I grin back as Mrs. Daly comes down the stairs and we stand to greet her.

"Did you guys have a nice evening?" I ask.

"We had dinner on the veranda," she says. "Jude was in good spirits, it was lovely. Isn't your"—she glances behind her—"*mother* here?" Jude must not have told her the truth yet, and it's not my place to, so I say, "She's on her way."

"That's good. I'm glad you're coming, Regan."

I let the bellhop take my bag as Mr. Daly appears. "This is my friend Micah. He got to know Jude, too, and he wanted to say goodbye. Where is Jude?"

"Just finishing his packing," Mr. Daly says. "Why don't you go on up?"

I leave Micah with them and climb the stairs to Jude's room, noticing the way my heart speeds up and my stomach tingles at the thought of seeing him again. After a few hours. "Jesus, who *are* you?" I mutter to myself, but I can't keep the smile off my face.

"Jude?" I rap lightly on the door. Then a little harder. "Jude?"

I push it open. The room's the same as it was when I stormed out of it two days ago, except it's dark now. Outside, the moon is still low in the sky and cold light streams in through the window and onto the bed.

But Jude's not here. The bathroom door is open but that room's empty, too. I look back down the hall and whisper into the darkness, "Jude?" but the fizzing in my stomach is becoming a sickening churn. "Jude, are you up here?"

I turn on the light, and the moonlight vanishes to reveal two crisp white envelopes lying on the bed.

Regan,

    You said you'd let me do this however I liked, so I hope you'll understand. And forgive me. You were right, some lies are well-intentioned.

    God knows how it will happen and I won't risk you or anyone else getting hurt. I have to be alone when it comes. Don't worry about me. I'm not afraid, and even if this week didn't go exactly as I planned, it turned out to be perfect. You can live a full life in a short time, you know. You can live a full life in a single day.

    If you're reading this, then I guess you've

packed and said your goodbyes already. You've imagined a new life for yourself. That's the hard part over. Don't waste it. Just go. You can do this. You can do anything.

I thought if I let you in, you'd be another person I'd have to leave behind. But that's not how it works. I'm taking you with me. Wherever. Always.

Jude.

"Mrs. Daly! Mr. Daly!" I take the stairs three at a time and almost tumble into Mr. Daly's arms at the bottom, thrusting the other envelope at them, gasping, choking on my own heart. "He's gone! He left! He's gone!"

"What? What do you mean? What is this?" There's a second of stunned silence as they scan his letter to them. They could barely have read it, but they don't have to. They know. We should *all* have known. There's no way Jude would ever have gone through with this ridiculous plan. He'd never risk anyone else getting hurt in whatever accident is about to happen to him. He's gone off by himself to keep everyone safe.

"Oh God. Oh my God!" Mrs. Daly starts to panic. "How did we let this happen! We should have . . . How could we have believed . . ." But people will believe all kinds of things if they want them to be true.

Micah takes my hand while Mr. Daly tries to put his arms around Mrs. Daly. He's as pale as she is, but she pushes him away, reaching for her phone. "We have to find him. We have to call the police. We have to instigate a search." Mr. Daly speaks urgently to the bellhop, who runs for the driver.

"He's not answering his phone," Mrs. Daly says, trying again.

"This is all my fault," I whisper. "This is all my fault." It is. He did all this just so I'd have the guts to leave town. Even his goodbye note was about *me*, not him. But he never wanted this. He wanted a peaceful, dignified death surrounded by his family. What will happen to him now?

"No, it's *my* fault," Mrs. Daly says, hanging up on the call and already dialing another. "I should have known. I should have . . ." She bursts into tears, and Mr. Daly takes the phone and folds her into his arms.

"It's no one's fault," he says. "Jude is headstrong. He knows what he wants. He's always known."

But she's shaking her head, pushing him away again. "No. *No!* I am *not* letting him do this, do you hear me? I could let him go, but not like *this*. Not *alone*. Someone has to be with him. *Someone has to be with him!*"

Mr. Daly nods. "All right. It's all right. We'll find him. We will. There's time. He couldn't have left more than thirty minutes ago. Regan, do you have any idea where he might have gone?"

"I . . ." My brain is a frantic mess of unintelligible thoughts. None of them useful. I force myself to breathe. To think. He barely knows the resort. And there's nowhere he could hide; everyone knows who he is. Everyone in the resort will be . . . It hits me in a flash of certainty. "The ruins."

"What?"

"The ruins of the *old* resort," I tell them urgently. "They're up the mountain a little way; you can walk. No one goes there. There's plenty of places to hide." Even as I'm saying it, I'm picturing the precarious buildings, the dark overgrown paths, precipices where you don't expect them, rattlesnakes, bears. I hear sheets of glass crashing to the ground and Jude saying, *You like to live dangerously, huh?*

"Call security!" I shout, grabbing Micah and pulling him to the door. "Call Dr. Lawrence! Tell them to start in the ruins. I'm going there now."

Chapter 16

"REE, ARE YOU SURE ABOUT THIS? WHAT IF HE'S NOT IN THE RUINS? He could be anywhere!" Micah pants as we run for Staff Town. "And he's smart. If he doesn't want you to find him, you won't find him."

"I have to!"

The air fills with a violent, percussive sound and I realize a helicopter has taken off from the helipad on the Lakeside roof, blades slicing the air and searchlights combing the ground as it sweeps toward the black silhouettes of the mountains. The security staff is likely on their way up there already. Maybe the police, too. I don't know if that's a good thing or if it'll drive Jude deeper into the ruins. It's after ten p.m. already. After midnight, it'll be the Date on his arm and anything could happen. Mrs. Daly was right—someone has to be with him. But not some random cop or security guard.

"OK, OK, but"—Micah grabs my arm and pulls me to a standstill—"let's be smart about this. Let's think."

We stare blankly at each other, gasping for breath. *Thinking* doesn't come naturally to either of us. Ironically, Jude would know exactly what to do. He'd have some clever idea that would give us a lead, narrow down the options. He'd know that you can track someone through their phone or their credit card or . . .

"Cameras!" I gasp, grabbing Micah's hands.

"What?"

"CCTV! You have to go through the resort to get to Staff Town. He must have been picked up on a camera somewhere. It could tell us which way he was headed."

"OK, but how do we check? There must be hundreds of them."

I shake my head, trying to clear it. "There are. The hotels have them. And the beach. And they're outside every nightclub in town, to protect the bouncers, and . . ."

We stare at each other, and say at the same time, *"Dante."*

When we reach Inferno, we sprint in through the iron doors before anyone can either hold them open or tell me I'm banned. They clang behind us. Inside it's loud, hot, heaving with dancers, the air muggy with sweat and hormones. Dante is in the DJ booth on the balcony, getting the crowd revved up. We fight our way through, spilling drinks, and race up the stairs beside the bar to reach him.

"Where's your knight in shining armor? I could sue him, you know." He works his swollen jaw for a moment, wincing.

"We don't know where he is! He's missing. We need to see your CCTV footage. We need to track him."

"I'm sorry, I must not have heard you right," he drawls, leaning against the side of the DJ booth and folding his arms. "Did you just ask me for a favor?"

"Dante! This is serious!"

"Oh, so it's serious when *you* want something. Where's the information *I* want?"

"I'll get it for you. I promise. Please," I beg, surrendering all dignity. I swore I would never need to ask Dante for anything, but right now I'd get on my knees. I'd hack Fort Knox's computers if he asked me to.

"You're a liar, Regan." He shakes his head. "I know they're about to leave town. I did tell you you'd regret not helping me."

"Dante, he's all alone! It's almost midnight. Tomorrow's his Death Date. Anything could happen!"

"And that's my problem because . . . ?"

I stare at him. Appealing to Dante's humanity was never going to work. I know how he thinks. Because he was right, we're not so different. I straighten my back, take a step closer, and level a steady gaze at him. "Look. Be smart about this, Dante. You can use it. If you help find him, the Dalys will be *so* grateful. They'd do anything for him. *Anything*. Make them happy and you'll get what you want."

That gets his attention. He arches an eyebrow, considering, then says, "You know, Regan, that's not such a bad idea."

• • •

"Everything's controlled from my desktop. I can access every club from here," he calls over his shoulder as he leads us to the top floor, to the roped-off part of the balcony where his office is.

"The CCTV?" I ask, hurrying after him.

"Cameras, sound system, stock levels. Everything." He unlocks the heavy, soundproofed office door and we hurry through. There's not much in the room—filing cabinets, a desk with his laptop on it. Dante opens a drawer and rummages in it for something while I bend impatiently over the computer.

"He could only have left thirty or forty minutes ago. He'd have reached the resort center twenty—" But I don't get to finish the sentence. Because Micah is suddenly shoved violently past me, his face smashing into the wall, while a hand reaches around me, jerking me backward until I'm pressed against Dante's chest, one of his muscular arms restraining me while he presses the tip of a blade against my throat.

"Ree!" Micah's voice is weak and muffled as he slumps to the floor, holding his hands over his bloody nose.

"Micah! What the fuck! Let me go!" I yell, trying to kick Dante's legs, stamp on his foot, wriggle out of his grasp. He only tightens his grip.

"I'd advise some manners at this point." He presses the knife harder and I go still, leaning my head as far to the left as possible as cold metal sears my hot skin.

"Don't hurt her! Please don't hurt her!" Micah begs.

"Calm the fuck down!" Dante snaps. "No one's getting hurt as long as everyone does what they're told."

Micah nods quickly. The musky smell of Dante's aftershave fills my nostrils; his ragged breathing is damp on my cheek.

"I told you we'd make a good team, Regan," he says, his voice slithering unpleasantly into my ear. "And I told you that you didn't have a choice about helping me. Didn't believe me, did you? Well, here's your next assignment." He jerks his head at Micah. "Take her phone out of her pocket," Dante orders him. "And don't even think about trying anything funny."

Micah edges toward us, eyes on Dante, and reaches at arm's length into my jacket pocket to take out my phone. My heart is thumping so hard I'm sure Dante can feel it. I hate him knowing how scared I am.

"Now take a picture," Dante says.

"What?"

"A picture! Just her face. And the knife."

"Micah, don't!" I beg.

"Do it!" He jabs the point of the knife harder against my neck, and I cry out involuntarily.

Confused, Micah fumbles to open the camera, blood-stained fingers shaking. He raises the phone and presses the shutter.

"Show me." He turns the phone so Dante can see. It's fuzzy and there are smears of Micah's blood on the screen, but it's clearly me with a knife to my throat—pale, wide-eyed, frightened.

"Now type the message *Come to Inferno immediately. Come alone.* And send it to Daly Junior."

"No! Micah, *no! Don't—!*"

"Shut up!" There's a sting at my throat as Dante jostles me, pulling me harder against him, the muscles in his arms bulging as he tightens his grip across my chest, and I struggle to breathe.

"Ree!" Micah says helplessly.

"Type it!"

"No! Don't!" I whimper.

"Fuckfuckfuck," Micah whispers as he types, Dante watching to check what he's written. Down in the club, the crowd roars at something, distant behind the thick door of the office.

"Why are you doing this?" I ask, desperate to stop him before Micah hits send. "What do you want with Jude? It's not like you need money! Do you have any idea how powerful the Dalys are? They'll lock you up for the rest of your life if you hurt him!" My voice shakes pathetically as I deliver my threats.

He barks a laugh. "Well, that's just it, sweetheart," he says. "The rest of my life isn't much to risk."

"What?"

"What would you do in my position? What *wouldn't* you do, if you only had a few years left?"

"W-what? You mean—?"

"Three, to be exact. Three years, four months, nine days. Not much, is it?"

"But—"

He leans down so his lips are right against my ear and I close my eyes, squirming. A metallic taste fills my mouth and nausea rises in my throat. "I know they have information," he says. Up close I can hear the edge of desperation in his voice, and it sends chills through me. I knew he was ruthless when it comes to money, but money is nothing compared to this. "They have information about the Survivor."

"They don't!"

"They canceled their kid's procedure. They know something; they've found a way."

"No! No, that's not . . . they don't know anything!"

"We'll find out, won't we? I wanted to do this civilly. I was prepared to pay like anyone else; I don't want any favors. But they won't even answer my calls. Well, if they want to do it the hard way, then we'll do it the hard way." He adjusts his grip on the knife and I feel a trickle of something warm and wet pool at my collarbone. "Their kid won't survive his Date anyway if they don't tell me what they know."

"Just help us find him! They'll give you whatever you want!"

"Oh, just hope they'll be generous? You're a fool, Regan. But you're right, they *will* give me what I want. Because I *am* going to find him. I'm walking out of here with all their files and a one-way ticket to the Maldives. You can't be extradited from the Maldives, did you know that? Send the message, Micah."

"No!" I struggle harder, the blade making cut after cut

in my skin. If he nicks an artery, it's game over. Micah just watches helplessly, his hands twitching to help me, afraid to make it worse. "Jude canceled for *me*! So we could have another day together. He never believed there was hope; he did it for me!"

Dante laughs again. "You're good, Regan, but you're not that good. Send the fucking message."

"So what makes you think he'll even come?" I demand. "Why would he, if I'm nothing to him?"

"Because he's a fucking boy hero, isn't he?" Dante works his bruised jaw and I hear the bones click. "Send it, Micah!"

"No!" I struggle against him, but he's too strong, and trickles of my blood are running down his arm now.

"I'm so sorry, Ree," Micah whispers. What can he do? He presses send.

As soon as the text was sent, Dante threw me into the corner, took both our phones, and left, locking us in.

We spend ten minutes battering on the door, screaming at the top of our lungs, but there's no way anyone can hear us over the music in the club. Maybe if someone was right outside, but this part of the balcony is closed off.

"Fuck!" I lift a stapler and throw it at the door in frustration, then pace the room, looking for something, anything to help. There are no windows. No phone. No spare key in a drawer. For all the lavish decoration in the club, the office is sparsely furnished. Just the desk, drawers,

two chairs, a fire extinguisher, and some stained coffee mugs. I try the laptop on the desk, but it's password protected. I wonder if the device Dante gave me could have hacked it, and I regret destroying the fucking thing.

"Maybe Jude won't come," Micah says hopefully. "He ran off so he wouldn't be putting everyone in danger. Maybe he'll stay away. Or call the cops."

But that's the worst part. He will come, I know he will. He'll come because it's me.

No. No, I'm not going to sit here and let this happen.

"Micah, we have to stop him. We have to get out of here and stop Jude from coming back." I look at him. "Don't you get it? *This is how it happens.* It's not the ruins, it's *this.* Dante is ruthless and Jude's going to end up dead. It's after eleven already. If he comes back here, *this* is how it ends." It has to be. I don't think I really believed in Jude's death until now, but knowing how it's going to happen makes it so real.

But it's also the seed of another thought. If this is what's going to kill him, then *this* is how we cheat Fate, isn't it? *This* is the one thing that needs to be different. All we have to do is stop him from coming back here. This is how we save him.

Except the door is locked and we're running out of time.

I take Micah by the shoulders. "*Think!* How do we get out of here?"

His poor battered face scrunches in concentration. "Maybe . . . what if . . . is there something we can use against Dante? Some information? What do we know about him?"

"Nothing," I realize. I've known him for years, but he never talks about personal stuff, never lets his mask slip. The only personal detail I know about him I learned in the last five minutes when he—

I freeze. Then I dive for the laptop on the desk. "We know one thing about him."

The password box flashes up. "Three years, four months, nine days. Right?"

Micah realizes what I'm doing and starts mentally calculating, figuring out the Date three years, four months, and nine days from today. I type it in and look up at him while he bites his bloody lip beside me. It's such a long shot, but if Dante's this obsessed with it . . . I hit enter.

The laptop unlocks.

The Wi-Fi connects automatically and we message the police through their emergency website. But how fast can they get here?

"We still need to get out. I need my phone. I need to contact Jude," I tell Micah, searching the laptop for anything that will help us. I could email Naomi or Luis, but how soon would they see it? We've got *minutes*, not hours. I don't have contact details for the Dalys without my phone. We need to get out of here before Jude gets anywhere near Dante.

I search the files frantically. But there's nothing in here that will help. Outside the door there are a thousand people, but we have no way to let them know we're here.

"The music!" Micah gasps.

"What?"

"For the club. He said he can control everything from his laptop!"

I slide over and Micah hunts around for anything with *music* or *sound* in the name. He finds a Club Settings app and within it, "Sound System." When he opens it, there's a bunch of controls that look like they're for speakers. Bass, Treble, Fade . . . There's one for Master Volume, and when he drags the arrow all the way down, the pulsing beat from outside the door stops dead.

Our screaming is immediately drowned out by the roar of disappointment from the crowd, demanding that the music be turned on again.

"They can't hear us!" Micah pounds on the heavy door and I grab his arm.

"Stop! Stop, it doesn't matter. There might be another way."

Sure enough, within thirty seconds, we hear the key turn in the lock. "What the fuck do you think you're playing at!" Dante rages as he throws the door open. I'm ready for him, fire extinguisher raised above my head, poised to smash it into his face. As I bring it down, he raises both hands to intercept it and wrestles it from me, barely breaking his stride.

But that's all we need.

While his arms are in the air, Micah, waiting behind

the door, launches his whole body at Dante's back, sending him crashing headlong into the desk.

He's up again immediately, but it's enough time for us to run past him and through the open door onto the balcony, just as someone in the DJ box manages to get the music pumping again. The crowd roars and the bartenders blow celebratory fireballs over their heads.

Dante staggers out behind us, grabbing Micah's collar before we can even reach the stairs. I throw myself at him, lashing out at anything I can reach, my screams inaudible over the music as Dante seizes my wrist and twists it hard. I sink my teeth into his hand while Micah aims a lucky punch at his bruised jaw. His hold weakens for just a second, but it's enough and we run for the stairs. He follows, makes another lunge, but I grab Micah's hand and yank him out of Dante's path. Dante slams into the balcony rail instead, unbalanced by the momentum, and is propelled headfirst over it. For a long, slow moment he's in the air, flailing through four stories of strobing light, and then he smashes down on top of the huge wall of bottles behind the bar, launching a shrapnel bomb of shattered glass and high-proof alcohol just as one of the bartenders tosses his lighter onto the bar top.

The wall of flame leaps so high, Micah and I instinctively lean back from the balcony rail, clutching each other as heat licks at our faces. It catches the gauzy white fabric panels wafting above the bar and spreads quickly from one to the next. Bottles are still falling, exploding as the fire catches them, and the bar staff is trapped, doused in alcohol, wings alight. A high-pitched wailing alarm replaces the music while sprinklers start spraying jets of water from above, but they're no match for hundreds of bottles of high-proof liquor. Through the rolling waves of black smoke, we can make out Dante's unmoving body on the floor behind the bar, his head smashed open. Dead. Three years before his Date.

And suddenly no one's Date means anything. The club erupts in total panic. There must be fire exits, but no one can think clearly enough for that. There's just a mob. A thousand-headed beast thinking one collective thought, pushing as one for the main doors.

The elevators have shut down automatically, and Micah and I rush for the stairs, along with everyone on the three levels of balconies below us. But the stairs are beside the bar and the bottom of them is engulfed in flames. We gather on the lowest balcony, unable to get any farther. The smoke is thick, acrid. My eyes are streaming and the girl beside me is struggling to breathe. My throat is raw and I'm lightheaded as the current changes direction, the crowd pushing us along with them toward the front of the club now, above the main doors, though there's no way down from there. The biggest guys are lifting chairs and tables, trying to smash the only windows in the building, but the glass is too thick. Skinny sixteen-year-old kids are crying, screaming, being crushed against the walls or trampled underfoot. By the time Micah and I get to the windows, pounding uselessly on the glass with our fists, we can see onlookers gathering outside, watching with hands over their mouths or helping the clubbers stampeding through the doors below us. I hear sirens, but there's no sign of the fire department yet.

And then I see something worse. My fists fall helplessly to my sides, my screams die in my throat, and for a moment there's nothing—no smoke, no screaming, no sirens—nothing but the figure running down the street toward the club, barreling through the crowd and then through the front doors.

"Jude! *Jude!*" I turn away from the windows to scream over the balcony, but my voice is a rasp and the screams and shouts from below are deafening. I can barely see him through the blur of tears in my stinging eyes. He's heading for the stairs, the office, the only person trying to get into the club through a sea of people trying to get out. Micah and I battle our way back there, the balcony bouncing beneath the weight of the panicking crowd. The smoke is thickest here and I feel woozy. Things start to seem unreal. A guy topples against Micah and sinks to his knees, passed out as others step over him. Remnants of burning fabric drop from the ceiling onto the crowd and the bar is still alight, preventing anyone from getting down the stairs. Our narrow strip of balcony is overloaded, and there's a screech as the metal complains beneath us.

Below, Jude starts barking orders and within a minute he's got three guys training fire extinguishers on the flames, their collars pulled up over their mouths, and he's wrapped his own coat around his head and run through them, up to the balcony, where I throw myself at him and he says, "Oh thank God, thank God, are you all right? You're bleeding, are you hurt?"

With the stairs cleared, the crowd starts pushing their way down. But everyone on the four levels of balconies is rushing for that single exit. The metal screeches again and there's a sickening lurch as the whole structure tilts beneath us. I scream, the shock shaking me out of my woozy state.

"There's too much weight!" Jude yells. He's right, the whole balcony is pulling itself free from the wall. But we can't all get down the stairs at once. We're above the bar, where the smoke is worst, and more figures are slumping to the ground and getting trampled.

"Go!" Jude pushes me and Micah toward the stairs and we start down them, my limbs shaking and my head light. But when I turn to look back, Jude is still up there, heading the wrong way, picking up unconscious bodies.

The open doors are right there, the current of the crowd carrying me toward them.

I don't even think about it. Micah is ahead of me, and without telling him, I turn and push my way back up the stairs.

"Regan, what the fuck are you doing? Get out!" Jude yells when I reach him. He has a girl in his arms, barely conscious. He gets her to the top of the stairs and hands her to another guy to carry down and goes back for others.

Some have been injured in the crush, some passed out from smoke, and probably some who were too drunk before the fire even started to get themselves out.

"There's someone over there!" I squint through the smoke and tears to where I can just make out a figure huddled beneath a table. Jude runs toward him and I follow. The balcony judders with every step. I can see bolts wrenching out of the wall and the whole thing is tilted so sharply we have to walk at a slant. I hear smashing glass and then jets of water are spraying through the windows at the front, and when I look down the fire department is inside, yelling instructions.

The boy is curled in a ball, conscious but panicking, sucking in lungfuls of smoke as he hyperventilates. Jude takes one arm and I take the other.

"Regan, please, you have to get out of here."

But I shake my head stubbornly, straining under the boy's weight. "I'm not leaving you."

"It doesn't matter about me!" His expression is agonized as he says, more gently, "This is it. This is how it's meant to go."

"But—"

"You know that. We both know that."

"I—" I stretch my other hand toward him. My hand, eyes, everything pleading. But I nod, blinking away tears. "I know." I get the boy's arm around my shoulders and start walking. "I'm still not leaving."

We get the boy to the stairs and he stumbles gratefully down them as Jude and I go back to where a girl has fainted. We've almost made it, he's just reaching for her, when there's a final, piercing, metallic groan and the entire balcony lurches away from the wall.

Jude grabs for the inside rail, and I see panic on his face as we hang out over open space. I reach for him with one hand, the rail with the other. It's no good, though; the rail is coming with us, the whole balcony swinging out from the wall as the supports beneath us buckle.

And then we're falling. Jude's pulling me close, wrapping his body around me, but there's nothing we can do except brace for impact. When we hit the ground, his body ricochets so hard I'm thrown off him, and I lie there on the dance floor for a moment, dazed, gasping. Everything hurts. I can't locate the source of the pain. I pull myself up and crawl over broken glass, twisted metal, and bodies to get to where he lies.

There's blood. There's blood everywhere, and I don't know whose it is, where it's coming from.

"Jude? *Jude!*"

The emergency services are fighting their way to us, and water and smoke and shouting all blur confusingly together. My chest aches and there's ringing in my ears. My head swims and my vision flickers like a strobe light. I try to shake it all away, but it feels like everything's getting darker.

"Jude?" His eyes find my face as I lean over him. He tries to lift his head, but it falls back and he groans in pain.

"*Jude!* Don't move! They're coming, help is coming!"

And it is, but they're having to find people under chunks of metal now. *"Help! Help him!"* I scream. But everyone's screaming, and my voice is so weak.

"Regan." I see Jude's lips moving, but I can barely hear him, barely feel his breath.

"Jude! Jude, please! Stay with me. Stay with me." I lean over him, holding his face in my hands. There's a stabbing pain in my ribs, another in my leg, and hot, wet blood is pooling beneath me. The shouting and screaming seem to be getting farther away, the fire crew moving in slow motion. "Jude." I rest my forehead on his, trying to stay focused. I can feel his breath on my lips now. Short, shallow gasps.

"Go," he whispers.

But I just shake my head against his head. I won't leave him. I won't let him leave me.

"*Go.* You're not supposed to be here."

"I am. I am, it's my job," I whisper back, and I feel his breath huff a laugh.

"It's not your time," he says.

"I don't care. I love you, Jude," I whisper, tears falling onto his face.

His lips twitch beneath mine as he whispers, "You can't fall in love in five days." It's my turn to laugh, but I don't have the strength.

"I'm here. I'm here. I'm here," I tell him, over and over, as I slump down and my head finds his shoulder. I shut my eyes so the world narrows to the rise and fall of his chest. To his heartbeat stuttering beneath me.

"I'm here," I tell him, praying we'll both lose consciousness before I hear it stop.

I wake in the same place I always wake. The recovery room at the clinic. One of the back rooms the families never see, where I can let the effects of the tranquilizer from my "procedure" wear off. It's so familiar it takes a stab of pain in my chest to tell me something's not right.

I hear a voice, my own, murmur, "Mom?" and there's a movement from the other side of the room, and then Naomi and Micah are frowning down at me in concern.

"Don't try to move, sweetheart. You've busted some ribs. It's gonna hurt like hell. Your mom will be here soon; Dr. Burgess went to find her. They're going to take you to the hospital. They're using the clinic rooms until they can get enough ambulances over here."

Her words wash over me. "What?" I try to say, but barely a whisper comes out. My throat burns like I've swallowed acid.

"You lost a lot of blood from your leg, too. Piece of metal right through it." Naomi winces and Micah squeezes my hand.

"But you're going to be OK, Ree," he says. His face is bruised purple, grubby with soot and dried blood, and his voice is gravelly. My head feels like it's full of smoke. I can't think. Can't get my thoughts to line up in the right order. It's like they're all stampeding for the same narrow door, and I want to close my eyes and go back to where it's quiet.

Something circles the edges of my brain, like the shadow of a bird that won't land.

"You were so brave, Ree," Micah says.

"You were, sweetheart. They said you got lots of people out. Both of you. All those kids trapped on the balcony. If it hadn't been for . . ." They glance at each other, and suddenly the world comes into focus.

"Jude!" I try to sit up, and the pain punches me back down with an iron fist. "Jude . . . is he . . . where is he? *Where is he?*"

Naomi rests a hand on my forehead and strokes back my hair. "He's gone, sweetheart. He's gone."

Chapter 17

Julia Daly
London
18th July

Dear Regan,

Thank you so much for your letter and for the beautiful photos. They practically breathe. That frown! I laughed when I saw that one. And then I cried at the one of him smiling. We've been looking at old photos a lot, it's like watching him grow up again. A few years make such a difference when you're young. A few days can make such a difference. I know his last week did, and I want to thank you for that, too. I know it wasn't "real," whatever real is, but I think he did fall in love. With his life perhaps.

I never did tell Mrs. Daly the full story. It was impossible to put into words, and anyway, I promised Jude my silence. I don't know if we ever really fooled her, though; she's a very smart woman.

I stroke the thick paper with its elegant handwriting before tucking it back into its envelope and sliding it inside one of my folders. It arrived a few weeks after the fire, and I've read it so many times, I know it by heart. I read it when I'm not strong enough to read Jude's.

Outside it's still warm, and kids are squealing and laughing down at the lake. But it's September now and there are signs everywhere that fall is here—a dryness to the rustle of the leaves, a crispness to the mornings, shorter days, an evening chill. For everyone else, fall means the onset of darkness, but if you live in the woods, fall brings back the light. The shade beneath the trees brightens and warms as the canopy turns fiery. The leaves peel away, the sky finds us again, and the resort staff walk to work over carpets of gold.

As you insisted, we've donated your fee to Jude's foundation. I hope you'll accept this gift from Jude, though. It arrived not long after we got home with instructions to pass it on to you.

I fold up the new tripod Naomi gave me and pack it carefully in my backpack. She gave me a scarf and matching hat, too, with instructions to "wrap up warm." Marta, the stylist, gave me a beautiful waterproof coat. Mom and

Micah chipped in for a zoom lens, and Dr. Burgess sent me the hiking backpack I'm packing everything into.

The camera, sent by Jude, has barely left my neck all summer. I've hiked for miles around the Catskills, making new paths through the undergrowth, taking photo after photo. At first, they were angry, brutal, ugly images about the damage people do, how nothing lasts and even the grandest things fall to pieces. But after a while, they became quieter, subtler. Stronger. And now I think maybe they're about recovery. Resilience. How even the smallest weed can break up concrete.

I chose my favorites and sent them to Yvette Scholes at *Zeitgeist*.

I didn't expect her to even read my email; it felt like writing into the void. But I told her there are old vacation resorts like this all over the Catskills, and people who remember what it was like to work here. I said I wanted to travel around and interview them, collect their memories, and take pictures of them. The things and people left behind. I told her I have zero experience, zero qualifications, but that I'm the only one who can tell these stories. Because it's my story, too.

She wrote back to say she loved the idea and they'd like to commission a piece for the magazine.

*I'm still getting emails and letters from people
Jude helped to escape that night. So many of them.
I wish it had all happened differently. I wish so
many things had been different. I wish you hadn't*

I check my backpack one more time—camera, lenses,
Mrs. Daly's letter and Jude's, my photos of Jude on top,
so they'll be the first thing I unpack when I arrive—then
I snap the fasteners before leaving it by the front door
and heading into the resort for my last session with Dr.
Burgess.

"So. Our last session. I think you've made really good
progress, Regan." Dr. B leans back in her chair and cocks
her head. "What do you think?"

"I think *I* want a job where you just sit there for an
hour saying practically nothing and getting paid for it."

She smiles, says nothing, and I smile back.

Even though I don't work for them anymore, Dr.
Burgess said I'm still entitled to counseling. At first I
didn't talk about Jude. I didn't talk at all. But she waited—
she's good at that—and one day I started talking about my
mom. And then my dad. And then all the other clients I've
had. I think I talked about them as a way of *not* talking
about Jude. But it turns out that talking about those things
helps, too. And that counseling actually works when you
stop lying to your counselor. Who knew?

"I heard they're renovating Inferno," I tell her. "And
renaming it, for obvious reasons."

"How do you feel about that?"

"I thought I'd be upset. But that place had nothing

to do with Jude really. It's where he died, but . . . it's not where he lived."

Four people died that night, including Dante and Jude. Apparently it was just after midnight when the paramedics got to us. Like the news channels, I spent a lot of time trying to figure out how it happened, whose fault it all was, what one decision I could have made differently. But like Mrs. Daly says, there were so many things. If the Dalys hadn't been researching Death Dates, if Dante's Date had been different, if Dr. Lawrence hadn't paired me with Jude, if the Survivor hadn't happened, if Jude hadn't canceled his procedure, if I'd given Dante what he wanted . . . Jude was right, *Romeo and Juliet* isn't a love story; it's a tragedy. Because it could so easily have gone another way. Because trying to be together was what tore them apart. Because they did it to themselves. You can walk away from sad things because you have no control over them. But tragedy you carry with you, in the muscle memory of your own hands. It was everyone's fault, and no one's.

"Mrs. Daly told me the last email Jude sent was to his foundation," I tell her. "To set up the Bergman Midsummer Fund to allow teenagers to throw a big party for their last midsummer." I grin at the thought of it. I don't want some sad sculpture or plaque on the site of Inferno. I can't think of a better tribute than kids dancing, laughing, and probably making very stupid decisions every midsummer's night, all in Jude's memory.

"That's a lovely idea," Dr. Burgess says. "I see the

Dalys are helping the police to prosecute the 'Survivor.'"
She puts the word in air quotes. Everyone does now.

The Survivor was a hoax, of course. Very clever, but
totally fake. It became obvious when he started trying to
sell interviews and guides to how he'd cheated Death. The
whole thing was crazy. But people don't believe things
because they're believable. They believe them because
they want them to be true.

"Yeah. They're closing the Daly Research Institute, too.
They're putting everything into Jude's foundation instead.
I think he'd be happy about that."

"I think you're right. Are you all set for your trip?"

"Yep! I have to get going actually; Mom's making a
farewell brunch. There's been elaborate planning. It's a
whole thing."

She laughs. Then asks, "Are you nervous about the
trip?"

I take a deep breath. "Fucking terrified."

"But you're going."

I shrug. "Life is short."

Of course the Survivor was a hoax. Because your Date
is your Date. And everyone's got one. It's what you do in
the meantime that matters.

When Dr. Burgess found Mom and brought her to the
hospital that night, she'd been drinking. The shock of seeing me in a hospital bed sobered her up pretty fast, but
she just kept crying messily and apologizing for not being
there. I couldn't deal with her drama as well as everything

else, so I just closed my eyes and Naomi took her home.

When they discharged me, Luis drove me back to our cabin in his pickup, and then I went to bed and didn't get up for a week. Mom didn't say much, just brought me food that I didn't eat, put on movies I didn't watch, drew me baths I cried in. It was almost a month before I lifted my head long enough to notice she'd been sober the entire time.

We still didn't talk, though. I didn't have the energy, and anyway, I'd seen her sober up before. I was wary of trusting that this time was any different. Why should I put myself through that? I'd been through enough.

But this time, she didn't ask me to trust her. Didn't make any big plans or promises or demand any praise for how well she was doing. She just quietly got on with things.

And the days passed. And then the weeks. And now here she is, fussing around the kitchen like Betty Crocker, saying, "I've got literally every possible thing you could put on a pancake!"

I marvel at the array of toppings. "Mom, I'll be home in a month. You don't have to feed me enough calories to last until then. Although the cookie dough looks weirdly appealing."

"What do you think of the candy corn, chocolate chips, and caramel syrup? Too much?"

I laugh. "You should suggest it at Bean Street."

"I might!"

Mom's working there now. Kristen put in a good word

for her before she left. She actually likes it. She likes chatting with the customers. She even likes the dumb dance routines and she keeps making up new ones. I think she got my grandparents' performer genes. Despite waiting tables and looking after me, she seems younger than she did a few months ago. Less tired. Her eyes are brighter, her posture straighter.

"Here. Put some banana on that. That makes it healthy," she says, ladling banana slices into a lake of syrup.

"Mother of the year." I grin, and she curtsies.

We sit down to eat and she asks *Did you pack this, do you have that, did you remember those other things . . . ?* I get up to check and recheck a bunch of times, but everything important is there. Camera. Lenses. Letters. Photos of Jude.

"How was your session with Dr. Burgess?"

"Good. She says I'm doing well."

"You really are." She reaches out tentatively to squeeze my hand. "I know it's been tough, but . . . I'm proud of you," she says, then makes a face. "I don't know where you get it from, but it sure isn't me."

I don't know about that. I watch her pour the orange juice, add milk to her coffee. Same things she'll be doing all day for hundreds of strangers for a paycheck that'll never stretch far enough. Mom wasn't wrong; it *is* harder for people like us, it just is, and I don't feel like judging her anymore.

There's a moment of silence, and then I ask, "Do you miss him?"

She looks up, surprised. But she doesn't need to ask who I'm talking about. She sets down her fork.

"I barely knew him. I miss who I thought he was. I miss who *I* used to be, I guess. Why do you ask?"

I shrug and tell her, "I found the roller rink."

Her mouth falls open. "You did? I knew it still had to be up there somewhere."

"The path had disappeared."

"You'll have to take me sometime. I guess it looks different now."

"It's not safe. The roof's falling in."

She's disappointed. "Man, that's wild. Seems like only yesterday I was up there." She reaches for her coffee, exhaling deeply. "Time just *flies* by when you get older. On the outside. On the inside, you feel exactly the same age you always did."

"What age is that?" I ask.

She shrugs. "About eighteen. Maybe your brain stops growing when you're eighteen or something. Maybe that's why. I don't know."

"God, you mean I'm going to be stuck like this forever?"

She laughs. "Be great if it was the other way around, wouldn't it? You stay eighteen on the outside, and inside you get all wise and mature. But it doesn't work that way."

"So you're an overgrown eighteen-year-old, that's what you're telling me?"

"Basically."

"Makes a lot of sense actually." We grin at each other.

It *is* harder to be mad at her if I think of her as an overgrown eighteen-year-old. Eighteen-year-olds do all kinds of dumb shit. I would know.

I toy with my pancakes, the sugar going to my head already. "Do you ever think about the future?" I ask. "I mean *your* future, not mine." Her brow knits like the concept has never occurred to her. "You know, like, your life. Your Date."

"Oh, that." She sighs and pokes a bare foot out from beneath the table. Her Date is sloped right across the arch, like the strap of a sandal. She'll be sixty-eight. And she still won't have done a fraction of the things Jude did. "Like I said, time changes as you get older," she says, tucking the foot away again. "When I was a kid, I thought my Date was *so* far away. And then, as I got older, I thought it was pretty young. And now I'm forty-one and some days I think it'll be a miracle if I make it that far, and others . . ." She sighs again. "It feels like a bus that was due ages ago." She shrugs. "You just gotta do your best with the time you've got, right?"

I nod. Maybe she and Jude would've gotten along fine. I get up impulsively, drape my arms around her shoulders, and hug her. Her clothes smell like my childhood and I inhale, aware that however shitty these last couple of months have been, someday I'll look back and wish I could do them all over. Just for a little more time with my mom.

"You're doing great," I whisper, and I feel her breath hitch as she squeezes me back.

I'm not naive. I have no idea if she's going to be OK while I'm gone. But I also know that if this time doesn't work out, it doesn't mean she can't try again. I guess that goes for both of us.

Micah and I follow the trail out of Staff Town and onto Bergman Road toward the bus stop as limos and sports cars swish past bringing new guests to the resort.

They've given me expenses and six weeks to take the photos, do the interviews, and write the article, then Yvette will help me edit it. I'm more terrified than I was doing skydiving or bungee jumping or rock climbing. But more awake, too. More alive. And I'm sadder than I've ever been in my life, and at the same time, roaming around the ruins, thinking about my article . . . I'm happy. I thought happiness meant noise and buzz and parties and adrenaline. But sometimes it's a quiet thing, happiness. Like a little creature in the busy undergrowth of your day, easy to miss.

"Now remember, this ruined-building stuff is good and all, but I want you to focus on portraits of the hottest guys in each town. Preferably nude," Micah says as we stagger down the road under the weight of my bags. Luis offered to drive us to the bus stop, but we wanted to walk.

"This is work! I'm going to be a serious artiste, Micah, not make soft porn for you."

"No. Fun. At. All," he huffs. He hasn't dated a guy since Carlos, actually. When he's not hanging out in the ruins with me, he's spending time with Luis or helping

Elena in the salon. When they came to pick him up after the fire, Elena was hysterical, and I think that was the moment Micah finally accepted that they're never going to kick him out. That they love him.

We reach the bus stop in good time and collapse on the bench, watching the long road the bus will come down while I check my bag one more time. Camera. Lenses. Letters. Photos of Jude.

Micah leans his head on my shoulder and I put my head on his. "Maybe I should stay. I mean, what are you going to do without me? Who's going to be the responsible one?" I'm only half teasing, nerves creeping into my gut as I watch for the bus. I thought that by the time I had to leave, I'd feel more confident, but I really don't.

"Are you kidding? I was always the responsible one. Look at this, I'm even reading a book." He draws a dog-eared paperback out of his pocket. *The Picture of Dorian Gray* by Oscar Wilde.

"Where did you get that?" I laugh.

"Jude," he says, and my laugh fades. "It came in the mail. A few days after . . . He wrote something inside."

I run my thumb over the illustration on the cover. A picture of a young man with a beautiful face and a vulnerable stare. Inside, Jude has written, *"Humanity takes itself too seriously. It is the world's original sin. If the caveman had known how to laugh, history would have been different." —Oscar Wilde.* I smile, remembering Jude and Micah, weak with laughter outside the Moroccan Lodge.

"Any good?" I ask him.

He nods. "I've read it twice now. Probably the first thing I've ever done that *wasn't* on Jude's Bucket List of Time Wasting. Elena's reading it, too. Saturday nights are a *riot* around our place now." He snorts a laugh, but I know this is big for him. He doesn't go to the resort on Saturday nights anymore. He's been seeing Burgess, too, every week since the fire. He's stopped drinking and smoking and he's even let Luis put some shelves up in his room, as if he might be staying.

The bus appears in the distance, and the nerves in my stomach start to bite. This is a mistake. I've never been away from home. I've never written an article; I've never interviewed anyone. What makes me think I can do this?

"What if I forgot something? What if my photos suck? What if no one will talk to me?"

Micah draws his head back and arches an eyebrow. "Regan Blythe, if there's one thing we know about you, it's that you can charm the pants off anyone. They're going to fall madly in love with you. Everyone does." He takes my face in his hands, fixing me with a serious expression, and says, "What would Jude say? He'd say *get your scrawny ass on the bus, you fucking idiot.*" He shrugs. "Or something inspiring in a sexy accent."

I laugh through welling tears as the bus pulls up and the doors hiss open. I hug him and climb aboard, promising to call soon. I throw my stuff onto the first empty seat, and Micah appears at the window next to me, waving and blowing exaggerated kisses. I laugh, but the bus is drawing away already and I watch as he stands there with one hand raised, and then we're around the corner and he and Elite Elect and Staff Town and Bergman Road are all out of sight and I am suddenly alone.

You're a special person, Regan. I know this because Jude never spent time on anything that wasn't important. Let me know if you ever need anything. Though, having met you, I think you probably have everything you need already.

I wish you luck and joy and purpose and, most of all, love. Grab it wherever you find it. Like life, it doesn't always last long, and isn't always easy, but I think it's always worth it.

Your friend,

Julia Daly

My heartbeat slows as the resort recedes behind me and I check my bag one last time. Camera, lenses, letters. Photos of Jude. Then I turn to face forward in my seat and tell myself to calm down, it's fine, it's all there. Everything I need is coming with me. Wherever. Always.

Acknowledgments

It took me about sixteen years to find all the component parts of this unholy mash-up of a book, but I'm glad I waited because it ended up being the most fun I've ever had at my desk. I wrote most of it thinking, *This is completely crazy, no one's ever going to publish it.* But apparently crazy goes down well in children's publishing, and for that reason, I feel lucky to be a part of it.

Love and thanks to everyone at Walker Books for their unwavering support and enthusiastic cheering; I can't imagine a friendlier team. To Jack Noel, Clo Tartinville, and Sivan Karim for the very cool cover. To Frances Taffinder for stepping in at zero hour. And especially to my editor and friend Lucy Earley for such skillful guidance and insight, and for her development not only of this book but of me as an author over the years. I really don't know what I'd have done without you, missus!

To everyone at Candlewick Press, especially Audrey Iocca and Lindsay Warren for such sensitive editing, Maria Middleton for the swoony US cover, and copyeditors Julia Gaviria and Sarah Chaffee Paris for turning my trousers into pants, my holidays into vacations, and my dodgy punctuation into something that makes me look quite smart.

To Kirsty McLachlan at Morgan Green Creatives for her always levelheaded advice.

To my ever-supportive critique group, especially Jenny Ireland for cheerleading skills Regan would be proud of. Every time I had a confidence wobble, Michael said, "Don't make me phone Jenny."

To Evan Vellis for enduring many WhatsApp conversations about American English, hangover cures, and Gatorade.

And to Michael Bell, who did bugger all for this book, but it's become a tradition to mildly insult him in the acknowledgments.

Regan's "ruins" were inspired by the real-life Borscht Belt, a resort destination in the Catskills popular with American Jewish vacationers from the 1920s to the 1970s and now largely abandoned. I would like to acknowledge and recommend the stunning photography and wonderful essays in *The Borscht Belt: Revisiting the Remains of America's Jewish Vacationland* by Marisa Scheinfeld, Stefan Kanfer, and Jenna Weissman Joselit, which I found invaluable in bringing these scenes to life.

As always, thanks to my mum and dad for being my most enthusiastic readers and for a childhood spent at quite a lot of American theme parks when I should really have been at school. Excellent parenting, guys.

And to Michael. You can fall in love in five days. You can also stay in love for thirty-two years (and counting).